SIDEWAYS GLANCES

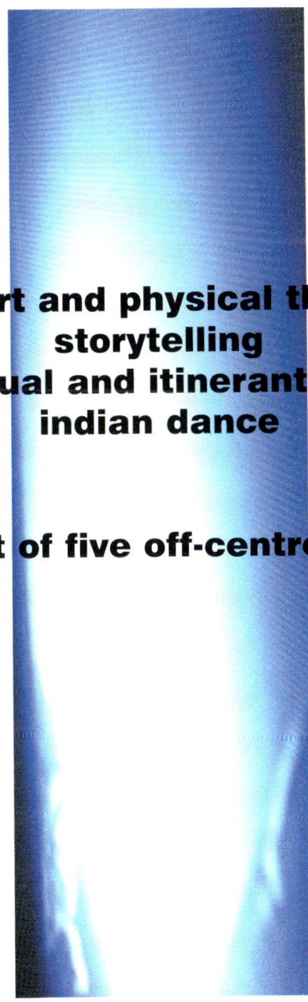

webart and physical theatre
storytelling
visual and itinerant art
indian dance

exploring the art of five off-centre artists in wales

TREFN *1*

SIDEWAYS GLANCES

edited by

Jeni Williams

PARTHIAN

parthian
the old surgery
napier street
cardigan
sa43 1ed

www.parthianbooks.co.uk

first published in 2005

isbn 1-902638-45-X

editor: jeni williams

typeset by type@lloydrobson.com
cover design by marc jennings

printed and bound by dinefwr press, llandybïe, wales

parthian is an independent publisher which works with the support of the welsh books council and the arts council of wales

british library cataloguing in publication data – a cataloguing record for this book is available from the british library

At times we think
we know ourselves

in time, when all we
know is a sequence
of fixations in the
s p a c e s
of the being's
stability –

a being
who does not want
to melt away, and
who, even in the
past, when he sets
out in search of
things past, wants
time to suspend
its flight.

In its
countless alveoli
s p a c e
contains
compressed timc.

That
is what space
is for.

Gaston Bachelard

CONTENTS

INTRODUCTION

Meandering, walking, without necessarily a plan to arrive, to take in the scene, to explore, to experience. This is what this book is about. It's an attempt at a sideways glance at the cultural activity bubbling under the surface, deliberately choosing five very different artists, whose vital, off-centre work benefits from being produced away from the pressure of the dominant metropolitan culture.

The five artists couldn't be much more different:

Eddie Ladd is a well-respected physical performance artist who has worked with internationally respected companies Brith Gof and Volcano. She has made shows incorporating American film and a live rap band. Recently she has developed into an award-winning web-based artist;

Although Megan Lloyd is a charismatic teacher, graphic artist and storyteller, her greatest passion is for the traditional Indian dance she learnt as an adult. She now performs as a principal dancer with India Dance Wales;

As an international storyteller, Daniel Morden works with words, drawing equally on traditional folk tales and classical texts like Homer's *Iliad* and Ovid's *Metamorphosis*. He has performed in places as diverse as a Haitian village and London's Science Museum;

Peter Bodenham explores the way that modern travel affects the contemporary Western experience of place, performing a kind of modern pilgrimage. He sees himself as a 'maker,' his quiet, thoughtful work reclaiming artefacts from the degradation of the heritage industry;

The final artist, Neale Howells, is an artist who chooses recycled materials, seeking out and exhibiting in derelict urban spaces. The violent energy of his surfaces becomes a form of performance in its own right, rejecting rational communication for dramatic effect.

Despite the evident differences between them, all five are concerned with finding space for their art work at the edges of an officially sanctioned idea of culture. This variety gives a sense of the rich fluctuations, the oddity and creativity that exist at every level of a Welsh culture in the midst of change, its boundaries caught between stories of the past and the constructions of the future, fed by traditions from distant cultures as much as native myths, by folk tale or by the urban art of America as well as by the Welsh industrial past, by rural industries in decline, by the internet, by modern technology.

After thinking about the choice of such an eclectic mix of art and artists, there are two other aspects to note about this book: the first is the choice of commentators, and the second is the layout. Both rest in an assumption that engaging with art should itself be a form of art; that it cannot be done through analysis alone but is a kind of conversation, even a performance. This is most evident in the chaotic pages devoted to Eddie Ladd. As a speaker of a marginalised language, Welsh, Eddie challenges the apparent objectivity of English as a mode of communication. Her section deliberately disrupts comfortable assumptions of its transparancy and makes its readers struggle between different codes of expression, drawing them to the visual rather than to the literary as a way of thinking about her work. These pages were created in a three-way collaboration between Eddie, the Cardiff-based designer, Anne Cakebread, and writer and film maker, Sarah Broughton. The other four sections, by contrast, being less concerned with the politics of communication, employ a more personal response. Each of these four sections was individually produced by writer and text operative lloyd robson.

For the book is not a standard study of non-conventional artists. It seeks also to be a beautiful and extraordinary art work in its own right. This is not a book that depends on the judicious selection of figures or art works of genius – it is no star-struck paean to the 'best' as if they emerge from nothing. It is not a sociological analysis in which the various artists are treated like symptoms to be analysed, or assessed. But then, neither is it a survey of Welsh art like that of Hugh Adams's excellent *Imagining Wales* – short, informative summaries of artists crammed into a small book. It is, in Eddie Ladd's words, 'a performance on paper' in which the layout reflects the work of the individual artist; seeking, in the chapter devoted to Daniel Morden, to mimic the way a story tells the storyteller who speaks it, or to demonstrate Ladd's own intense exploration of creative space, the slow unfolding of Bodenham's theoretically-informed, meditative projects, the shapeshifting qualities of Megan Lloyd, the vulnerability and paranoia of Howells' graffiti. This is a modern Wales, as fluid as any other contemporary culture, defined by its vibrant internal differences far more than by the artificial restrictions of any single tradition.

Jeni Williams

!!+!:

words, images & eddie ladd

sarah broughton
design: anne cakebread

SB: Can you tell me when you became interested in theatre?

EL: I think I said when I was four that I wanted to go on the stage – I mean God knows how you'd know at four...

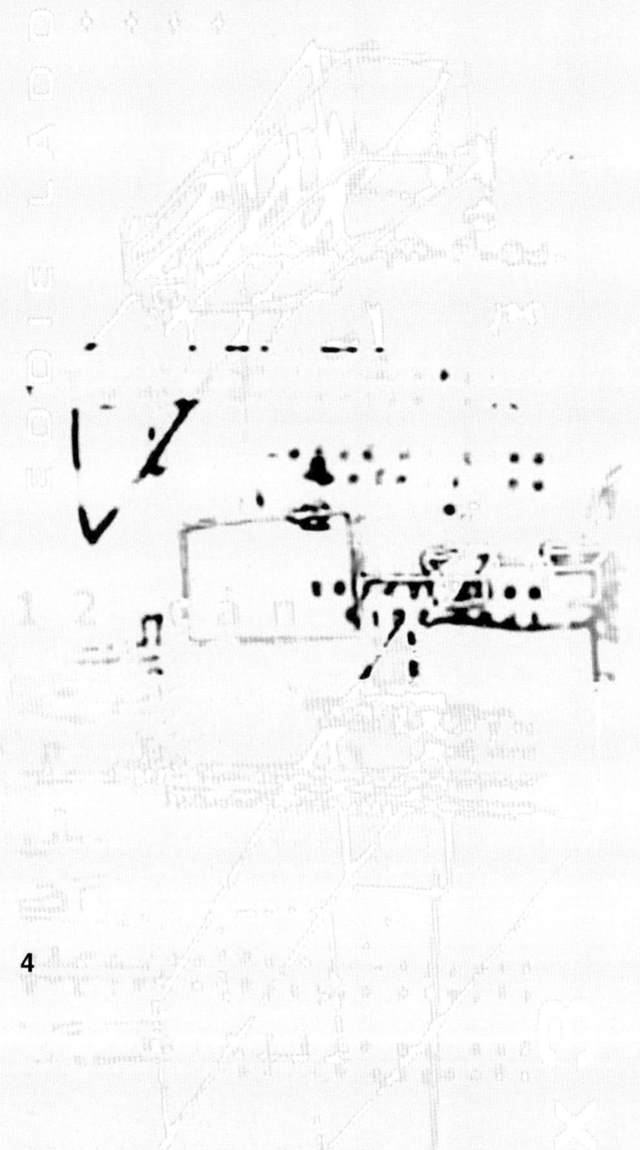

SB: Was it originally more conventional? Did you see yourself going on to have an acting career?

EL: No, it was television. The late 60's and early 70's were full of television specials, all the London Palladium stuff was on and that's what I thought entertainment was. I didn't have any concept of theatre or drama it just didn't figure really. We did go to theatre sometimes – but that would have been really late on and that would have been the result of doing English in school or something.

SB: Shakespeare?

EL: I didn't see a Shakespeare until I got to college, I doubt if I'd have seen anything like that. My ... experience of doing and watching would have come from chapel activities and choir and a little bit of eisteddfod but not an awful lot. Anything that involved things that were not acted actually. I did see Welsh plays around but they were really, you know, people that we knew in them and they were gorgeous, they were fantastic because there was no illusion there either – you could really see people doing an act even though they were proper written plays, comedies in Welsh....the lady from the farm down the road was in one of them and to see her in a slightly vampish character – it was very strange! So there were plays but I don't think I saw anything in English until very late on.

SB: So it wasn't 'go to drama school'?

E: That didn't exist, I had no idea about it. It's not that I was in a stupor and didn't know. Film was the thing that I was aware of as a dramatic form and that was films on television because we never went to the cinema either. **Star Wars** when I was 12/13 was about the first time. American films, British films and Welsh local theatre – not even Welsh professional companies.

SB: So you did the drama at university and then from that it was your route to the palladium?

EL: It was Cinzano ads! That was my idea of the future. It was going to be like that. And record covers – you know those classic ones of Mary Hopkins in a field, sitting playing a guitar on a wire chair. That was the atmosphere.

SB: But when you did drama were you made to actually act there?

EL: We had a real interesting mixture right because.... I remember sitting in the Castle Theatre in Aberystwyth and they said now who's going to do Welsh medium and who's going to do English medium? And I found myself sitting in Welsh medium and I thought – oh god, shall I do English medium and I can't believe that I was even in any doubt! You know, for the image that I've created about my identity and my culture that I was actually thinking 'I should be on the other side with the English speakers'!!! And so I stayed on the Welsh medium side and because of that then, we met BRITH GOF – they taught us in the first year! So there was Mike Pearson and Liz Hughes Jones and they were the ones who took us all the way through the first year. Every week, week in week out.

SB: So there was no equivalent of doing the Welsh version of Noel Coward or Alan Ayckbourn – you were immediately in to physical theatre?

EL: In the second year we had Emily Davies who was a classically based actress and we did Shakespeare with her, in Welsh. Then we had more physical-based stuff with Charmian Saville .... Then we had another guy who came to do Grotowski with us and - he said well you've got a lot of energy actually - and as you go on you become aware or people tell you things about what they see and you don't see that in yourself at all.

SB: As soon as you began working with Mike and Liz did you immediately think 'this is me'?

EL: I couldn't connect it with naturalistic acting which I had seen as film. I couldn't connect it with the idea of standing and being a character, standing and speaking script because they did all sorts of physically based things – biomechanical cat!- I would think why is she working physically? What does that help you do? I had no idea! And of course you can't have the answers at that time and you just do things and think it may become apparent later. But the thing was then that they showed you the culture that you'd come from and I'd no idea what this culture was, I'd no idea of how special it is or what its characteristics were.

SB: You stepped out of it in order to be able to see it?

EL: That's right, yes and ironically through someone like Mike Pearson who is from Lincolnshire and learnt Welsh and was being part of the solution not the problem.

SB: Did you know though that when that was happening, that's what was happening – or is that in retrospect?

EL: Retrospect! I had no idea at the time because I was so bound up in what they look like as people and their authority and they looked incredibly serious as well – the real deal, they really were!

SB: And you could see it as a path you might follow?

EL: No because the crunch moment there, although I didn't know it was a crunch moment at the time, was I was working with Geoff Moore, we were doing **Romeo and Juliet** and it was pretty much the first commercial job I had after college – after a period of not knowing what the hell to do and not knowing how to get into the profession.

SB: But wanting to?

EL: I was in a daze – I didn't know what I was doing! And working with him, I said well if I say it like this – how's that? And he said – well no – he said stay away from that because that's kind of naturalistic and really you don't need to do that, you're really that kind of actor and that the first time that I'd thought 'I'm not that kind of actor? Oh my God what shall I do then?'

SB: Was that a way out for you or was that scary?

EL: It was scary because I thought I can't do anything else. I don't know what else I can do, but then all the companies that I went in with were all community based or education based where that kind of naturalistic acting wasn't their currency.

SB: Was it quite soon after that that you became involved in BRITH GOF?

EL: '86 was when I came to Cardiff and worked with Geoff and with his company MOVING BEING. I'd never seen any of their work, I'd seen a poster of theirs in the Green Room in Aberystywth and it was obvious they were quite experimental and stuff that I had no experience of. So I knew their reputation and I knew I was working with that kind of company and I was delighted to be even though we were doing Shakespeare, and then I worked for several years with people like HIJINX, I did one with VOLCANO, I did two or three with TALIESIN and then I auditioned for BRITH GOF in 1990 and thank God I did because I nearly didn't you know and these opportunities don't come that often and the people they took in that intake they worked with for the next six, eight, ten years! They didn't take on many more performers after that even though they did look around for people.

SB: There was no thought in your mind about making your own work at that point?

EL: No, not between '86 and '90

SB: So at what point did you form JESUS & TRACY [a company]? Was it formed for the Callas show?

EL: I can't remember now! I think it was formed for a piece called **C D E** which was about pianos. It was a scrapbook of work really, with an organising form of the scale of the piano – C D E F G A B C.

SB: Was this done in quite an informal way – or were you thinking then about getting grants and venues?

EL: I don't think we thought grants at that time, but we did approach Chapter and say can we do our show? And they gave us a little bit of money to make something. I don't think it went down particularly well at all – I remember someone saying it was clever (laughs). Nobody thought it was good. And after that we went for a grant, we went for **Callas** [opera house version] – that's why we applied.

SB: So there wasn't a collection of people? Just basically you...

EL: I think it was me wearing out people along the way, actually, come to think of it! Why am I a solo performer?!

SB: So were you simultaneously working in BRITH GOF at that point?

EL: Yes. We had just done two **Paxs** – we did one in Cardiff and one in Glasgow and straight after Glasgow we then started working on **C D E**.

SB: Through all of this were you becoming more aware of the importance of your own background in terms of how that was later going to be absolutely vital?

EL: Not then, no. Because I went into a complete denial detour (laughs). Which is weird because I was working with BRITH GOF who are high politics and yet immediately after I went and did a show about Maria Callas which had nothing to do with... of course it had everything to do with female power and strength of female will which is why I was so attracted to her. And then I did a show about Leni Riefenstahl which is about the position of the artist in society so you can kind of see that it's all circling around certain issues but it was during the Leni Riefenstahl show that, because we used six tons of corn to perform in, we had to rehearse it at home – you couldn't rehearse that in Cardiff – there's nowhere that's going to let you stick in six tons of corn and leave you to it for 6/8/12 weeks or whatever so we did it at home in the potato shed.

SB: So there must have been a shift of focus – from Callas to Rienfenstahl...

EL: A lot of these descriptions you come to through art-speak, by having to describe your ideas to the Arts Council, or even to a journalist or to journalists who don't exist who you might have to talk to! So you say – it's about the position of the artist in society and you think that probably is why I've chosen this person but I mean a lot of them were kind of instinctive...but then you think well why did I choose Maria Callas? Because I was absolutely obssessed with how do I function as a woman – it was a huge concern at the time, you know – it just was.

SB: But you picked a singer to embody that concern.

EL: Yes, God knows why!

SB: But that must have been another really strong internal connection.

EL: Yes, yes it was. I suppose my voice was pretty shot by then – it had been shot for the best part of a decade by that time so maybe that was a psychological reason for it – but it was the power thing really. Because I thought – well how am I going to live then? How am I going to live in Cardiff? What am I going to do? You know? What am I going to do in the 40 years I've got? Next? You know it's just like – yeah it's a period of showing yourself and forming your identity.

SB: Can you take me through the process then – of how you go from that to Once Upon A Time in the West?

EL: I think we were doing Rienfenstahl late '94 but by about May '95, I started writing **Once Upon A Time in the West** - I knew there was something somewhere – but not what. I'd heard of **Shane**, didn't know much about it and... then it confirmed exactly what was happening to my auntie – I mean! You know? So in the film's story there is a huge cattle ranch operation threatening the existence of a small homesteader. And there was at the time Welsh Water saying that my auntie had mismanaged her land and that, or there was some allegation, that the cause of the St Dogmaels' landslide was my auntie's mismanagement of her land – where as we always thought they'd – on the site of an ancient landslide – What was the question?

SB: The process....

EL: It might not have happened – but it was that thing that grabs hold of you and makes you sit down for 3 weeks and write. That slightly obsessive side was good because it keeps you sitting there staring at the paper when you can't think of anything. But it drives you into all sorts of other obsessive areas as well which is what the following year was about! (The worst time! I was 200% mental and awake all the time). End of '95 I got work with BRITH GOF again and that's when Cliff and me were working together [on **Tri Bywyd**]. And because I'd worked with Cliff on that and it had worked really well, I went up to his flat one day and said 'You've got to help me!' And he said yes. Christ was I lucky, was I lucky!

SB: You know you need to make that work and you need that person to help you do it.

EL: Yeah, you're just looking for help you know - I was so happy with that show because it really pushed things on.

SB: You needed to be pushed through the next door?

EL: Yeah, kind of, yeah – I knew I couldn't organise **Once Upon A Time** by myself and I knew that formally, I hadn't got a clue and I did feel lost, by the time I'd written it I felt completely lost you know?

SB: What was that like - to make something so personal?

EL: It was fantastic! I just felt something about it. You borrowed all those mythic elements from the film - here comes the revenge, here comes the shootout – you've borrowed all those kind of feelings which add to your real experience, and that feeling, which I kind of mistrusted at the time but kind of went with as well, of making a myth of family people – you know – making them as big as the screen.

SB: What did that do in terms of how you started to look at home and culture and language – because that has informed you ever since, hasn't it?

EL: Yes it has – I mean you know, you'd think I was like that from year dot but I wasn't.

SB: That's why I'm so interested in those very early shows.....

EL: My light-ent phase!

SB: Exactly! You could have been lost to Butlins!

EL: Lena Zavaroni – those were the influences.... She was the same age as me and how eaten up was I by absolute envy and desire. Olga Korbut! Showbiz and celebrity and celebrity sport. But **Opportunity Knocks** was the format, you know, that was the format! Why would you want any more than that?

SB: So this was about going into a new period with a sense

Callas sings mad scenes at Craig-y-nos

Callas sings mad scenes
1993

callas sings mad scenes_o **recit** 3 hyd **aria** 6_dau ohonom yn ymddangos fel Madame Butterfly mewn "spacewrap" arian a sgidie ar flocs pren_yn datod gwallt clwt gwyn ac yn ei daflu rownd pen i drac Nirvana Smells like teen spirit_'nghodi â rhaff 12 troedfedd yn 'r aer mewn ffroc parasiwt wen debyg i ffroc Callas yn Norma_pys sych yn cwympo o'r nenfwd_Callas yn trial canu/**aria**/a'r angel yn ei thaflu ar "crashmat"_â chwaraewr recordie ar 'y mhen â chanddo record o Callas arno croesi'r llwyfan a symudiade'r corff yn amharu ar sicrwydd y llais_y/**recit**/ar farwolaeth Callas yn cael ei chwarae at gamera ben pella'r llwyfan_ni yn sefyll o'i flaen a'r llun yn cael ei ddangos ar deledu bach reit ar flaen y llwyfan

Yr un "semi-opera" gafodd ei llwyfannu yn y tŷ teras yng Nghaerdydd ar ei newydd wedd yn nhŷ opera Adelina Patti ger Abercraf_tŷ hyfryd euraidd baroc yr olwg gyda bwa proseniwm ag enwau'r cyfansoddwyr mowr arno_llwyfan draddodiadol â drws trap yn llawr_chwaraewyd cerddoriaeth y sioe gan ddwy feiolynydd yng ngherddorfa'r tŷ_y cyfansoddwr Geoff Haines yn arwen_Ian Rowlands a ? yn ishte yn y gerddorfa yn cyfieithu ar y pryd_y gynulleidfa yn derbyn cyfieithiad Cwmrâg neu Sysneg_deunydd gwahanol i'r sioe dŷ wedi ei seilio ar goreograffi butoh

Callas Minister St
1993

Gwaith we'n i'n ei ddisgrifio yn "semi-opera" wedi ei lwyfannu mewn tŷ teras, 5 Minister St.+Cathays+Caerdydd_wedd y darn ar ffurf whech recit ac aria ac yn disgrifio bywyd Maria Callas_y gweithgaredde yn gyfuniad o waith byw a gwaith fideo_y perfformwyr yn gweithio o flaen camerau (gosod a symudol) a phopeth yn cael ei ddangos i'r gynulleidfa trwy gyfrwng tri teledu wedi eu gosod yn y rŵm ffrynt_y testun wedi ei sgrifennu mewn "Eidaleg" wedi ei ddethol yn uniongyrchol o'r geiriadur_cyfieithiad ar y pryd i Gwmrâg a Sysneg fi'n meddwl_y gynulleidfa yn derbyn y cyfieithiad a thestunau erill drwy ffônau pen (lliw oren)_ddim yn cofio a wedd y gerddorieth wedi 'i sgrifennu i gyd_sgrifennu'r testun nadolig 1992 ar 'y nghwrcwd o fla'n tân letric getre yn rŵm canol_tair ohono ni yn y sioe_Siân Richards+Ri Davies+fi

5

of discovering your identity?

EL: Yes.

SB: And you knew at the time you were doing this – or is this all retrospective?

EL: I think at the time I did know that, by that time, definitely.

SB: So Once Upon A Time was an up, your life all around it was an up – in the wrong way! manic! – so was the next one a down?

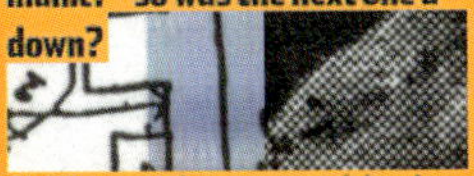

EL: The next show was much harder to do - in a way **Lla'th** was almost goodbye to something and I knew it was at the time, I mean I was – what how old by then? 33? I knew I was leaving that period behind at that time and this was a show that was all about death. Three deaths! How many more do you want? You know! I didn't feel physically older but I just felt as though something here – you know. Once I got to 32 that was definitely the cut off point – I'd spent from 18 to 32 being about 25 years old and I knew things were changing. What was **Lla'th** about? It came out of reading things as well – I was reading Norman Mailer **A Fire on the Moon** and all the Russian cosmonauts came into it and…I knew I wanted to make something.

SB: So you forced the subject matter?

EL: Yes, I forced the subject matter on that one really. But there was some fantastic connections came up – I was just thinking of my background and of farming and it turns out that the American Mercury astronauts – quite a few of them, and a few after, were farm boys, because it was a career move. You went into the army to advance yourself and professionals would not go into the army - professionals did not become astronauts - they were really like farm boys who'd become something. And Yuri Gagarin was the son of peasants on a collective farm and so… there were all those things in the same space at the same time – there is no clear narrative there but…

SB: But you are the link, aren't you? You find the connection…

EL: …you have to make it clear, you can't just say – isn't it obvious? And although you go through all phases with the show thinking that's no good and that's no good, looking back at it now I think the first version of **Lla'th** was miraculous – we made it in Penlanwnws which is a disused farmhouse just outside of Felinfach and, as far as I can work out - because I never saw the show - it looked beautiful you know because it was banks of monitors – 10 monitors, for each room in the house and the yard – it's a fractured narrative…

SB: So…

EL: I can tell you what happened next? I went to Glasgow as a kind of artist-in-residence. And I worked in the biology department in Paisley University, and so I ran after all sorts of scientific ideas, which I'd no idea about, and eventually **Scarface*** came in at that point. A drop – boom – from somewhere? I don't know, but that would have been the end of '97 - boom – somehow!

SB: And when you say it dropped in?

EL: I suddenly heard of the film **Scarface**, maybe it came out again or it was being name checked in rap tracks or… I don't know how it came into my head – did I watch the film? But I'd pretty much decided to do something about **Scarface*** before I even saw the film.

SB: So there wasn't an immediate connection, as in Shane and your auntie's house, Scarface* came in and this was something you wanted to work on?

EL: Yes…**Scarface*** is a violent film, so why are we so attracted to violence? And then I got drawn into the narrative of the film, got drawn in to Al Pacino and the choreographic bravura he has in the film and tiny practical things happened like how am I going to rehearse this? What am I going to do? Where am I going to do it? … again this is a slightly down period because the work was really getting difficult – it was obvious I wasn't going to get any more work, and nothing was moving. But I still wanted to make stuff – and how many times did **Scarface*** get turned down for project funding? It got turned down outright first, then we put it in for the second time but that was only in the year 2000 – that was two years away and even then it only got half-funded because that was the bad year in the Arts Council, so it was kind of just making the work on spec again really.

SB: So how were you actually living at this point?

EL: I think I was just burning up the

Unglücklicherweise_**ail gwarter**_sefyll ar stôl a neidio i'r llafur fel yn **Olympia**_palu trench o un ochor o'r strwythir i'r llall drw'r llafur_hanner gorwedd yn trench a chanu/ **Ich will dir bei mir stehen**/ fel deuawd_datod cynfasen wen o'i rhwyme reit ar ben y strywthir a'i hongian fel sgrîn sinema_tynnu rhaff yn dyn o un ochor i'r llall_ dangos darn o **Triumph of the will** tra'n croesi'r gofod yn hongian a llithro gyda help y rhaff_Rog yn dangos sylwadaeth wleidyddol ar garden ar yr un pryd_dechre cau part bla'n y gofod â bêls a chreu pedwarydd wal

U n g l ü c k

Set tair wal wedi ei hadeiladu o fêls gwellt. Y set yn dal tu fiwn iddi whech tunnell o lafur. Teledu i ddangos y gweithgareddau trwy gamera wedi i'r wal flaen gael ei chau. Rwy'n credu fod hyn yn asio gyda bywyd aralliedig Riefenstahl wedi'r rhyfel.

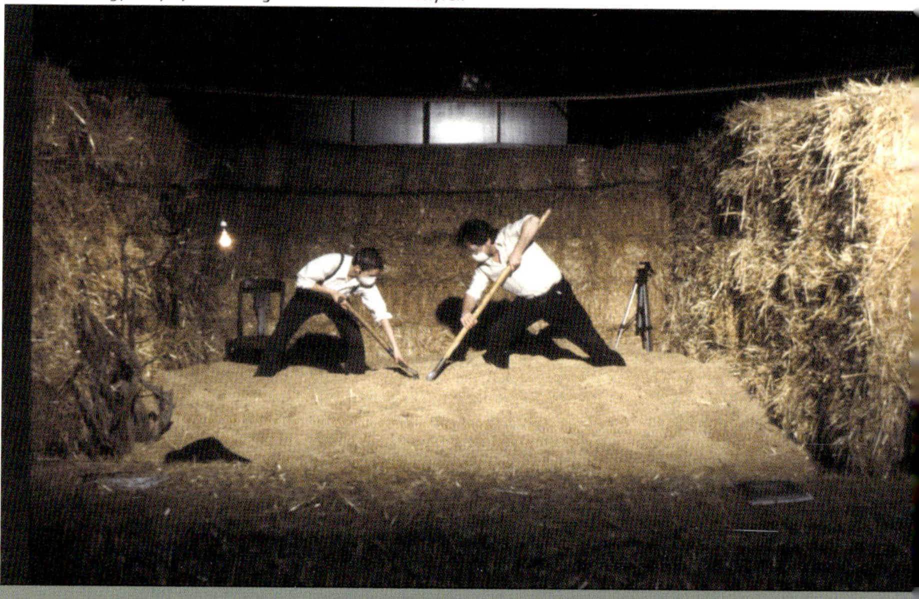

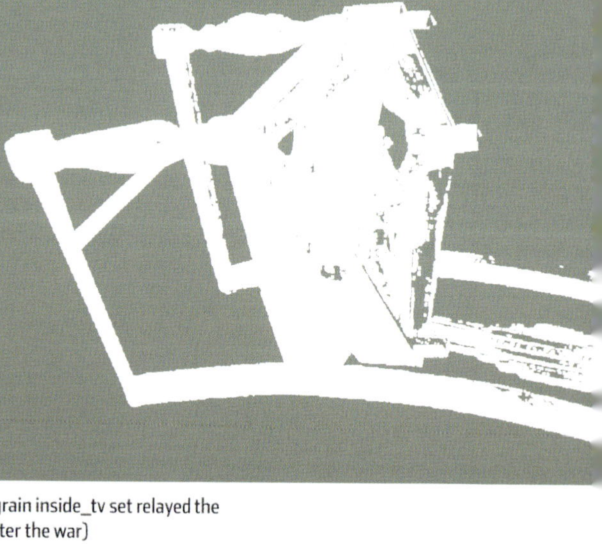

three-walled set built of straw bales_a container for the six tonnes of grain inside_tv set relayed the action when the open wall was closed for a while_(Riefenstahl's life after the war)

Roger Owen/Owen Trefere (brawd/brother)

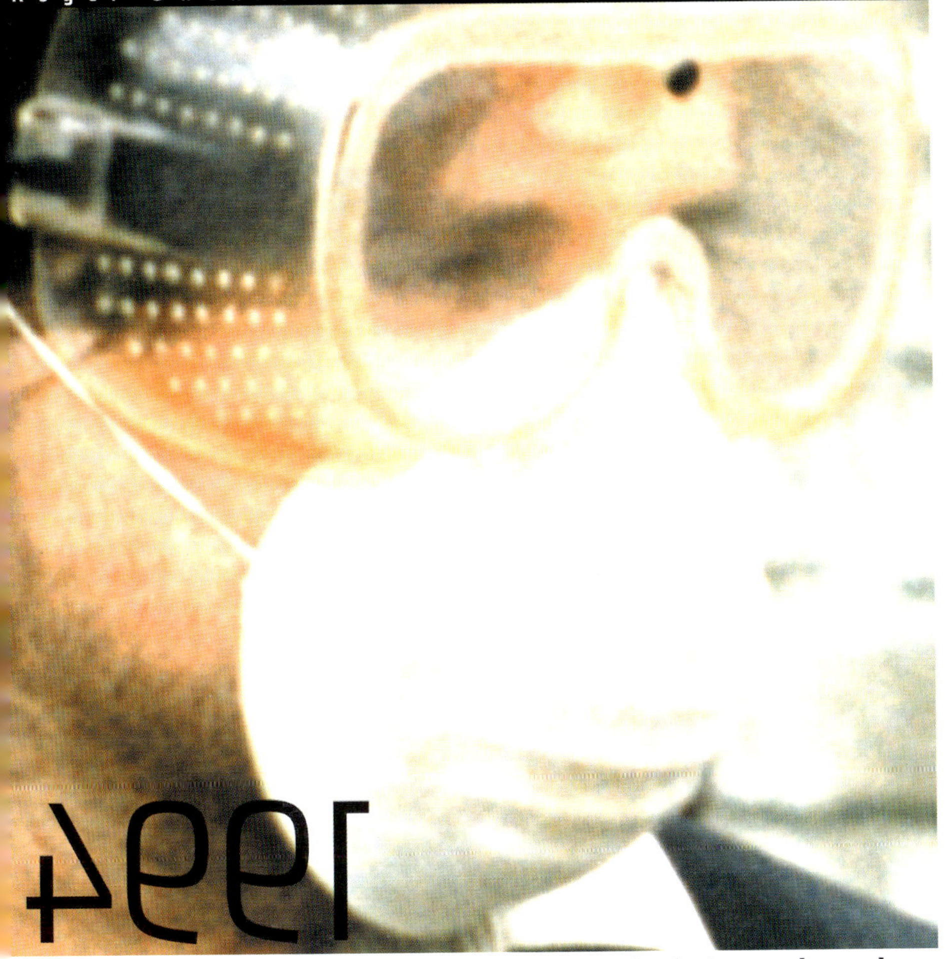

bywgraffiad dethol o fywyd Leni Riefenstahl

selected biography of Leni Riefenstahl

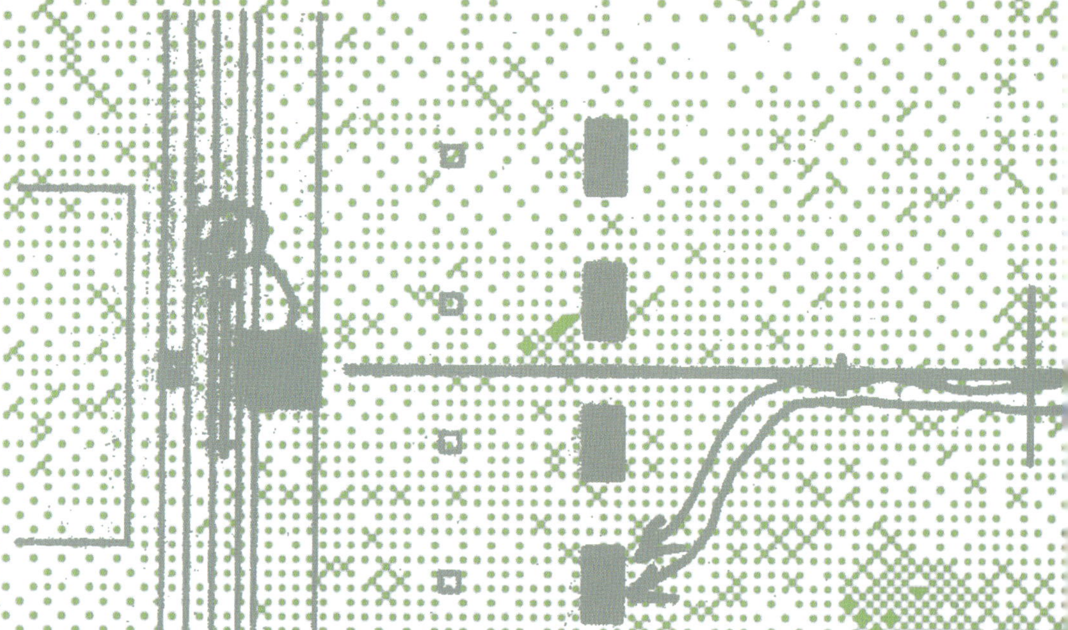

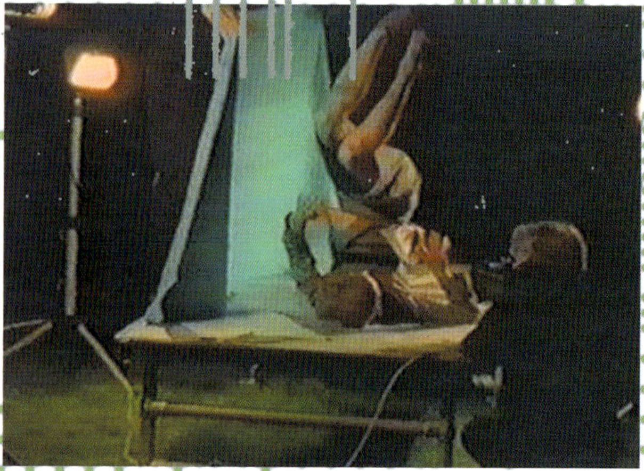

once upon a time

once upon a time in the west_**o 268 price ymlaen**_symud lawr y parc o'r reilen glwmu gan ddefnyddio y ffigwr codi a suddo_taenu canu/**I Galfaria**
sgrîn_adrodd y testun cyhuddo o blatfform y fedyddfa_dawns dangos 'n fam yn eira 1947_'n ôl ar glawr y fedyddfa+tynnu siaced a gwisgo ffroc ●●
cyn dechre saethu_aros am y pedair ergyd dryll_gwthio'n hunan i'r whith lawr i'r dŵr_gadel 'n anadl mas a gwthio'n hunan i waelod y pwll a dal 'n
o'r goreograffi reit lan hyd 'n ôl at y reilen glwmu_marchog y ceffyl 'to a mas o'r parc_Suzanne wedi gosod y tanwydd yn trench a'i gynnu_llinell tân

Sioe mewn parc yn cymathu hanes tirlithriad Llandoch ym 1994 (a rhan 'n fodryb Caryl Davies ynddo) â ffilm **Shane**_y ddau naratif yn ymwneud a
neu deledu_gwaith coreograffig+testun+delweddol_testunau wedi eu dethol o gyfweliadau gyda'n fam a'n anti+sgript y ffilm+digrifiadau o ●●●●●
drowser menyw

Dechreuodd y cyfnod "cysylltu" yma gyda **Unglücklicherweise** oedd wedi ei ymarfer getre ac oedd yn dwyn elfennau gweledol o'r ardal_dyfnhawy

Site-specific show performed in a field featuring linked accounts of a landslide in St.Dogmaels in 1994 and the film Shane_small elemen
from interviews with my mother and auntie+Shane film script+scene descriptions+geomorphological reports_costume was a copy of Al

Unglücklicherweise rehearsed at home and draws on its visual elements_process goes further in **Once upon a time in the west**_home

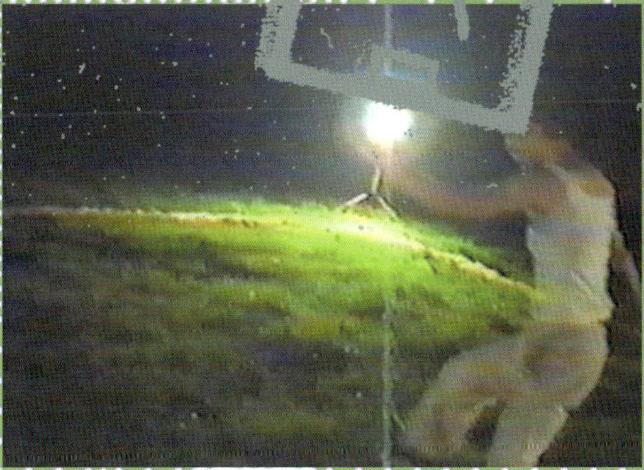

in the west 1996

•• **trof fy wyneb**/dros fynediad Jack Palance o'r paith i'r dre a saethu Elisha cook Jr yn farw_llosgi model o'r tŷ ffarm a'i ddangos yn fawr ar
•• briodas tra bo Rog yn tynnu'r clawr i'r dde i ddangos y dŵr_tynnu'r meic radio+disgrifiad o Alan Ladd a Jack Palance yn y salŵn yn llygadu 'i gilydd
•• hunan yno â 'mreiche_gadel fynd a saethu bron i'r wyneb_Rog yn gafel yndo fi a 'nhynnu i'r lan_ni'n dechre wmla_diengyd a dechre ail whare darne
•• reit ar draws y parc

• elfennau bychain yn wmla cyrff a chwmniau mowr_gweithio'n fyw a thrwy gyfrwng camera_y gwaith at y camera yn cael ei ddangos ar sgrîn sinema
• olygfeydd y ffilm+dogfennau geomorffolegol_gwisg yn cynnwys copi o siwt leder lwyd Alan Ladd_"costiwm" sef siaced a sgyrt_ffroc briodas_siwt

•• y broses yma yn **Once upon a time in the west** oedd â'i bwnc yn uniongyrchol ymwneud â chynefin.

•• v. large corporations_working live and to camera_camera work shown on a cinema and tv screens_choreography+text+imagery_text
•• Ladd's grey buckskin suit_skirt suit_wedding dress_women's trouser suit

•• area is the subject matter

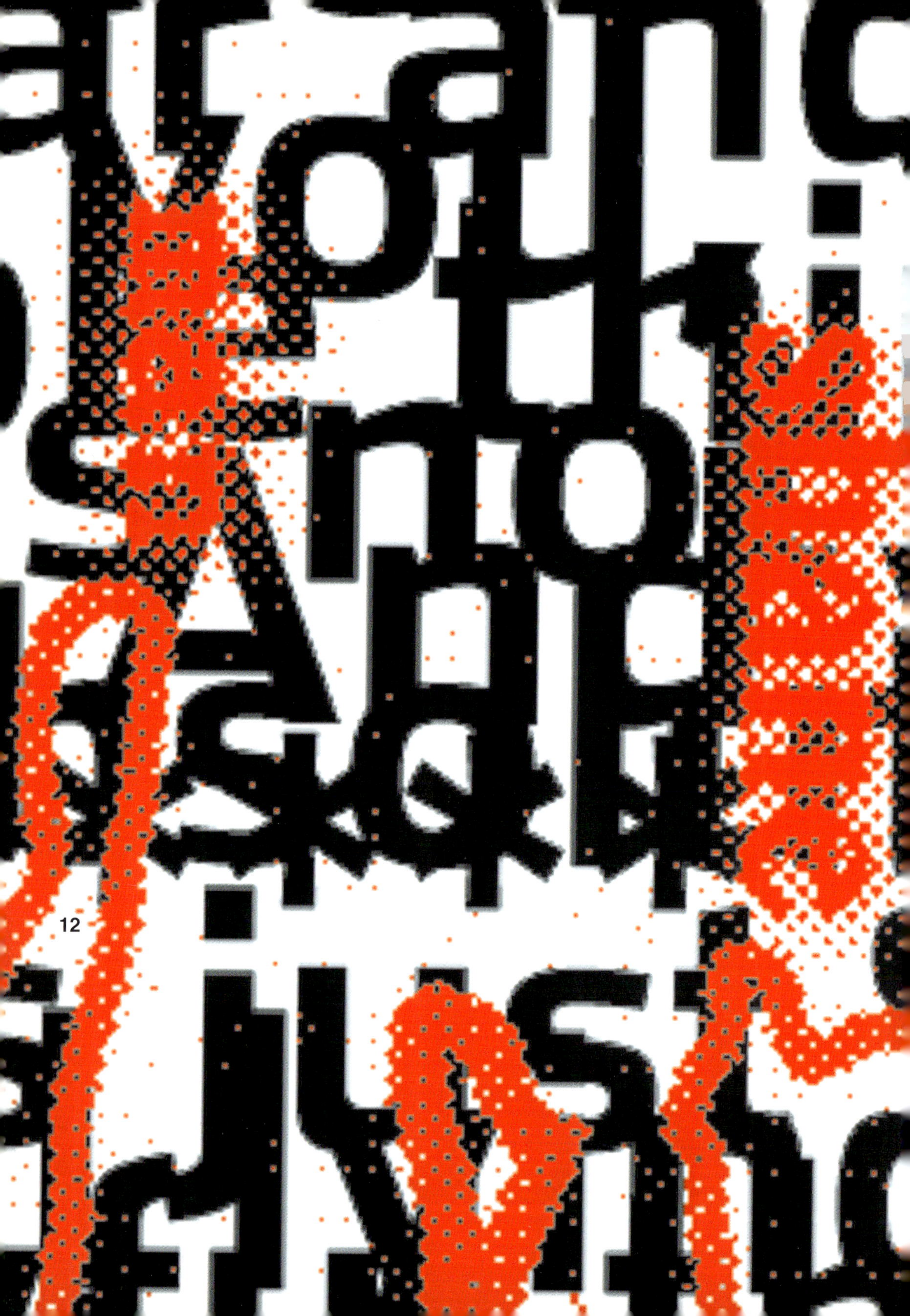

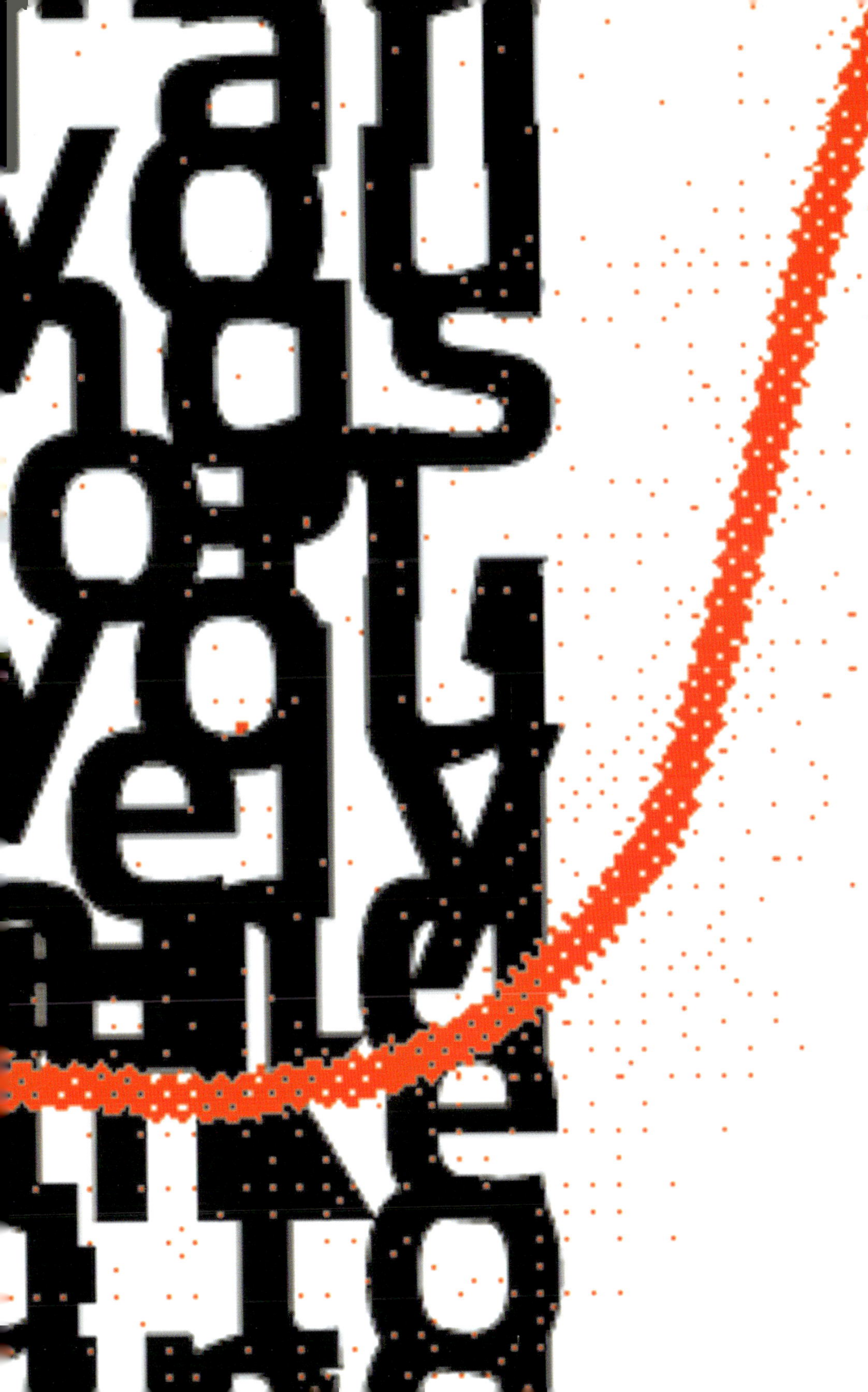

once upon a time in the west 199E

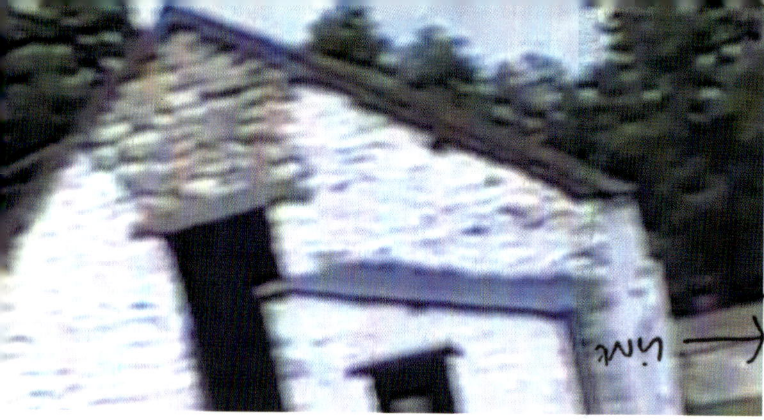

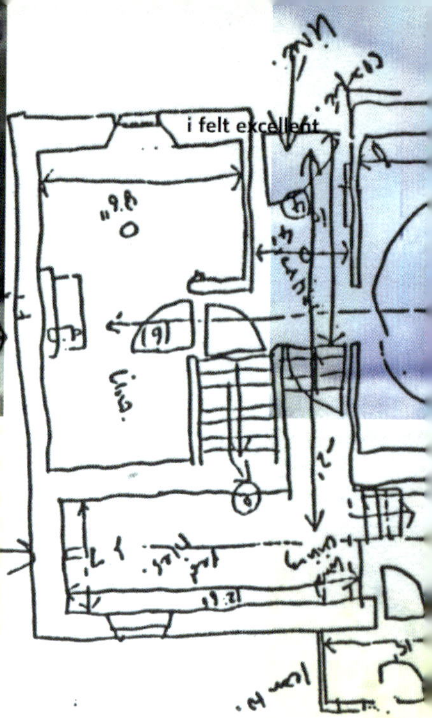

Penlanwnws
gosodwyd naw o gameràu o amgylch y fferm (y clos a'r tŷ)
roedd y gynulleidfa yn gwylio'r perfformiad ar naw sgrîn deledu yn un o'r tai mas

three-narrative show

**on: David Finch
: Yuri Gagarin
: passion of Christ**

EXCELLENT

sioe ag iddi dair naratif

**hanes: David Finch
: Yuri Gagarin
:
dioddefaint Crist**

[lla'th [mowr] 1997-8

sioe ar safle arbennig   site-specific show

Penlanwnws
nine cameras around the farm relayed the action to the audience
which was sat watching nine tv screens in an outbuilding

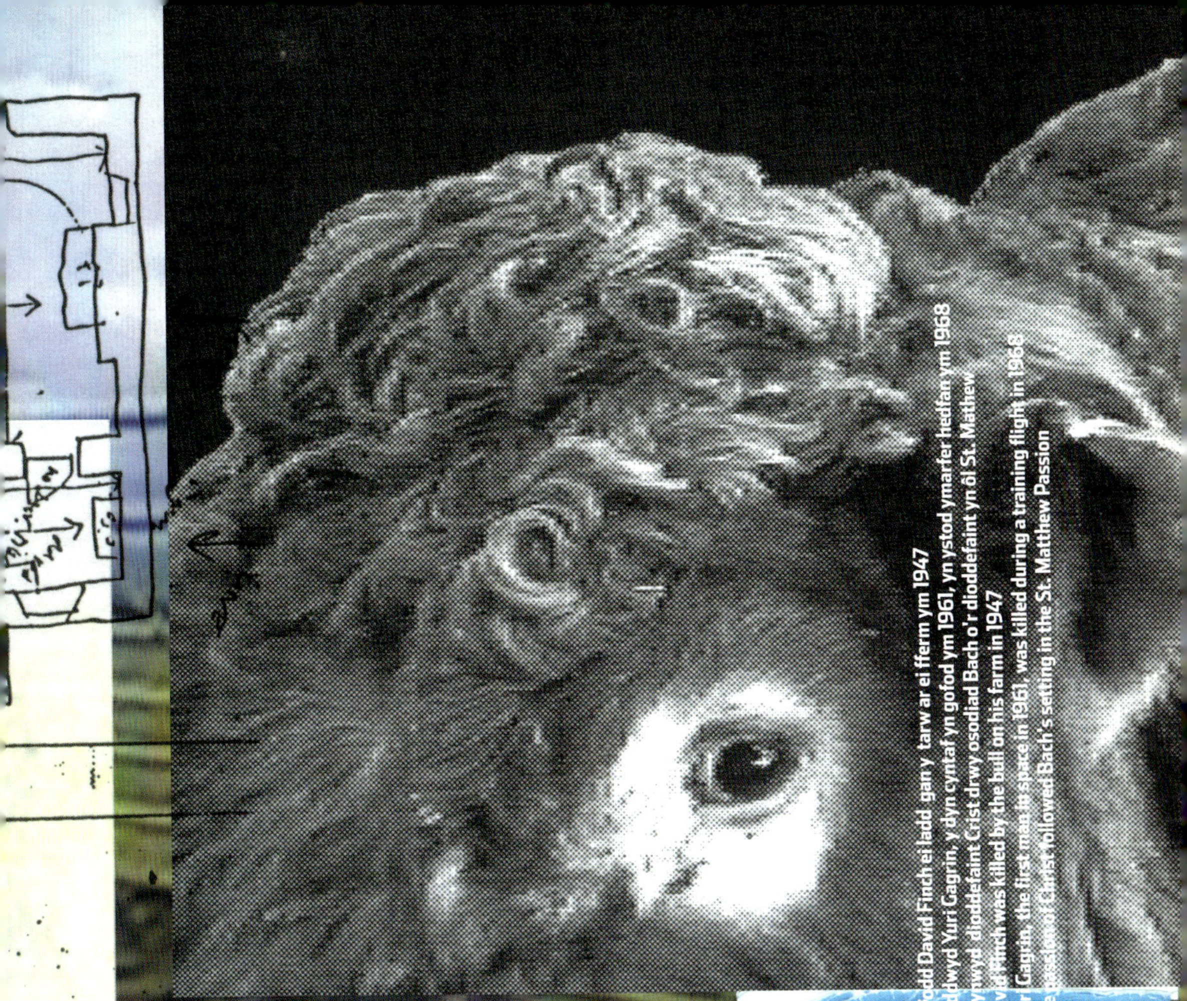

cafodd David Finch ei ladd gan y tarw ar ei fferm ym 1947
lladdwyd Yuri Gagrin, y dyn cyntaf yn gofod ym 1961, yn ystod ymarfer hedfan ym 1968
dilynwyd dioddefaint Crist drwy osodiad Bach o'r dioddefaint yn ôl St. Matthew
David Finch was killed by the bull on his farm in 1947
Yuri Gagrin, the first man in space in 1961, was killed during a training flight in 1968
the passion of Christ followed Bach's setting in the St. Matthew Passion

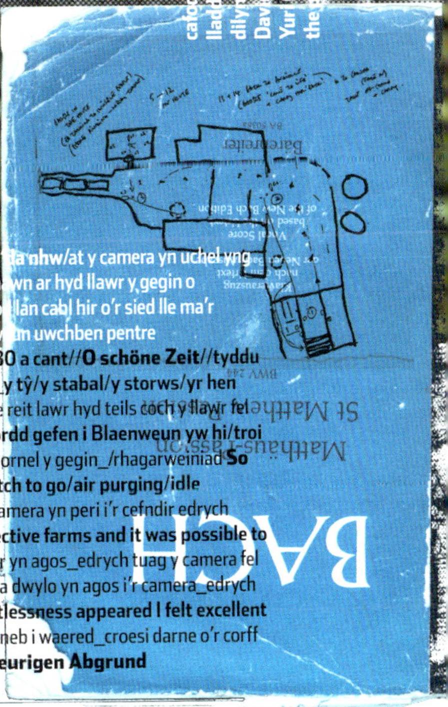

Am Abend da es kühle war

lla'th [mowr]_**hediad Yuri Gagarin**_agor y drws i'r gegin_gneud/**we shorthorns** ma nhw/at y camera yn uchel yng nghornel y gegin_darn o waith stepio (answyddogol) a thestun_dechre sgwario mawn ar hyd llawr y gegin o dwmpath yn cornel_/**Am Abend da es kühle war**/yn dechre whare_y sain yn dod lan cabl hir o'r sied lle ma'r gynulleidfa'n ishte_creu tirwedd ar y mawn gan ddisgrifo nodweddion ffarm Penwaun uwchben pentre Llandoch_/**tyddu blode ma'r bobol sy' 'na nawr/ffarm o biti 80 acres/rhwnt 80 a cant//O schöne Zeit//tyddu popeth/gwair a llafur/tir pori/peth green crop/tato/**_gosod goleuade+bocsus_**y tŷ/y stabal/y storws/yr hen stabal/y catch lle ma'r tarw//Sein Leichnam kömmt zur Ruh**//rhedeg rhyche reit lawr hyd teils coch y llawr fel ffyrdd_mas i ben rhewl/troi fan hyn/bwrw am Croes-y-frân neu Trefigin/**y ffordd gefen i Blaenweun yw hi/troi fan hyn ar bwys Brynheulwen/wedi do' lan o Llandoch o Aberteifi**/symud at gornel y gegin_/rhagarweiniad **So ist mein Jesus nun gefangen**/_dechre clwmu'n hunan â bache at y rhaff_/**switch to go/air purging/idle run**/_tynnu'n hunan lan i'r gornel reit i'r nenfwd_/**y roced wen yn codi/cccp**/_y camera yn peri i'r cefndir edrych ymhell i ffwrdd_//**Sie führen ihn**//**I could see clearly the big fields of the collective farms and it was possible to tell which was ploughed and which was meadow/y tir coch/y tir pori**/_y ffigwr yn agos_edrych tuag y camera fel mewn capsiwl yn gofod_/**es ist gebunden**/_troi wyneb i waered_hongian traed a dwylo yn agos i'r camera_edrych yn ôl ar y tirwedd bell i ffwrdd_cadw symud_disgyrchiant yn llacio_/**when weightlessness appeared I felt excellent //Sind Blitze sind Donner in Wolken verschwunden**/_cadw symud_troi wyneb i waered_croesi darne o'r corff ar draws y camera_aros am y saib_/**verschwunden**//excellent //**Eröffneden feurigen Abgrund**

Я ПОЧУВСТВОВАЛ

i f e l t e x c e l l e n t

СЕБЯ ОТЛИЧНО

yuri gagarin

lla'th [bach] 1998

lla'th [ba

18 UN DEG CHWECH

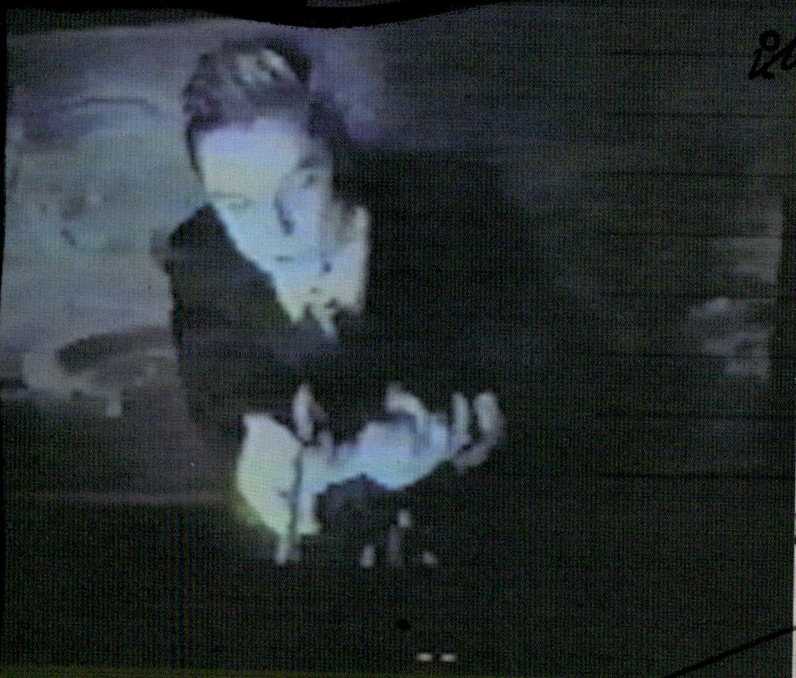

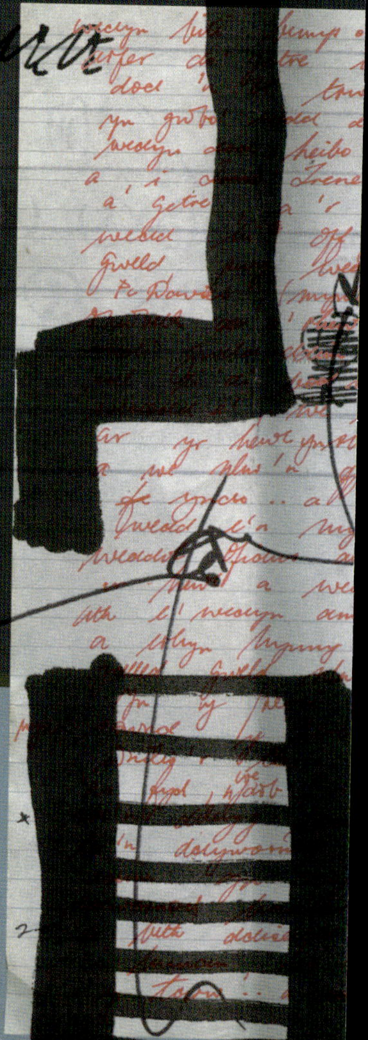

Sioe ag iddi bedair naratif_cyflwynir y sioe mewn stiwdio neu theatr fach_fe'i llwyfennir ar ac o gylch i ford 8m o hyd â'r gynulleidfa yn ishte bob yn ochor iddi_felly fe all y gynulleidfa fod cyn lleied â 26_tair naratif yn ymwneud â'r un pynciau â Lla'th [mowr] a'r pedwarydd yn disgrifio gosodiad Lla'th [mowr] ar y fferm

A show with four narratives_ presented on and around an 8m table with the audience sat at the table_ audience number could be as little as 26_three narratives are on the same subjects as the site-specific Lla'th_ the fourth narrative describes a performance of that show

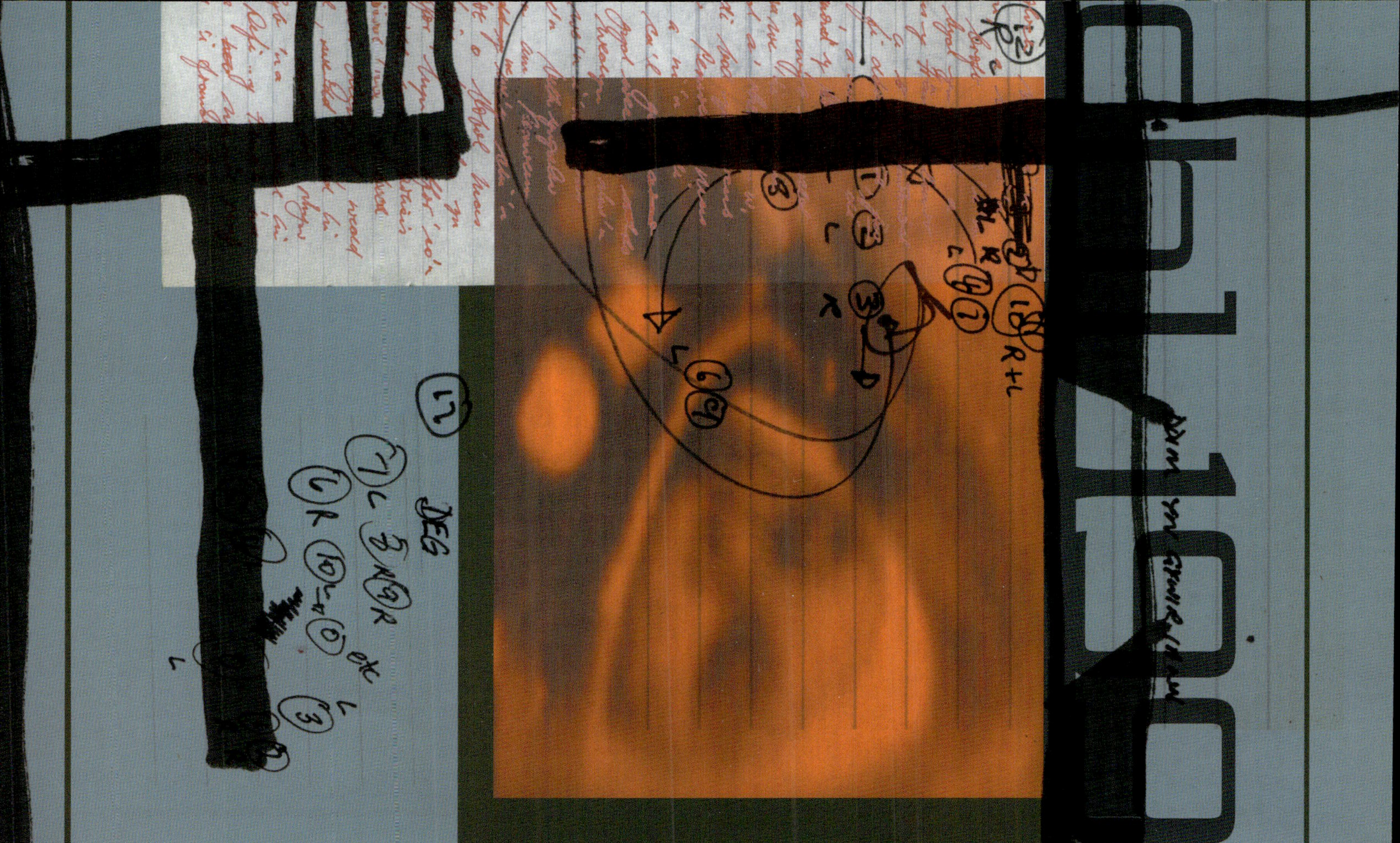

ricordiad yn y man a'r lle

lla'th bach**_o'r pasej hyd shorthorns**_clymu bache at 'r harnais a suddo at wyneb y ford_gwisgo'r menyg oren_iwso dwylo a'r tra'd i hofran uwchben y ford_/ricordiad yn y man a'r lle o fi'n anadlu yn neud gwaith tebyg ym mhasej tŷ ffarm Penlanwnws/yn adrodd **enwau cosomonauts** o Rwsia sgrifennwyd ar y walydd/_symud rownd y ford mewn ffurf 'u' bedol ambell waith wyneb i waered_trial dod at 'n stôl a datod wedi/**Svetlana Savitskaya**/_adrodd yr **adnod** wedd ar ben stepse'r llaethdy gyda'r trac_newid y caset sy' yn y mishîn a'i roid i'r neilltu_dangos lle 'y ni yn tŷ trwy ei ddangos â map dwylo ar ford_/**lan lofft/lawr i'r llaethdy/ miwn i'r gegin**/_peri i'r naratif lithro wrth greu map tebyg ar ford i ddisgrifio lladd David Finch_/**yr Italian yn rhedeg i ben stepse'r storws i drial tynnu sylw'r tarw/y tarw yn gadel y clos/yr Italian yn trial dragio Defi miwn i'r tŷ/y tarw yn dod 'n ôl miwn i'r clos/yr Italian yn rhedeg i'r tŷ**/_nôl 'n siaced_'i gwisgo ac ishte_edrych ar y gynulleidfa_newid cywair y perfformio eto wrth siarad yn uniongyrchol â'r gynulleidfa_gofyn a odi nhw'n deall beth sy'n mynd yn ei fla'n_esbonio os na_dringo 'n ôl ar ben ford i ddechre/**we shorthorns 'da nhw**

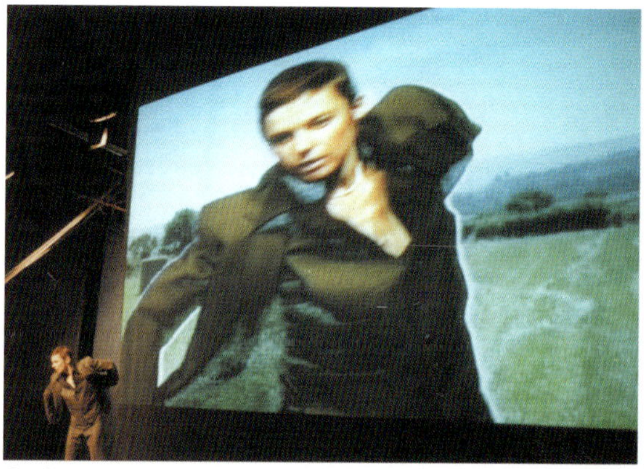

Scarface*

A tribute to Brian de Palma's 1983 classic and to its lead Al Pacino.

The show is played against chromakey (blue screen). Eddie Ladd stands in for Pacino, performing to camera throughout, her image locked to a series of backgrounds and a better-than- the-original soundtrack by John Peel favourites, Tystion. Everything then is put up big on a cinema-sized screen. It is an epic on the cheap, the action relocated to the west Wales that is the performer's home and as cynical and shiny as de Palma's own remake.

◂ listings copy

Sawn-off Scarface*

A duet and a (semi) ironic tribute to Scarface, Brian de Palma's notorious 1983 film classic, starring Al Pacino. Performed to a short, tough synopsis of the plot, and on something close to a sticky, wet nightclub floor, it reduces nearly three hours of film action to twelve minutes. A no-technology attempt on filmic effects and the glamour, cynicism and homoerotics of the gangster genre.

SCARFACE*

+scarface* bach

[sawn-off scarface]

2000

Ok alright Tony

scarface bach_**killing frank**_gosod 'n hunan hanner ffordd ar yr ochor whith ar ymyl y carped_darllenydd yn aros_darllenydd yn tynnu anadl_wrth glywed yr anadl fi'n codi 'nwylo o bob yn ochor i fi at ganol 'mryst gyfer yr arwydd cynta'_/**Ok**/_ffurfio 'o' gyda bawd a bys cynta'n llaw dde+tri bys arall ar ongl 45° uwch eu pen_troi'r byse trwy 180° bron+agor 1+cadw 2 ar agor+cau 3 a 4+cloi tu ôl gyda'r bawd+gosod 1 y llaw whith tu ôl 1 a 2 y dde i ffurfio postyn y 'k' _/**alright**/tynnu'r llaw whith rownd o'r cefen i'r blae'n_cau'r llaw yn ddwrn ar wahan i 2 yn agored_cau'r dde yn ddwrn ar yr un pryd_cyffwrdd cwgn 2 y dde â 2 agored y whith_cyrraedd erbyn __**right**_/**Tony**/_2 y dde yn arwain_llunio siâp calon o waelod y sternwm+lan hyd dwy fodfedd o bont yr ysgwydd+'n ôl_penelin dde yn tynnu'r fraich at 90° at yr ysgwydd_1 a 2 y dde yn ffurfio siâp fforch_arwain yn ôl lawr i dorri siâp fforch trw'r galon [tatŵ Tony Montana]

scarface*_**colymbians**_gosod 'nhroed whith tu fiwn i'r tirongl whare_ cadw gweddill y corff rhag y camera_dechre'r gerddorieth am yr olygfa newydd_**/Ma nhw'n dreifo lan y stryd ac yn troi'r car rownd/**_tynnu'r corff miwn i'r shot_gweitho nawr yn llwyr o fla'n camera_disgrifio Tony a'i ffrind Angel yn mynd i hotel y Colymbians i brynnu cocain_y sgwrs letwith gyda Hector y gwerthwr_gwylio'r monitor mwyn gweld y cefndir yn dechre troi o ddrws rŵm canol i'r ffenest a thuag at ddrws y gegin_**/Ti moyn i fi fyn' mas a jocan bo' ni'n dechre 'to?/**_cadw edrych ar y camera_yn erbyn y cefndir rwy'n ymddangos fel se mod i'n cerdded am 'n ôl trw'r drws i'r gegin_**/Man pulls a gun on Angel/**_unwaith heibo'r ffrâm dechre troi'n araf i'r whith_**/Marta from under the pillow pulls an enormous gun/**_a dechre dangos 'y nghefen i'r camera_**/Hector fetches a chainsaw/**_troi 'r un cyflymder â'r shot a fi'n ymddangos yn symud nawr trw'r drws i'r porch_**/They're tying Angel to the shower rail above the bath/**_ymylu'n nhraed ag ail linell y triongl whare mwyn cadw 'nghorff mewn cydluniad â'r hyn sy' o'm hamgylch_rhy bell tua'i gefen a fe fyddai'n rhy fach yn erbyn yr amgylchfyd_mas yn clos_troi rownd yn sydyn_**/Tony won't relent/Angel gets sliced/first the head/**_codi breiche+gwthio top y corff tuag at y llawr_**/then the leg/**_plygu'r goes whith+ishte ar ei phen+neidio'n ôl o'r llawr

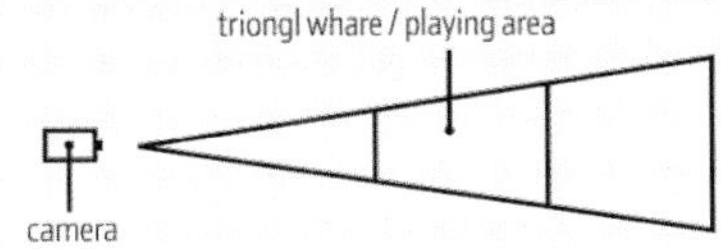

SCARFACE*

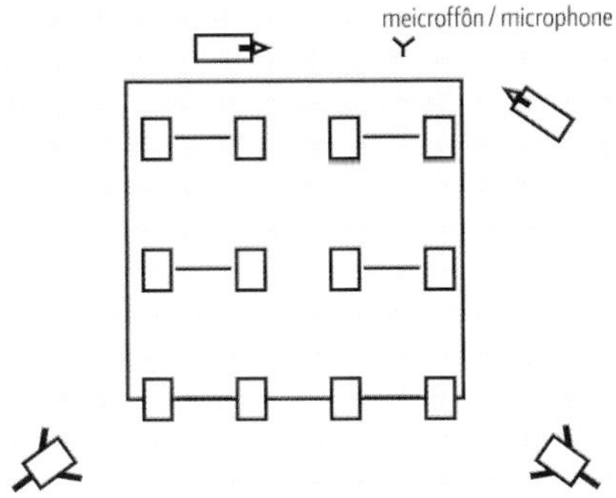

SCARFACE* BACH

SB: What about Scarface? No that wasn't...?

EL: No I wasn't. That was alright. That was just normal stupid mess

SB: The usual...

EL: Yeah, and also because Scarface, by the time I got to Scarface I hadn't been funded for six years so I felt like a right idiot. I was going to say twat

SB: Twat!

EL: I felt like a twat

club luz

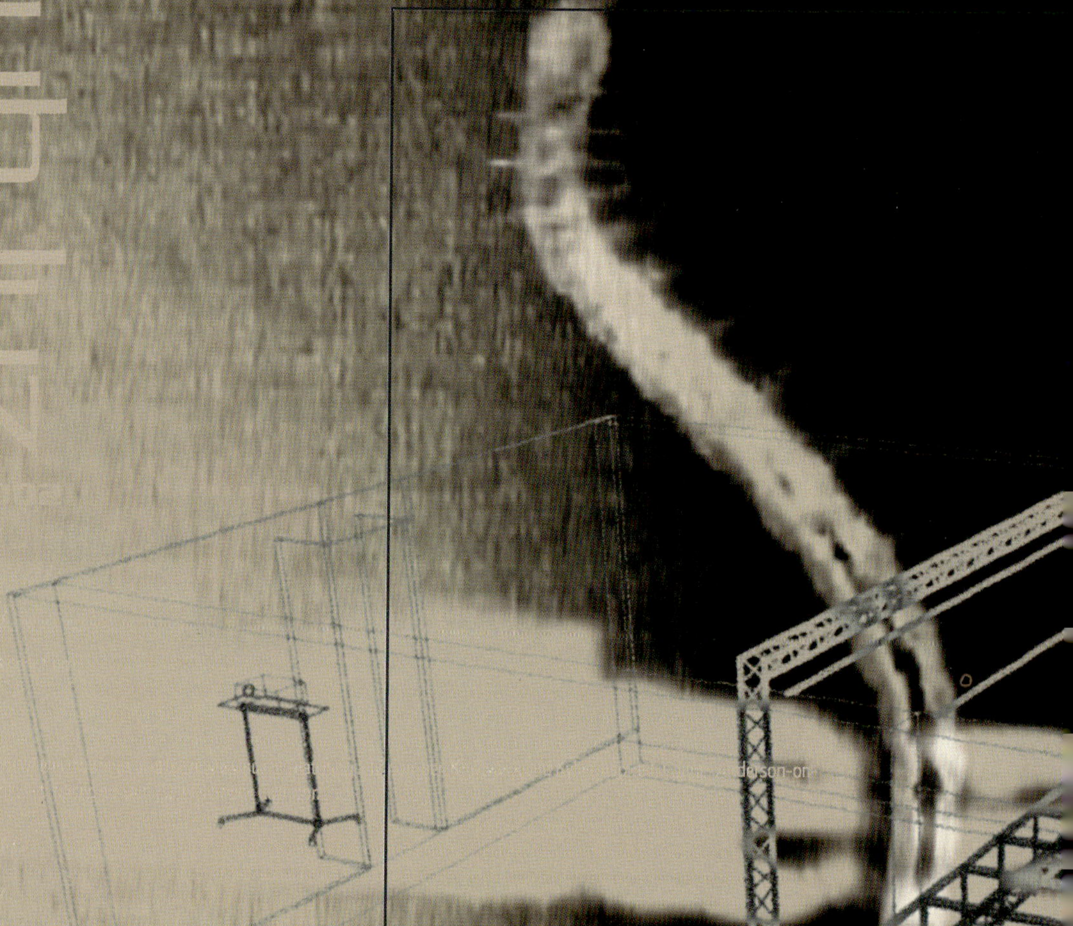

... and choreography. Shock Corridor is the set, 12 numbers

... who believes he is white and a member of the Ku Klux Klan.

... expression of a self-loathing learned on the wrong side of

... at the lone microphone leaves the film behind and ...

... grief, extreme solutions and the redemptive power

... hunan- ...

... ffilm ar ôl, llunia ddilyniant, o dan ysbrydoliaeth

... sy'n olrhain aralliad, ymgais, galar, eithafiaeth a phrynediagaeth canu pop.

... gan Rheinallt H. Rowlands a'r gwaith ffilm gan Chris Nurse.

... yng Nghaeredin yn ystod yr ŵyl ar ymylon yr ŵyl fawr yno, a chipio gwobr Total Theatre, a gynnigir gan

... am waith theatr/dawns arbrofol.

180° stop 180° flip short life automatic/spiral 1 spiral 2/imaginary pink link component/dumb friction free motion/max torque bore and stroke/high line replica/german car/german car/yn symud/yn llonydd/ hofran cynnal paratoi

Club luz_**7.chrome machine_180°**/_troi o'r llawr ar y dde a chodi reit lan i sefyll_stop/**stop**/sydyn iddo wrth iddo arafu gyda'r droed whith_sefydlu_/**180° flip**/_troi a cherdded_/**short life automatic**/_falle 4 cam i'r dde_sefyll_/**spiral 1**/ plygu'r coese_cyrcydu_penglunie'n cyrraedd y llawr_traed yn sythu o dan corff_gwthio chydig ar y dde i godi'r clunie o'r canol mwyn ishte ar y dde+phwyso ar y llaw dde_corff yn cadw fynd_/**spiral 2**/_penglunie yn datod wrth i'r traed ddisgrifio 180° gan symud o o dan y corff mas i'r whith+sythu_trosglwyddo o'r glun dde i'r whith_glanio ar y whith+y fraich whith wedi cyrraedd i gadw'r corff o'r llawr trwy gwrlo o dan yr ysgwydd_pwyse ar y glun whith a'r penelin whith_/**imaginary pink link component**/_y fraich dde yn cyrraedd_y fraich whith yn sythu a thynnu'n ôl_y canol yn tynnu'r coese fiwn_y llaw++fraich dde yn symud o'r llawr_yn tynnu am 'n ôl ychydig i gydbwyso_gosod y droed dde ar bwys penglun blyg y goes whith_y fraich whith a'r goes dde yn angor i'r goes whith sy'n ymestyn â'r droed yn arwain yn bell mas yn syth ar hyd y llawr ac ochor fas y glun yn rhedeg ar hyd wyneb y llawr_yn tynnu'r corff ar ei hôl_yn ei achosi i droi eto i'r cyfeiriad arall ar y bola_/**dumb friction-free motion**/_corff yn tynnu 'i hun bron at gwrcwd llawr_breiche yn gwthio cyn cyrraedd a'i osod ar y glun dde_ei defnyddio fel man troi i chwipio'r coese 180° eto i'r whith_rhòl+glanio_/**max torque**/_y fraich whith yn syth mas o dan pen_y dde yn glanio'n blyg o fla'n corff i gryfhau'r gosod_trosglwyddo'r pwyse at y fraich dde gan ei defnyddio i godi'r corff a rhyddhau'r whith_y whith yn symud trwy 90° gan wthio/llithro dan y dde_/**bore and stroke**/_mas i gyfeiriad y gynulleidfa_gorwedd pen ucha'r corff_/**high line replica**/_y benglun dde yn plygu a thynnu'r goes dde lan at y fraich dde_ennyd o gronni egni_y goes dde yn gwthio+sythu am 'n ôl ac yn tynnu'r corff gyda'i_yn achosi'r corff i ddod i'w ishte a throi_cadw'r traed o'r llawr_troi o'r glun whith i'r dde a'r dwylo++breiche yn trosglwyddo o'r whith at y dde i'w wthio rownd_ail wthiad gan y fraich++llaw dde yn gorfodi'r corff i godi ar 'i benglunie_cadw'r clunie'n syth_cwarter tro i'r whith_gadel y corff suddo i'r whith+gosod y brieche i'w droi eto i'r whith_y man troi yw'r benglun whith yn ffafrio'r dde chydig cyn diwedd_wedi tro a hanner suddo ar y dde a'r fraich whith yn cryfhau'r gosod fel uchod_gwthio â'r fraich dde i godi'r corff drwy dro tri chwarter i'r whith_y goes dde sy'n ei wthio bron at godi'n llawn_/**german car**/_suddo'n ôl i'r llawr ar y whith a chyrraedd fflat y cefen yn gyflym_plygu'r corff i ddod i'w ishte_troi ar y pen ôl i'r whith_/**german car**/_gosod y traed_/**yn symud**/_gorwedd yn ôl gan adel y coese'n blyg_gadel i'r coese suddo i'r whith ochor yn ochor i'r llawr_/**yn llonydd** /_sythu'r coese a dechre gwthio mwyn troi'r corff yn rhòl i'r whith_cadw droi hyd i'r law++braich dde orfodi 'ddo beido_gwthio'r corff i ishte â choese syth sy'n anelu i gyfeiriad cefen llwyfan_/**hofran**/_plygu'r coese a rhòl i ddod i'r ishte ar ben y coese plyg yn wynebu'r gynulleidfa_/**cynnal paratoi**

Club Luz

Shock Corridor set
12 numbers based on Sam Fuller's 1963 film, Shock Corridor

1. ysbyty 1/hospital 1
split brain
2. breuddwyd/dream
3. B3
being an alien
4. esprit de corps
being in/out
5. mary/david
segue
6. those were the days
national song
7. chrome machine
trad. electro machine song
big and dumb
8. montana
moroder, 2 national icons and a corrective persona
9. scarfacebach
extreme solutions
10. ysbyty 2/hospital 2
last song
11. surf's up 1
still here/not
12. surf's up 2
walkout music

money to the end. It was the end of Slate money – it was burning to the end. And I'd pick up work in Glasgow...

SB: So the big push on Scarface* was '99 then wasn't it - And got some of it funded in 2000?

EL: Yeah – kind of after the event really!

SB: So did you feel with Scarface* that again, from the outside again, that felt like it was another leap?

EL: Yes – I don't know what kind of leap it was but it's the show that's been best received you know because, I don't know... it had that fantastic gimmick! And I think because it's got a classic narrative...

SB: It's already got that familiarity...

EL: You know this narrative already even if you've never seen the film, you know what's going to happen. But it's the physicality of Al Pacino you know – because part of my thing on stage is not to be there at all, because part of me is introverted and quite inward and yet I'm in a job which asks you to be outward – it's the corrective in some way! But I think his physicality made me think about my physicality for the rest of the next three years. It's pretty active and outwards, pure will power – the world will not get the better of him! And none of his moves are inward at all, he doesn't bow his head, it doesn't roll down into his chest, the shoulders... he's out in space all the time and that, I think, filtered in and answered something... because I began to think about my physicality which can be a retiring one or an ambivalent one where I show something and refuse to reveal it at the same time and a lot of people have said about my work – it's elliptical, obtuse and you're kind of not telling us what you mean, because I didn't want to, was scared to as well. And I think is that a characteristic of this nation where you have been so intruded upon, where it has been so insisted that you are included and that you are included through the operation of the English language you know – whether you want to or not – you think well maybe it's not surprising that we keep something in reserve here, that our outward actions are kind of cloudy sometimes?

SB: There's a kind of veil between?

EL: Yes – the necessary veil really. Why would you give out any more! Because it won't ever be used for your benefit, it's just more information.

SB: So you keep the maximum to yourself?

EL: Yes. So in a way Al Pacino became the corrective model. You could do anything through him! People would say 'oh you look like him' you know and I didn't look like him but you adopt the icon and you adopt the physicality and the physicality was not difficult to adopt that was the strange thing – so it's obviously in there.

SB: Maybe that's the thing then? It's opening out – having gone from opening out in Once upon....

EL: I wasn't bothered by physicality in **Once Upon A Time** and I wasn't bothered by physicality in **Lla'th**, I think by **Scarface*** I noticed a tendency...but definitely the idea of his physicality revealed something, I think.

SB: Do you think that's changed forever now?

EL: I think once you have the awareness you can't undo the awareness. I can't undo1996 and **Once Upon A Time** showed my feelings for the culture and the next two shows that I'm doing or did **[Club Luz** and **Stafell/Repulsion]** address physicality...your body and your physical and mental health. **Club Luz**, scurtling back to poetic narrative –– it's a meditation on the figure of Trent [one of the lead characters in Sam Fuller's film, **Shock Corridor**] and his condition and our condition as Welsh people. There are no parallels in the action after that.

SB: Did that idea occur to you during Scarface*?

EL: Yes. **Club Luz** was formed during the tour of little **Scarface*** – **Sawn-off Scarface** – because we were going round Europe you know and suddenly you're in a country where people speak four languages –... it was a kind of multi-lingual piece and it refers to David Bowie working in Berlin, Mary Hopkin, Dave Datblygu and American film and I think of it as a kind of Berlin show - a bit teutonic, as somebody said at the end of it, and it is – it's monochrome and I was in love with Kraftwerk and I loved being in Berlin. It was a European show. I'd made American shows up until then. And it was influenced by 9/11 and just everything because I began to think how can you be a small country in the world and do no harm to nobody and leave no shit whatsoever so I wanted to make a show which was about a virtual future in Wales – but I couldn't make it because I had to deal with current, pressing things and the current pressing thing is this feeling of self-loathing, cultural self-loathing. Which I'd started to address in **Scarface*** because it's obvious that the problem was that the narratives that you receive about your culture come from the outside, from big, massive outside – **Club Luz** went into exploring that but it went more into what that feels like – it wasn't so politicised in a way as **Scarface*** is in a tacky sort of way! But I couldn't deal with the future of Wales because I couldn't think of one. Oh God!

SB: Was that around the Anne Robinson time?

EL: All those things went into it but....

SB: This is just around 9/11?

EL: Since 9/11 happened you thought well there's only one subject now which is how you work as a nation in the world. How do you operate? You don't start from point nought on anything. But I couldn't sketch out what the steps would be even in an impossible way to achieving things. Then we were touring big **Scarface*** as well – we'd been to Kosovo. It was full of UN compounds. We had a UN compound straight outside the hotel. Garrisons of French, German, Welsh soldiers, Italian soldiers – everything, this is what their past has led them to and what was their future is going to be and I was thinking of all those things and we kept meeting officials, and I began to think I've got to make a Welsh 'desk set' – they don't exist - the Welsh flag and Welsh notepaper and all those things, that's the future then – that we have a seat at the UN – as Plaid Cymru said! But I just couldn't think beyond – the present. And then I saw Trent in **Shock Corridor**, I watched it because I liked the title. I looked at the film and thought there's nothing here. The I saw Trent and thought oh God I know what that is! [Trent is black but thinks he is white and a member of the Ku Klux Klan]. That's what it became then, in a way I grabbed the nearest thing possibly – but the more I looked the more I see right up until now how much of that is in still here – it's still in this country! Fuck, it's awful! It was invisible to me before. The work I'm doing now on the Nesta project is still that kind of – these behaviours which I've learned because of the relationship with the country next door – they show up on you, somewhere along the line.

[1] miriam delahunter [2] richard morgan [3] john rowley [4] janek alexander [5] steve vearncombe [6] giles parberry [7] edwina williams-jones [8] siân richards [9] rhian davies [10] geoff haines [11] rachel whitehead [12] steve fisher [13] jesse schwenk [14] 2 x feiolynydd [15] roger owen [16] sam owen [17] mary owen [18] ceri collier [19] sean tuan john [20] cliff mclucas [21] curig a jonathan [22] cathy [23] caryl davies [24] suzanne phillips [25] owen wright [26] richard [27] lowri jones [28] barney [29] alison woods [30] y ferch o'r iseldiroedd [31] euros lewis [32] technegydd lla'th mowr [33] trevor turton [34] gerald tyler [35] angus ford [36] lucy byatt [37] tystion [38] athina vahla [39] rob pleasance [40] leigh canning [41] james tyson [42] gordana vnuk [43] dan young [44] clive williams [45] guy passmore [46] john thorne [47] siôn williams [48] beryl davies-griffiths [49] marc rees [50] bets [51] andré stitt [52] dewi evans [53] chris nurse [54] sarah broughton [55] margaret ames

thought & memory: two conversations with daniel morden

jeff teare

THOUGHT AND MEMORY – TWO CONVERSATIONS

Daniel, in the introduction to your book, Weird Tales from the Storyteller you say, 'I have always been a storyteller'. Could you expand on that? For example, when did 'always' start?

I was a very bookish child. I was the sort of child who would devour books. I used to walk to school by myself and I used to tell myself stories as I walked to school. And I used to write them down, interminable stories....

You actually wrote them down?

They'd be drawing on what I'd seen on the television, what I'd read in a comic or what I'd read in a book so they'd range from Marvel comic heroes to Greek divinities, sometimes in the same tale. If I was making it up, I was always searching for a way by which the story, and especially the end of the story, seemed to be satisfying. So the question, 'What made a story satisfying?' was the question behind all that mumbling on my way to school. What made the resolution of a story fulfilling?

My parents gave me a copy of Norse Myths by Kevin Crossley-Holland when I was thirteen, and I remember reading about the god Odin who had a raven on each shoulder. One was called Thought and one was called Memory. I remember being very intrigued by that. So I tried to find out more about those images but, by doing so, very soon I ended up in an academic world that I was not really happy with or interested in.

So, I've always been a storyteller because I've always been telling stories as a way of exploring narrative form, as a way of 'unriddling' stories, as a way of trying to answer for myself what it was about an image that fascinated me. And that's really the major reason for my still doing it.

So, the next question has to be how did that 'bookish child' get to be a professional storyteller?

Well, I did an English and Drama degree, at Goldsmith's in London. I didn't enjoy the drama. It was a theoretical course, analysing theatre and drama more than I wanted to. I wanted to perform. And I didn't enjoy the English greatly as I found so much of what I was compelled to read just didn't have the richness of mythology and fairytale.

Anyway, I came out the other side and started my own theatre company, very much in the model of Gwent Theatre, trying to tour community venues....

there was a hunter.

Could you expand on that?

In my teens I went to Gwent Young People's Theatre and Gwent Theatre was, at that point, a TIE (Theatre in Education) company that would also go round village halls. I used to go and see their TIE productions on a regular basis in schools and I was always very impressed by the way they could transform school halls into, say, a jungle, purely on the strength of a few things they'd said. I loved the idea of taking accessible, enjoyable 'good night out' theatre to venues like village halls where nobody in the audience had come further than about ten miles – theatre as a social event. I started a company in London which attempted to do the same kinds of thing, but around Lewisham, not south Wales. We did a lot of street theatre and we toured round local schools and parks. Very soon it collapsed, because we were all in it in order to perform and nobody was in it in order to administrate. There was no money in it, it was more like a religion than a theatre company...

He had four sons and a wife whose belly was full with another child.

Yes, I've been in a couple of those....

So it collapsed. And also, I got disenchanted with the devising process. I always felt that the end result was what everyone would grudgingly agree on, rather than including any of the elements suggested along the way that were exciting or controversial. So then I tried to find a way of performing that didn't involve anything, or anybody, other than myself. I didn't want to be carting bits of set and a lighting rig around. In fact I wanted to find a way of being able to tour by public transport.

At that point I ran across a course at the City Lit in Central London which was a storytelling course run by Pomme Clayton. I went to that and she told a story about Baba Yaga, a Russian witch. In this one, three knights go by a girl who is walking into a forest; three knights ride past on horses. The first one is black, completely black – his armour, his horse, everything. The second one is red and the third one is yellow. They gallop past and she hides and watches them. Later on in the story, it is explained to her that the first one is the night, the second one, the red one, is the dawn and the third one is the sun and they are controlled by Baba Yaga. The image, and the idea that all of these three are in the command of this witch struck me with the same level of resonance as the image of Odin with the two ravens. I thought this was something that I could do. If one human being could sit in front of me and talk, basically in conversational terms, and reach that part of me that is very rarely reached, then I'd like to do that myself.

The hunter went out into the woods one day but he didn't come back.

Pomme was a member of a group called the Company of Storytellers, with Hugh Lupton and Ben Haggarty. They were terribly encouraging. They'd take me on tour with them and I'd start to do turns and they'd discuss what I'd done and give me advice, and then I began to advertise myself as a storyteller, around schools mainly. Schools were my apprenticeship and I still regard them as an important part of what I do, not just because of the children that are hearing the stories but also because I think that there is no formal professional development for a storyteller but if you're in front of kids on a regular basis you have to stay grounded. Kids are not polite so if they're not enjoying something they very easily display their displeasure. So it's a good training ground.

So how long have you now been a professional storyteller?

The wife and sons waited

Fourteen, fifteen years.

And now, well, I suppose you wouldn't have a 'standard week' of work but in a month, or a year, what range of stuff are you now doing?

and then searched,

searched

Within a month it would go from visiting a nursery school, to book-weeks, perhaps writing workshops connected to storytelling in a primary school. I might be doing a 'Talented Writers' Squad' which is active in this area (Gwent), where kids who particularly enjoy reading and writing will work with me for a day. Then I might also be doing adult shows at arts centres, literature festivals, etc. So the stories I might be telling might range from something equivalent to Jack and the Beanstalk to the Iliad.

searched,

searched

I know you work internationally; are there differences around the world to performance approach, to what the storyteller does?

then they gave up.

Europe is pretty homogeneous. I can go to a festival in Norway and perform there and the performers who are alongside me performing in their native language, their manner is not so different to what I'm doing. But America and Canada are radically different. They don't draw on the same material, partly because there's a big copyright issue over there. If you tell a story like Raven Steals the Light from the north-west coast of

America then what they say is that you're appropriating the story from another culture and it doesn't belong to you and you haven't got permission. Plus somebody else might have told Raven Steals the Light and actually copyrighted their rendition of it and then they are able to sue you for telling what is, after all, a traditional story. So, lots of people tell personal reminiscence stories; stories based on personal experience, which I do not do at all. And they are always astonished at how British storytellers are almost still when they are speaking, when they are telling, because the compulsion in America and Canada is to enact an awful lot. It may be to do with the fact that it's big business there, so they tend to be playing, at festivals, to thousands of people. That probably has had an effect on their performance style.

His wife and his sons forgot about him.

What about the more folk tradition of it all, when it is just one person telling a story to a few others in a pub or a kitchen. Do you ever come across that?

Yes, there's been an ongoing debate within storytelling in Britain which has culminated in a delineation between two different traditions, one being what's called the 'fireside' tradition, like the Seanachai in Ireland, the man or woman who everyone knows can tell stories so the community would visit them to hear stories. Then there's the performance tradition, which is the person who is paid to do something that others cannot. But the two traditions have always been communicating with one another. For example, the Turkish ashiks, the Turkish bards, do ostentatious displays of their skills. They might ask the audience for a theme, then they put a pin between their lips so that it's pressed against their upper lip. They begin to play their musical instrument, which is like a lute, and they improvise a song on the theme they've been given without using certain consonants because if they do the pin goes through the lip. So, that's ridiculously ostentatious as a display of skill. However, they do say that they learnt most of their fundamental storytelling skills from their grandmother in the village when they were children. So the folk and the performance traditions always have been communicating with each other, influencing one another and that still continues now in Britain. There are some venues that are still very much fireside venues. You, as the visiting teller, are expected to listen to the local performers tell their stories and then you tell your own. It's very small-scale and it's very folksy, very intimate. The organisers are proud of the sense of it being a community. And then, on the other side, there's the Hay Festival or Beyond the Border at Llantwit Major, where you're on stage, there's theatre lights, you've got a radio mike, the stage lights go on, the house lights go down so you can no longer see your audience and you hold forth into the void.

I've seen you in a village library near Swansea and 'performing' the Odyssey in a fairly large theatre, under lights, to a full house. Now, in my opinion they are, in essence, the same thing, if not in appearance, but it would be quite easy to say that they weren't. What do you think?

This is a conversation that people in the storytelling world have all the time. Lots of people like some things that I do and other things that I do they say are 'theatre'. But I'm trying to get to the same place in both instances. What I'm trying to do is vanish. What I'm trying to do in theatres, with my colleague Hugh Lupton particularly, is to try to create something in collaboration with the audience, so that I disappear and the story takes over. There are strategies that one must employ in order to reach that point and every room, every story and every audience influences what strategies I select.

Does that say something about your selection of stories per gig?

Well, the market influences that a lot. We have been stunned, Hugh and I, that there is a market for the Greek material that we do, the Iliad and the Odyssey. We started doing them because we wanted to and we've been very surprised by the size of audiences we get and the number of places that actually want that material. It's been wonderful because we started out doing them because, well, it made us feel like storytellers, we wanted to tell these stories. But there are an awful lot of other stories that I've never had the resources to explore in the way that I would like to. Mainly because I just don't see, effectively, where I'm going to find a market for them.

Eventually the wife gave birth
to another son.
And
the baby
grew and grew
until he could walk.
And then he began to make
– noises.
Then the noises became
– words.
And his first words were:
Where's my father?

The others remembered.

So there are stories you'd like to tell that you don't think that there's an audience for?

Yes.... No, no.... It's a strange thing. Ghost stories, for example. If you say you're doing ghost stories then sometimes you get a strange reaction. I did an evening last week in a remote church in Pembrokeshire, and it had been billed as ghost stories so I said all right, that's what I'll do. It was absolutely packed. The vicar stood up at the beginning and said that there were more people in the church that night than at a service for something like two centuries. So there are certain areas, like ghost stories, where you can immediately draw an audience. People are fascinated by them but ghost stories are actually very hard to tell. What people want is to be frightened but when you actually do that and frighten them, they're disturbed, and they're unhappy.

They went out into the woods again. They came to a clearing; in the green grass they saw glowing, bleached bones.

You give them what they want but they realise they don't like it?

The first of the four sons said: 'I could put these bones in their proper pattern.' So he did. They cut the grass and for hours he carefully reassembled his father's skeleton.

Yes, so it's very tricky, this business of whether there's an audience for something. Sometimes, if the audience is already there and you tell them a story they would not necessarily have chosen to come and hear, they very often love it, absolutely love it. So, the challenge is trying to present what it is you want to do so that the audience do enjoy it and think that they've had an exciting evening out.

To what extent, now, are you in a position where there is, for want of a better word, a storytelling industry, or at least a regular circuit?

There is a circuit growing, particularly as a result of the Greek material we're doing, around the literature festivals. The Greek material is wonderful because we can tell the Iliad and then at the end of the evening we can tell the organisers that next year we can tell the Odyssey. We've now got a mailing list of people who've come and enjoyed the Iliad and next year we can offer the Odyssey and now the year after that we can go and do Metamorphoses. What happens the year after that I don't know. We are getting to visit an awful lot of literature festivals, arts festivals. But generally storytelling is pretty poorly served. People, festival organisers, don't know much about the art form as such but if there's a story they can connect with, like the Iliad, the Odyssey, Sheherazade, then they'll say, 'Oh, we might get an audience for that,' but they're not programming the storyteller, they're programming the story.

Is there any storyteller around, other than your good self of course, who pulls an audience just on their own name?

I don't pull on my own name. The answer is no. There is nobody out there in Britain who, purely by dint of their name, is guaranteed a house, an audience.

Let's talk about what you're actually doing as a storyteller. Something you said earlier which interests me, as a theatre director, is that in the end you're trying to disappear and let the story 'be'.

Eventually they stood over the white bones on the brown earth.

Yes, that's right.

That seems to have a bearing on what you've just said that there isn't any star storyteller who can tell whatever they like, but it's the story that has to work for an audience. So is that actually the nature of the art form? Or is that too bullshitty a question?

It's an absolutely valid question; what I'm worried about is a bullshitty answer. I think every teller that you ask would have a different response to this particular question. But, for me, the answer is yes, that's what it's all about. It's about managing to purvey the story in such a way that it comes alive to an audience. That is a very delicate business, a very delicate business, trying to use techniques. Anyone doing anything really well makes it look easy. So what you're trying to do all the time is look as though this thing is happening in front of an audience in a tremendously simple and easy way, whereas, in fact, underneath the apparently calm surface there's an awful lot of hard work going on.

The second brother said:

'I could put flesh on these bones.'

Having seen you do a few gigs, Daniel, I think you succeed very well. I think you're very good at what you do. The thing that fascinates me as someone who's dabbled in theatrical storytelling; narrative theatre I suppose, is how do you personally choose your stories? I understand the market requirements, and so on, but where do you find the stories you tell and what exactly are you looking for? Or is it not as conscious as that?

And he kept a vigil for days, collecting herbs burning incense and whispering words in a clacking tongue.

Veins and muscles and sinew crept across the skeleton

No, it isn't as conscious as that, though I have tried to be more 'conscious' recently; I suppose more businesslike, because I want to go back to those venues that have had a great experience. I want to go back and reach those audiences again. So Metamorphoses was a deliberate decision. We wanted to find something with a classical theme and we began to look at Ovid. But if we'd found Metamorphoses to be tremendously dry and boring source material then we just wouldn't have done it.

The third one said: 'skin, it needs skin, and hair.'

But when you're doing your bread and butter stories, how do you chose them?

In that particular moment?

For weeks he sweated over a boiling pot
until a bitter taste congealed in the bottom of the cauldron.
He took it and smeared it over the head
the chest
the arms
the hands
the legs
the feet
of his father.

And hair and gleaming skin made

the fleshy thing

a corpse.

Well yes, but how do you get your repertoire together, and then how do you decide which ones you're going to do at any particular gig?

First of all, for the first eight years or so probably, the phone rings and somebody says, 'Do you know any Abyssinian stories?' and you say, 'Is that north Abyssinian or south Abyssinian?' and they go, 'Oh, er, north Abyssinian', and you say, 'Yes, I know some'. Then you put down the phone and go and get a book. But out of that will come some stuff that you think, 'Ah that's really good. Is there any way I can tell it outside of the context of this north Abyssinian project?'

And that's how the repertoire evolved, being offered things and then trying to make whatever is offered you work in different contexts.

I had this gig, for example, just up the road at the Ebbw Vale Garden Festival, walking around for six hours a day offering stories to anyone I met. I had this coat painted with scenes from the stories, and on the back it said, 'Daniel Morden, teller of myths, legends, ghost stories, riddles and

The fourth brother said: 'life, it needs life.'

fibs, stop me and hear one.' My repertoire absolutely ballooned because I had to find something that was right for the blokes at the bar, a bunch of infants on a school trip, a little old lady in the greenhouse.... I had to find something that would amuse and entertain everybody I met. That was a steep learning curve.

Is this all book-based or are there other sources, like on the net?

And he knelt and pushed breath between the lips of the corpse.

There are resources on the net and I do draw on them increasingly but I've got a huge library of books, and also, I just know a lot of stories now. It being a vocation, I try to go and hear whoever I can. When I first started out, practically everything I was telling I'd heard from somebody else. But after a while I became uneasy about that because I felt that the chances were I'd end up going to a lot of the same venues as the people that I'd heard the stories from. So I tried to broaden the repertoire a bit more.

You were saying in America that there's a copyright issue.

Yes, but there's no copyright issue here. By and large everyone is generous with the material because the assumption has to be that in three or four weeks of telling a story you will have made it your own; subtly reconfigured the whole thing. And that does seem to be the case.

But if on the one hand you're trying to disappear and let the story stand alone, but on the other hand you are constantly redefining how you are going to tell that story, then a common story will be diverging every time from an original source.

Yes.

To a point where, comparative linguistics or whatever aside, they are no longer the same stories. Is that 'the ownership' of the story?

If I understand your point, I don't see that there's a problem with that. I think that's what storytellers do, they're always editing and embellishing, according to the amount of time they've got, the audience they're telling to and what might have happened in the news that day.

Yes, I noticed yesterday when I was watching you, you were doing the story The Magic Well. The last two lines in your published version are, 'And suddenly her stepsister was lovely again. But this time she was lovely outside and in.' But, both times you told it yesterday, she wasn't already 'Lovely outside and in', but it would take time for this to happen.

That text has already made a very long journey from the text that I originally encountered, which is an incredibly convoluted nineteenth-century transcription of a story told by Abram Wood, a gypsy storyteller from north Wales. So already it's made a long journey. I am very uneasy, ambivalent about books of stories, of written-down versions of my stories, because I regard all the stories I tell as work in progress. They're all on a journey to somewhere else and committing them to paper is somehow fixing them. But, the advantage of having a book out is that the book can be reaching people that you can't reach physically.

Is the business of storytelling, in the end, that you have to publish?

No, not for me. I could make more money in a week visiting schools than I will make from a book. The money I got for writing Weird Tales from the Storyteller was dismal. But my feeling is that the book goes out there in the world. I can only be in one place at a time but the book can be out there reaching people in some form and trying to do some of the things that happen in a live performance.

Sweat trickled from the fourth brother's temple. He'd given something of himself that his father might live.

In your pamphlet for The Society of Storytelling, The Language of Signs, you write, 'Stories are the language of dream, symbol,' and you talk about how when you tell a story you're not just telling the story but that you're passing something on that is somehow 'beneath' the story, the 'substory' or the 'Ur-story' or something. That would appear to be essential to what you do. Can you talk about it? I mean, presumably it wouldn't be true of an episode of Eastenders?

The hunter's belly began to lift and fall.
fingers twitched.
eyes opened.

I think in any story there is plot and there is theme, and that would be as true of an episode of Eastenders as in the Mahabarata. This returns us to one of the other questions you asked: 'What draws a storyteller to a story?' It also takes me back to where we started because very often I don't know what it is about a story that intrigues me, the image of Odin with the thought and memory crows, for example. It's the process of telling a story which is the attempt to try to discover what it is about that story that intrigues. It's a bit like me putting my tongue in the gap between my teeth over and over again.... Storytelling is the means that I have whereby I am most likely to answer that question: 'What is going on in this story? What is going on under this story?' Reading dry academic texts does not do the job for me. Reading 'new agey' analyses of stories, extrapolating into our lives.... I always find them very unsatisfying.

The hunter said:

I remember reading Hero with a Thousand Faces by Joseph Campbell and thinking, 'Yer, all very well but....'

'Where have I been?'

Yes, Hero with a Thousand Faces is an important work; well, there's The King and the Corpse by Heinrich Zimmer as well, which is smashing, but Hero with a Thousand Faces is a bit of a clever book that keeps jumping around. Campbell will be writing about Greece or something and then refer to some obscure character in Mesopotamian mythology and immediately he's lost me. But, in the end, these more or less academic books are pretty good but I'd much rather be telling those stories than attempting to come to terms with what's supposed to be behind them, culturally or anthropologically or whatever.

So, how do you see your future in storytelling, Daniel? Where, as they say in job interviews, do you want to be in three years?

I did the Edinburgh Book Festival this year. I went to see Ross Noble performing at the Assembly Rooms. He was in the 630-seater venue, £12 a ticket, and he was on for an hour. Now, of course it's going to cost a bomb putting yourself on in the Assembly Rooms. His ad seemed to be on the side of every taxi you saw, and must have cost a fortune as well, but I did look at him and think, 'He's better at what he does than I am at what I do, but it's not so different.' I do think sometimes that if one of the big 'alternative' agents; managements, like Addison Cresswell or Avalon Management got to see some storytelling, somebody out there might think, 'There could be some money in this.'

At the moment storytelling suffers terribly from being branded as just hippy rambling, and if only it could get out a little bit more, onto a bigger stage if you like, then I reckon there's a tipping-point at which people would think, 'Just because I see a bad storyteller that doesn't mean I don't like storytelling: I just didn't like this storyteller.' Then the art form could really take off, and then we could be out there performing proper tours rather than what happens now when I do – I don't know – ten or twelve performances of a certain story a year. With so few performances you don't get to the point with a story that you need to get to because you're just not telling the story enough. I do believe that if we can get the right people to come to see the work and recognise its potential; at that point it could really take off.

Some of the personal viewpoint stand-ups that you see – I saw one last week – some of what she did is very close to what you do…

'You have been dead but now you are alive,' said his wife.

It can be.

She walked the hunter back to the village.

When they get into riffing about social mores, alcopops or whatever; well, a storyteller might not do that, but when they talk about something their mother told them or maybe they make up a story based on an observation.... Do you think you would ever have to shift more towards that? Is it the traditional nature of the stories that scares the stand-up comedy audience? It sounds like a folk club?

I think there is a danger of that. People think, 'What have these stories got to do with me? If this story is 3,000 years old what could it possibly have to do with me?' I'm going to do a festival in Vancouver soon where they've got me on with dub poets and performance poets and they are trying very hard to make the point that storytellers can be gritty and urban too. My point, which is in the Language of Signs pamphlet, is that just because a story is 3,000 years old doesn't mean that it's not addressing the same issues that we are now: gritty urban issues. I don't really think that we've changed that much.

Interesting thing; I work in a different area; I mean, last week I was working on a

He
At first he was weak; he couldn't walk for long.
He took to making.
He took a stick and carved images on it.
Images of his journey from Life to Death and back again.

Shakespeare workshop, Taming of the Shrew, but of course, if you look at how people do Shakespeare now, two or three of the plays are being adapted to Californian High Schools, including Shrew....

Yes, the play may be adapted to its audience, but the story of the play remains the same.

Doesn't that take us back to the nature of story itself – what is the story actually doing? To what extent do you have to keep the traditional trappings of the story or can you adapt it so far that it becomes almost unrecognisable? Many traditional stories are meant to be to do with rites of passage, for example. Well, I saw an episode of The Simpsons that had a certain essence of that; it was clearly about a rite of passage, in this case for Lisa. Do you think you'd ever go that far away, as far as Springfield even, from your traditional sources?

No, and I don't think it's necessary to do so. Inevitably one is adapting story and inevitably one is compromising the essence, some of the essential elements in order to purvey it to an audience. For example, in Homer's Iliad, no human being gets to make their own decision: gods and goddesses manipulate them into doing everything. For an audience member now, that is unacceptable, because it feels as though all the characters are just puppets and that world view is just not how we see ourselves. So we, in our version of the Iliad, have pulled back massively on the gods' meddling, the gods' manipulation. We allow characters to make decisions for themselves. But I am terribly wary of the business of making Gwydion of the Mabinogion into a scientist who constructs a woman à la Frankenstein. I've only ever seen it done clumsily. I think the baby goes out with the bath water. I can't see myself ever setting a traditional story in a contemporary milieu.

He attached a cow's tail to the stick.
It was a cow tail switch, for keeping flies at bay.

Daniel: you're at a party and someone asks what you do. You say, 'I'm a storyteller.' What reaction do you get, or expect?

All of his sons coveted it.

The hunter said: 'I will give this switch to the one who has done most for me.'

It's a great conversation starter, though it does make the conversation rather one-sided because then you get a succession of questions. 'You can make a living at that?' That's the first one. 'Do you have a book, a script, do you recite?' So then there's the conversation about how you know what story you're going to tell and how it's going to end but you're not quite sure what words you're going to use. And finally, very often, people ask for a story.

So, when us theatricals, artists or whatever, say that people do need stories...

Yes, we even make up stories in our dreams, we try to come to terms with our experiences, we do these fundamental things within a narrative, a sequence of events. Films, soaps: they're all basically trying to hook you into a gripping story.

Eastenders can bring back a dead character so what's so special about mythology?

True, but Eastenders is absolutely absurd in the respect that everyone goes through a major life crisis every month and then has to forget about it because they've got to have another one.

Which of his sons got the switch?

As I understand it, this essay about you, or conversation with you doing most of the talking, is part of a book about performance artists in Wales. Now I'm not entirely sure what a 'performance artist' is. A storyteller is obviously someone who performs, and is an artist, but do you see yourself as a 'performance artist'? I mean a guy, or woman who covers themselves in paint and rolls about on paper in front of people, that's maybe a 'performance artist' but do you see yourself as 'just' a storyteller? I mean, I know you're soon on the same bill as a rapper but…

Well, it's more a case of what others see as a storyteller. I'd be surprised if a rapper saw what I do as relevant to what they do. I'd be really chuffed if they did but I think they would assume that I was coming from a different culture. I see myself as part of, really, a literary movement. I would connect more with poets, like Catherine Fisher, than I would with a theatre company. I would feel more of a connection, more of a sense of kinship with someone who is trying to reach some kind of truth through a sequence of words on a piece of paper, rather than a collaborative art. There's something about the individual voice....

I remember years and years ago I booked Linton Kwesi Johnson for a gig at the Theatre Royal, Stratford East. He was appearing with a band but at least a couple of things that he did were stories that seemed to have some kind of traditional form. Could you ever see yourself moving in that direction?

I saw Linton Kwesi Johnson doing those gigs and I found it very inspiring. When I was sixteen, in my school Eisteddfod they had a poetry competition and I recited Five Nights of Bleeding in a Rastafarian accent. Mind you, I got through to the final and my drama teacher asked me if it couldn't be three nights... but I do find that crossover kind of work intriguing.

I think the televised stories I did for Double Yellow were an attempt to employ the techniques and rhythms of television to traditional storytelling. It is interesting to step over into other art forms. I dabble in theatre every couple of years, try to get on the television, do some stuff on the radio, because it throws what I'm doing into relief. For a start, if it's recorded, I can see it, or hear it, again. Because if you perform by yourself an awful lot, you can forget exactly what it is that you are doing. The books are another way of doing that, a way of using the material through another art form so I learn about my own.

So, maybe that's enough for today. Or perhaps I should prolong your agony... what's your next gig?

I'm launching a triple CD telling of the Iliad for children, at Key Stage Two, with a resource pack, at the British Museum. I'm very excited about that because children just don't get the chance to experience this material and it's our birthright. It's one of the two central, oldest epics in Europe. Achilles' Heel, The Wooden Horse... there are images that resonate across our culture. They've been touchstones for artists, writers, playwrights ever since. And it's wonderful to try to have a means by which kids can get reacquainted with all this story, so that all the other art referring to it actually means something.

Are you actually telling any of it on that day?

Yes.

I'd like to come to that.

Great, I'll keep you posted.

The fifth one, the youngest one. Because he remembered.

And you are only truly dead when you are forgotten.

Right, so: it's a few weeks later and I've seen the launch of your epic War With Troy at the British Museum, in the Reading Room, no less. Time for the second part of our conversation.

Daniel: we talked about your classic stories a bit last time. Do you, in your own mind, demarcate between, say, the Homeric tradition of the Iliad and the Odyssey and any other sort of story that you might tell?

In the sense of it as a story, no I don't; in the sense of a piece to perform, I do, if only because I take a deeper breath before I start the Homeric material. It involves a level of concentration and a level of thought that is greater than anything else that I do.

How many times have you done, say, the Iliad?

We do it probably ten to twelve times a year, and we started doing it in March of 2001.

And you've got the three big classics now: the Iliad, the Odyssey and...

The third one that's just come this year – Metamorphoses, which is drawing on Ovid. But, that has a very different structure to the other two, because the other two are continuous narratives, whereas Metamorphoses is an anthology. There's a frame story within which self-contained stories exist.

'Truth travelled among people.
Truth walked naked through the streets.
He wanted to tell them about himself.

And you were saying last time that Metamorphoses is, at least partially, an audience-development project, so that you could go back and revisit audiences who've enjoyed the Homeric stuff with another big classic story.

Yes, that's true. Like I said, if we perform the Iliad and it gets a good house then we can immediately go back to the venue and say, 'Look, that audience that you've now got on your mailing list enjoyed this performance. You could have an equivalent one next year with the same storytellers, the same format: the Odyssey, and then after that you can have Metamorphoses.' That's the thought behind it. And that's also why we've changed the Roman names in Metamorphoses into Greek ones. So Jupiter becomes Zeus, Minerva becomes Athene and so on. So far it's worked very well.

So this process: repeat bookings for classical storytelling, is already happening?

Yes. This week we're going to Newcastle, to the Live Theatre, for the third successive year. Last year we sold out the venue so we are really building up an audience for this material, which is very exciting. And what's more, the theatre is hired – the local storytelling group took the risk of hiring the venue and it's paid off for them.

The size of these stories raises the number one obvious question that I think I managed to avoid last time, 'How do you remember them?'

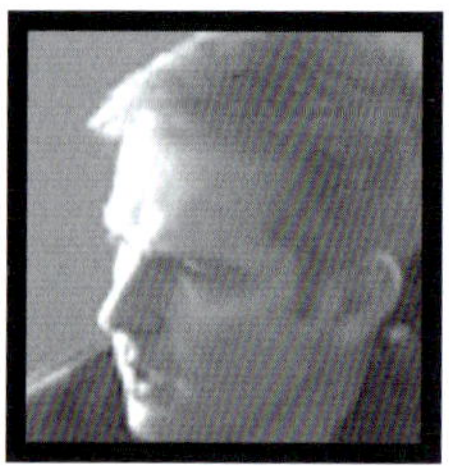
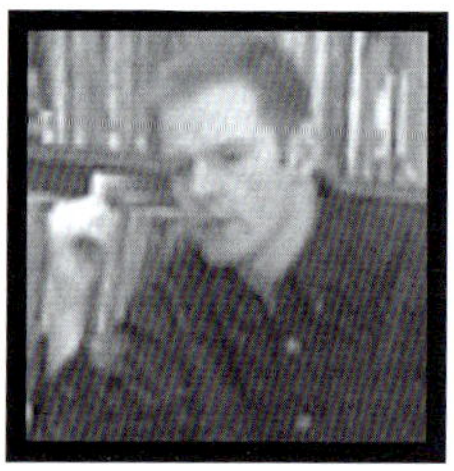
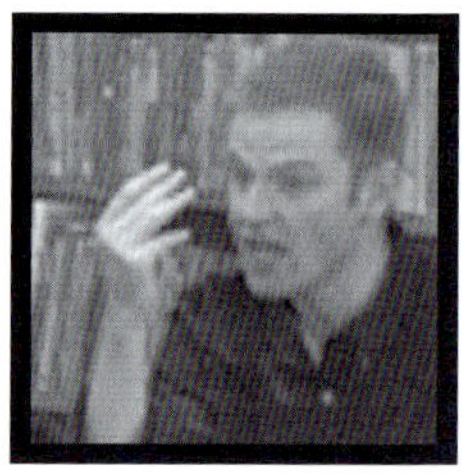

But they did not greet him as a friend.
The people would turn and run away.
Truth found himself creeping from shadow to shadow.

Well, let's take the Iliad as the example. It would be a lie to say that we never wrote anything down, but it's in the initial research process that we do work with a pen and paper, as a means of organising all the material. For example, moving the story's perspective from one point of view to the other, ie from the Greek perspective to the Trojan perspective. But as soon as we started performing it, any written text that we had, soon became redundant. We were soon nipping and tucking and nipping and tucking, and in some cases embellishing, so any written text we might try to refer to would only serve to confuse us. That's why there's no script as such.

Most of the memory work is done through a series of pictures. It's done like a storyboard...

But you don't actually storyboard, or do you?

No, my draughtsmanship is not good enough. I'd like to, I'd like to get to a point where I could start doing that because I'm getting more and more interested in producing books with lots of illustrations. The memory process, though, is to do with visualising the whole thing. A lot of the work on the Iliad, for example, involved Hugh and I mapping the terrain between Troy and the Greek camp and imagining exactly what the Greek camp would look like, and exactly what the characters would look like. Once that we'd agreed on that, so we had a shared world, then came the process of imagining each event very clearly as a sequence of pictures. Effectively what we're doing when we're telling a story is describing one image, and then moving to the next one. Inevitably, as in the original telling of the Homeric stories so far as we know, some of the rendition is very fixed. Even though I haven't attempted to memorise it in the way that I might learn a speech from a Shakespeare play, every time I deliver it it's close to the way I did it last time; yesterday, last month. But then there are also sequences that are pretty fluid and they rely on inspiration, my mood, the audience's response, what's been happening in the news, etc. All of these things will inform my telling of the story.

I'm very interested in what you say about how you and Hugh actually visualise the characters. Does that mean you create Odysseus in your own head? Or maybe he's just like that bloke who runs the café on the corner?

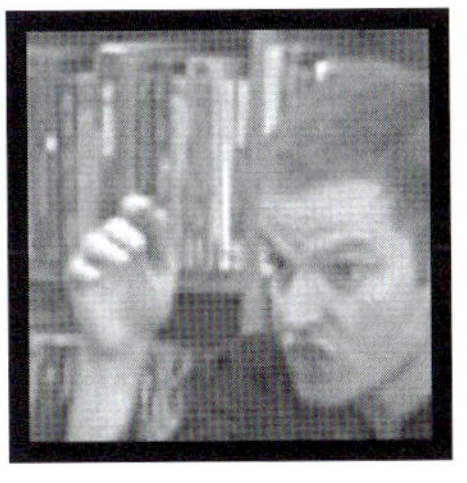

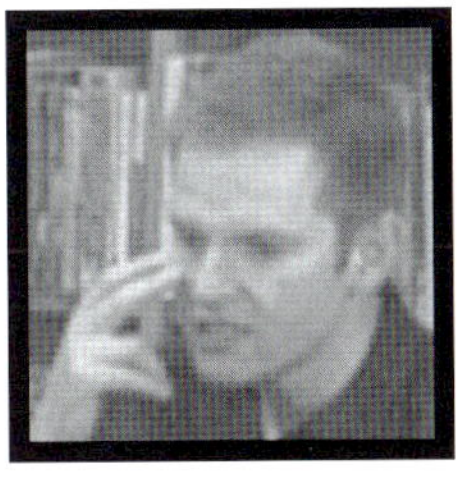

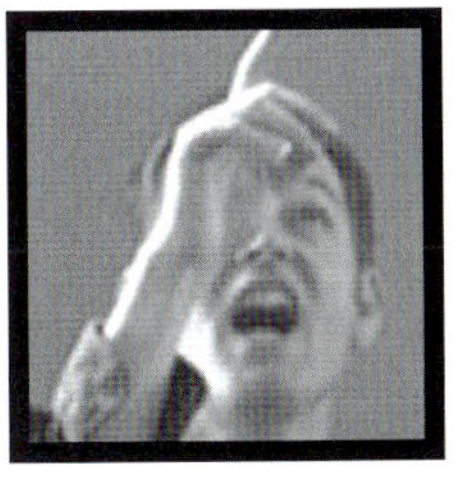

One day he saw a stranger enter the town.
This stranger was dressed
in the most beautiful, elegant clothes.
The people went to him as though he was family.

There's a fair amount of that. I remember having a long conversation with Hugh about how if we were ever going to make a film of 'my' Iliad it would be African-American. I can imagine Hollywood African-American actors playing the characters exactly as I envision them. Denzel Washington as Hector, Samuel L Jackson, who can talk anyone into anything, as Odysseus... but it isn't just the fantasy casting. As you say, there might be 'that bloke' who Hugh and I both know and because of one aspect of his character, we're reminded of a character in the story. Or it might be a character in another book, say in a children's novel.

So the storytelling process is perhaps more visual than most of us might think?

It is: the pictures come before the words.

So when you were talking last time about the image of the ravens, it's the visual image as much as anything that grabs your attention?

Yes, that's what stays with you after the story. If I've heard a story or read a story, what will remain with me are images. And the process of telling a story is the process of exploring those images.

Something else that comes up with the classic stories, but is true of many others, is the lineage involved behind the story. We were talking last time about how stories evolve and change but also how the core of a story, the fundamental image, remains the same? The Trojan Horse: that image is now over three thousand years old? Is that an issue to you? To be part of the passing on of that image, and therefore I suppose, part of the image itself?

Yes, I find that very exciting. It's like the children's game, Chinese Whispers, when you pass on messages, sentences. As they travel they change. I find it very exciting to think that I'm a part of a chain, though it's been disjointed by the stories being committed to a text and then restored to the air again, but a chain nevertheless. A chain that stretches back to when the story was first told.

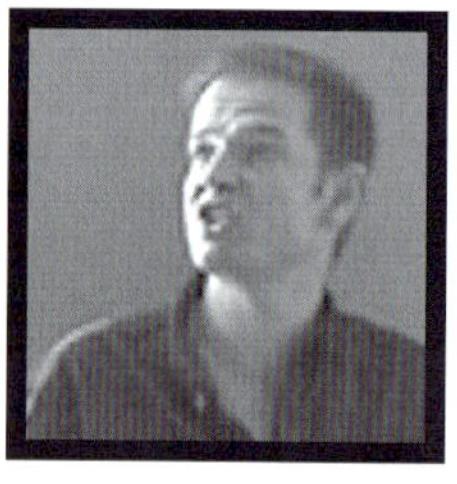

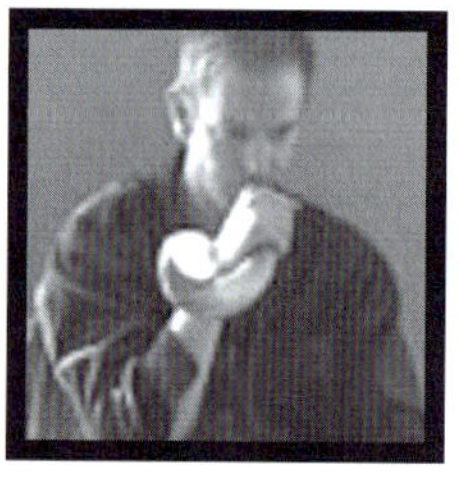

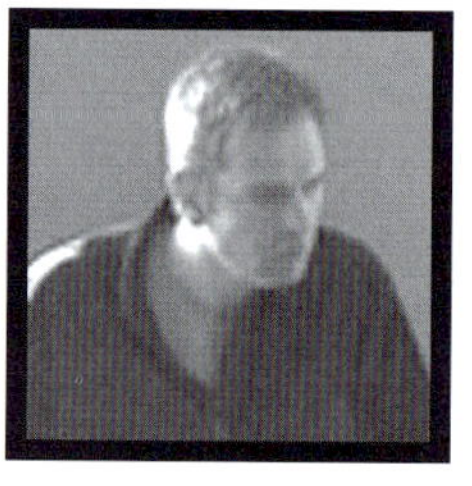

They gathered around him and listened to his every word.
That night Truth took the stranger aside

I was in the Yukon, in northern Canada, and there they are still telling stories of how to hunt and trap a Woolly Mammoth. I find it tingly to realise that that story has almost certainly been passed down orally since they were being hunted.

With these big, classic stories, there may or may not be a degree of historical truth behind them. I don't suppose there's a lot of fact – history – behind the Odyssey but there is a place called Ithaca. But the Iliad? 'Once upon a time' these were possibly real people doing and saying these things?

I remember going to a conference on Arthur, organised by the Welsh Academy. There was an awful lot of hair-splitting going on between the historians present as to who the 'true' Arthur was. I find it interesting that there's this place on the western coast of Turkey that's reputed to be Troy, and I'd like to go there, but the fact that the Iliad isn't just history is what excites me. An event occurred, somebody recounted that event to somebody else, that person went on to tell the story again but left out some details, added a few more, maybe by accident maybe on purpose, but the details they added made a better story.

Going back to Arthur, I remember hearing a history professor talk about how the Arthur story had changed. Every time a new addition, like the Round Table, or Lancelot, or the love triangle between Guinevere, Launcelot and Arthur was introduced into the story, this historian rolled her eyes. Every time, a new detail had arrived because it was relevant to the culture of that particular generation, but to the professor it was a corruption. I found the story more interesting with each new detail whereas she just thought it another deviation from 'the truth'.

In common parlance, if you call something a story it is not true...

Same with myth...

Exactly, so the kernel of the 'truth' of a story is not about the background or 'fact' of the story?

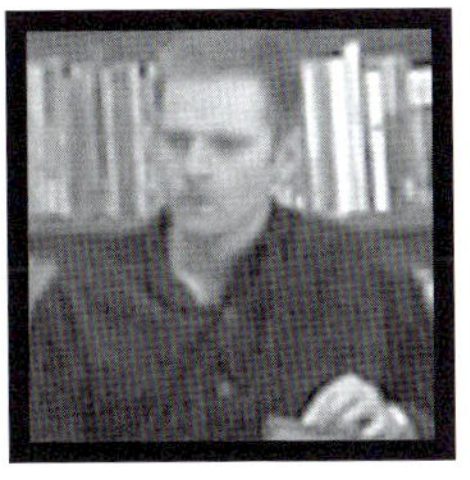

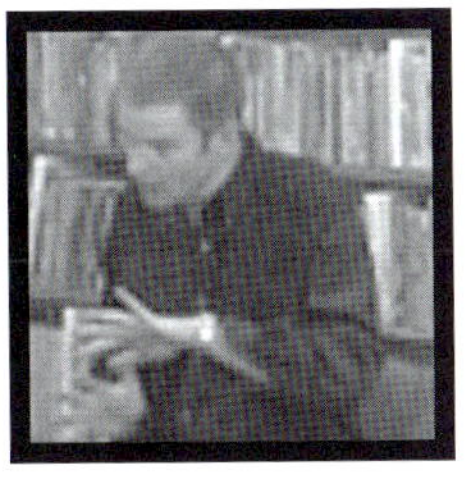

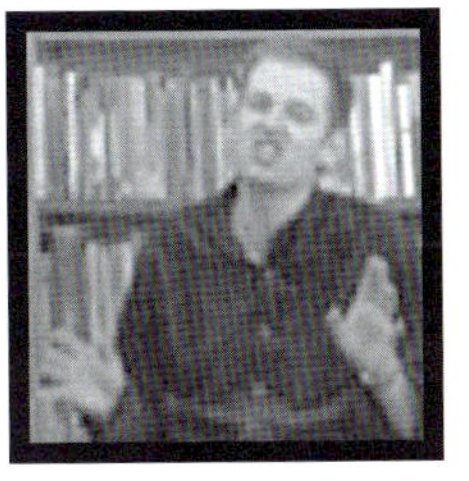

and said,
'Why is it that they listen to you but not to me?'

The kind of truth that interests me is the metaphorical truth. With the Iliad, there probably was a king, maybe even called Priam, in a certain period that had to go through certain experiences. But, what interests me are the accretions that have accumulated around his story. So, I mean, it's the symbol in the story that interests me.

At the British Museum you said that you'd contributed a little to the story yourself?

We wanted to tell the story for now, just as those people who added something to the King Arthur story wanted to tell it for then. So we had to agree on what it was about this story that made us want to tell it. And once we had done that we had to structure the story so that those things that we wanted to explore were emphasised. In the process of doing that we had to edit out elements that weren't relevant to the particular thread that we wanted to follow. We decided that we would tell the story of the birth, the life and the death of Achilles. So, in our version, the Trojan Horse, which takes place after the death of Achilles, is a brief episode. Because what is important in the story for us is Achilles' choice. From his birth he's been told that if he goes and fights in the war, although he'll win glory, he'll die young. This really struck a chord with us, the idea of young people being intoxicated by the idea of war without having any sense of the reality of it. I remember hearing an anecdote from the Second World War, when a sergeant-major stood in front of some troops and said, 'Eight out of ten of you won't come back.' And all these eighteen to twenty-one year-old young men; every one of them turned and looked at the chap to his left or right and thought, 'Poor bastard'. Nobody thought it would happen to them. At that age they thought they were invulnerable. Now Achilles, who is invulnerable, is told that if he goes and fights he will die, and yet he chooses to die. So, our version of the story effectively ends at the moment that his mother stands by his grave and says, 'You made this choice, you chose to die.' We do take it a bit further than that but that's the last big emotional moment. We've made our own journey through the material.

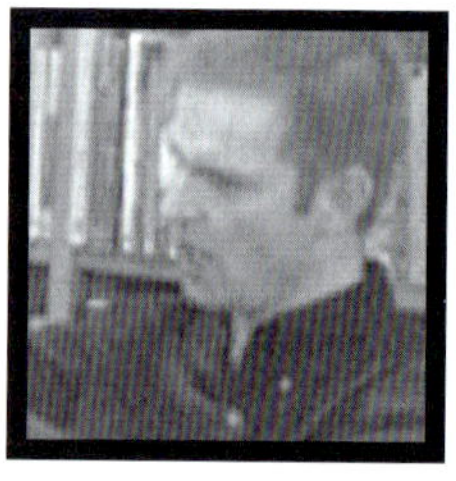

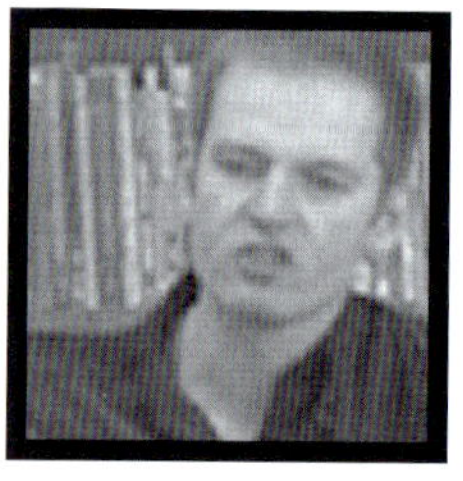

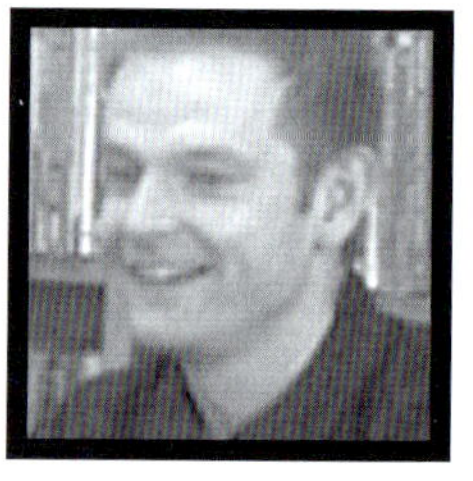

'I am story. Don't you know, my friend, that people can't take the naked truth? It's too ugly for them. Borrow my clothes.'

OK, so that's an editorial decision, that gives you shape. What about actual one-liners? I remember from working on a stage version of the Odyssey, we found it very useful to use verbal hooks like, 'Wine-dark sea...'.

Yes, in the Iliad we do lift self-contained chunks from various translations, so we do use the Homeric similes. For example, Priam looks out at the Greek camp and there's this description that the Greeks are like 'Flies around the cowshed when the pails are full of milk busy about their business'. This kind of image recurs across the whole of the Iliad and we use as many of them as we possibly can because we feel they serve a very useful function. Each one of them is a pastoral image. They give you a window for a few moments into this peaceful life, this pastoral life in the midst of this carnage. So they actually amplify the sense of the savagery of the war.

And perhaps they give you some context in which the story might actually be being told. The storyteller might be in a rich man's house but maybe you could see, maybe even smell, the cowshed?

Yes, it's a connection to the everyday, which would have been very useful then and is useful now.

Again, for the British Museum launch, you were asked about the first time you were aware of the Greek Myths. Now, last time, we talked about your reading matter as a kid....

Yes, my parents used to buy me these educational magazines, partly, perhaps, to wean me off comics. So we used to get World of Wonder and Look and Learn. Most of it was lost on me; all the science and all the maths, but among all that stuff there'd always be a serialised story, something like Treasure Island, or, in one case, the Odyssey. I remember being absolutely gripped, each Friday it would arrive and I'd flick past all the educational bits to the serialisation of the Odyssey to find out what happened next. I still have some images in my head from the illustrations that went with it. Even though I've made a long journey in my understanding of the story, some of those images are still lurking around in my hard drive....

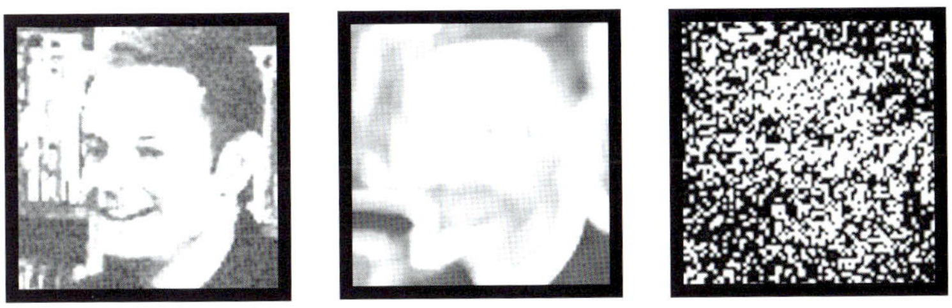

And the stranger took from a bag another suit of clothes, and Truth dressed himself in them.

Did you, then, make a distinction between the Greek heroes and comic characters? I know you read Marvel mags, so maybe like the Silver Surfer?

No, not at all. I used to make up my own stories, as you know, and Greek heroes and gods and Marvel characters would be completely integrated.

The Silver Surfer would be running up against Zeus, or Odysseus would be running up against Spiderman. In my mind they seemed to be just the same. Stan Lee, who started up Marvel Comics, used to say that myths, especially Norse and Greek myths, were his original inspiration.

Marvel did a 'Thor', didn't they? I remember his catch phrase: 'To me my hammer....'

Yes, and if he didn't get his hammer in his hands within sixty seconds he reverted to his human form. It was pretty rubbish, but the 'Loki' character was good. He had the right balance of mischievousness.

So are there any stories out there, big stories, that you haven't told yet that you want to tell?

Loads. I'd love to do an evening of Krishna stories.

I've got an Indian comic version of Krishna stories...

And the next day Truth found the people greeted him cordially, and listened to his every word.

I've got hundreds: it's one of my obsessions. I'd also love to explore the two great makers of Greek mythology, Daedalus and Hephaestos. They both seem to be the blueprints of scientists today – particularly Daedalus – because he always thinks, 'Oh, I could do that.' He doesn't think, 'I should do that.' So he makes things that actually cause great destruction and sorrow. It's the process of making things that excites him rather than their implications. I think that could be incredibly relevant to today.

This is verging dangerously on what I'm doing currently: getting kids to do plays about biomedical science and the social responsibility of scientists.

It's all there in the Greek myths!

There you go: good place to stop I guess. For now anyway.

And ever since then Truth has travelled in the clothes of story.'

the wandering eye and its resting place: looking at pete bodenham

jeni williams

Meditation I: looking at the inside from outside

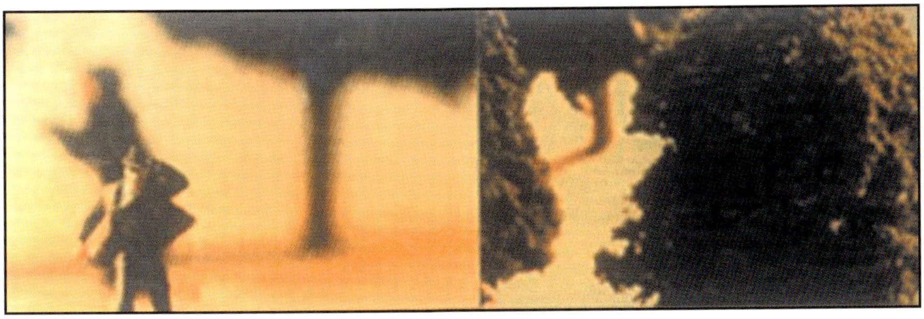

St. Dogmaels,

Cardigan: May, 2004. A large village in west Wales. As part of the fortnight of community celebrations that make up the first St. Dogmaels/Llandudoch festival of 9 - 22 May, someone has come up with the idea of asking local artists – whether amateur or professional – to display photographs, pots or paintings in their front windows. A lot of artists currently live in and around the village, many of them producing beautiful objects for the craft and heritage industries.

Although there is no local tradition that would provide the patronage, training and specialised exhibition spaces for a rooted fine art community, a quick internet search reveals how rich the area is in painters, potters, jewellers and stained glass artists, leatherworkers and woodworkers: all struggling to sell themselves and their work. So the suggestion is inspired, because for once it allows artists to produce work for themselves and for others without seeking sales. The community displays itself to itself, producing a kind of neighbourliness – as much as a licensed nosiness – as leisurely people walk past houses and peer in at photographs and images placed against the window-glass.

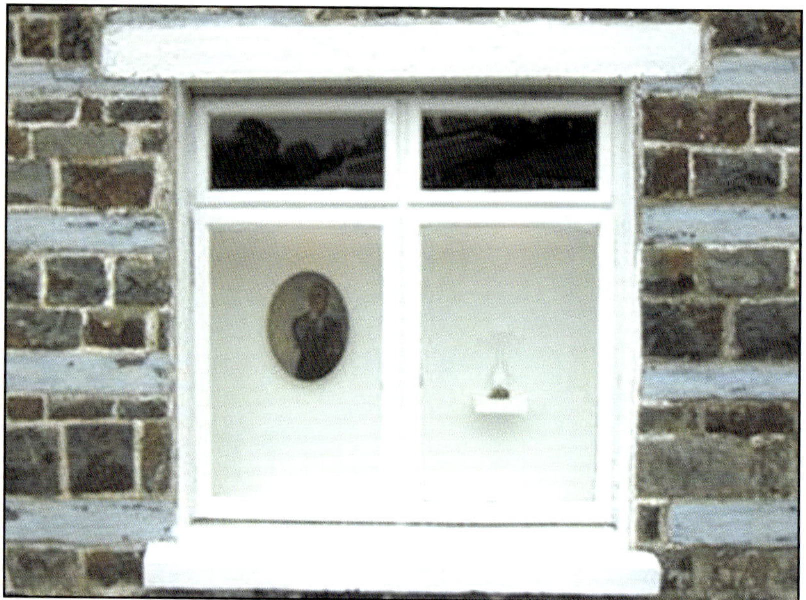

The front window of Pete Bodenham's terraced stone house plays with this opportunity to attract the eye. The interior is not visible because the white-framed window panes have been lined with white board and the two objects displayed are formally enclosed in the plain white space that results. Because this simple action plays deliberately with the way we look, it affects the way we interpret the space we see. On the one hand, it transforms the exterior of the house into a gallery space but, instead of the art works being inside with viewers walking (or peering) in to see them, they are placed on the boundary – the skin – of the building, with the viewers outside. On the other hand, by offering quiet, ordered, impersonal images in place of glimpses of a private life, it inverts the slide towards art-as-revelation or confession common to so many contemporary artists.

A similar careful play can be seen in the pieces chosen for exhibit: an oval shaped piece of wood impregnated with the faded image of a man is placed to one side while a tiny man carrying a ladder scales two stones under a small upturned wine glass on the other. An undecipherable portrait; a small construction that parodies heroic endeavour: these images intrigue in a quirky, downbeat way. And as poised and beautifully balanced moments they provide a kind of window through which we can look into Pete Bodenham's thoughtful work.

Meditation II: looking at the outside from inside

I sit at my desk and gaze at two photographs. In one of them, two men, seen from behind and placed off-centre within the frame, walk off into a blurry distance. It's a peculiar, dream-like picture. The two anonymous figures seem to be modelled in candlewax, more gesturing towards movement than in actual transit. The other picture is also strange. At first it looks like a long narrow photograph of a copse of trees. But the small landscape is equally dream-like. The trees themselves float like ghosts over the ground, lit by an eerie saturated light. On closer inspection the hazy trunks reveal the spiral threading of metal screws. The picture's simplicity is deceiving: these trees are tiny models that have been scanned, digitally modified and projected onto a plank of wood. The tawny light that seems to play over the image actually lies beneath it, in the reddish brown whorls of the wood grain. The eye flickers undecided between the image on the wood and its materiality, as what you see at first glance is turned on its head. Neither picture is 'about' what it represents – travellers, trees – but instead is concerned with the place and role of the imagination in framing and interpreting what is seen.

These two dreamscapes were amongst the first images I came across by Pete. They are older then the window arrangements but they share a similar interest in exploring how we understand experience and relate it to the world around us. They made me think about what counts as inside and what outside, about the kinds of attention we accord images, about what a photograph is and does – particularly in relation to scale, when what you think are trees turn out to be screws. As the tiny construction of the mountaineer beneath the wine glass demonstrates, such preoccupations characterise all of Pete's varied artwork.

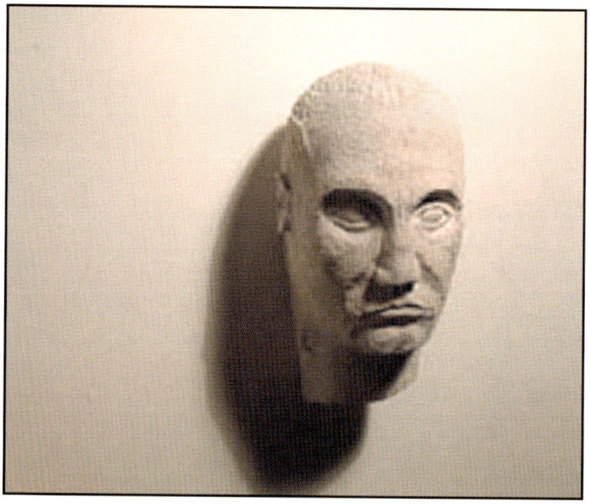

Journeys: confusing internal and external worlds

Pete graduated from Camberwell with a degree in Ceramics and 3D in the early 1980s. Given the time and place, it was unsurprising he moved into installation work, expressing an abstract interest in spatial relations; drawn in particular to rethinking scale – as in his illuminated jam covers. He returned to Wales and, after five years working as an artist and tutor, and with an interest in phenomenology, he took an MA in Fine Art and Critical Studies in Cardiff Institute.

An abstract interest in space is common among urban artists but for Pete, who grew up on a farm in west Wales and is deeply aware of the way that a lived landscape is shaped by human activity, space cannot be divorced from social and economic concerns. This awareness was sharpened by the theoretical slant of his MA and, on his return to St. Dogmaels he started relating his interest in space to the changing nature of his home landscape. Working primarily as a lecturer and teacher, he had become BA course leader and Lecturer in the History, Theory and Philosophy of Art and Design in the West Wales School of the Arts in Carmarthen by 2002. But he felt that his college commitments were taking over and that he had no time or energy left for his own work.

The turning point for him was meeting 'itinerant artist' Simon Whitehead, an artist who developed his early career in dance into a fascination with making meanings through movement in space. This meeting led to their joint project of autumn 2002 – 2mph. It also led him, at the relatively late age of 37, to give in his notice and commit himself fully to making art.

Following 2mph, Pete has produced a range of very varied work, both following a solo creative practice and working on collaborative projects. Many of these collaborations have been with Simon Whitehead and with a group of associated artists. He is, like Simon, a founding member of the 'Ointment' artist-led group. He explained the satisfactions of combining the two: 'working collaboratively creates challenging and inspiring levels of dialogue and creative exchange. The collaborative projects and works that stem from them have to be understood in the context of a collective body of

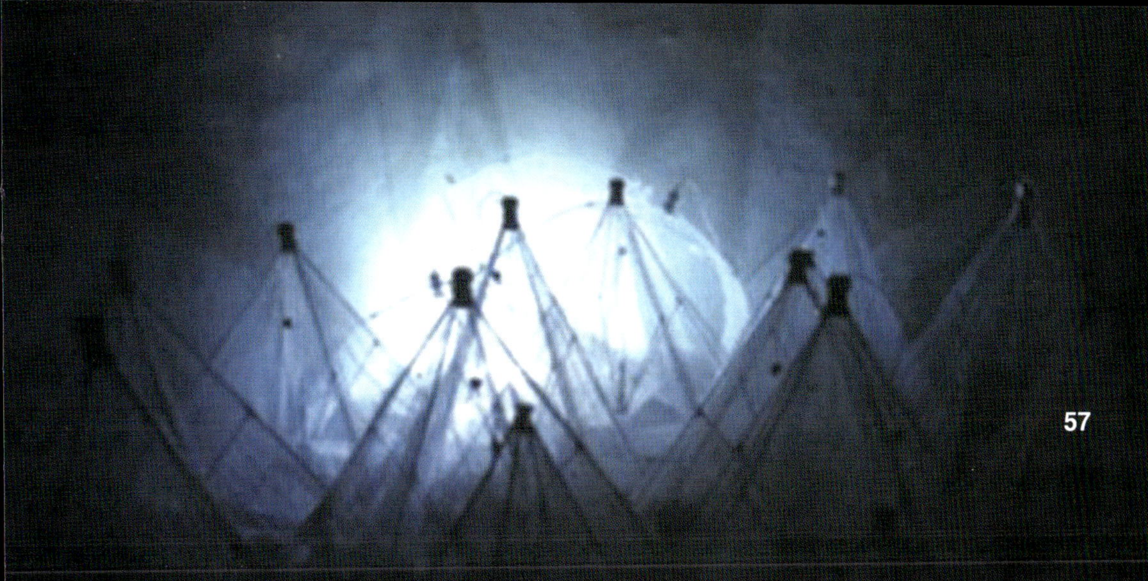

work shaped by the group. The painting and sculpture I produce as a sole artist deal with a more personal visual vocabulary and cultural concerns.'

I had met Simon Whitehead some years ago so I knew something of his interest in the politics of place and his practice of walking through landscape but the first time I heard about Pete Bodenham was when someone told me that he and Simon had walked from Cardigan to London pushing a stuffed duck. This was the project called 2mph. To be honest, it didn't sound groundbreaking though it seemed different from what I remembered of Simon's work. What was the point of the activity? Why take this particular route? Why walk for three weeks when a train takes a few hours? And why a stuffed duck? Or as it actually turned out to be, a stuffed goose?

Without an informing context, 2mph seems pointlessly self-indulgent. With one, however, it becomes both fascinating and significant. The project involved walking the 300-mile old drovers' road from west Wales to London, travelled one way by drovers taking livestock to market and the other as they returned with merchandise. Traces of this activity can still be seen in the place and pub names that line the old route but, sidelined by rail and motorway, the road is now half-forgotten, and big breweries are starting to rechristen the wayside taverns with trendy, ironic names that also, just incidentally, disconnect them from a sense of either history or place. The memories of the complex historical interdependence of city and countryside are disappearing fast. The gaps created by such lost memories are filled by new stories, in this case, by a reductive story that sets town and country in a baleful opposition. It's an opposition that continues to colour relations between the two at every level – whether in the urban misunderstanding of the rural economy that led to the mishandling of the foot and mouth crisis and to its political fallout in the emergence of the Countryside Alliance, or in the urban belief that innovative art can only happen in cities while the country is a backwater, only able to produce something lesser to be termed 'craft', and the response that any kind of radical art is a metropolitan irrelevance in the country where creativity is 'naturally' expressed by sustaining an (often illusory) tradition defined by craft. Behind such mendacious simplifications lies a kind of map shared symmetrically by both sides. Drawn according to the logic of the medieval mapmaker, it designates the unexplored space of the 'other' as an inexplicable place inhabited by incomprehensible monsters. As political histories of all kinds demonstrate, the construction of maps can exacerbate as well as contain divisions. It all depends what the maps are for.

Modern trains allow travellers to pass through places without noticing what is happening on the ground. So when Pete and Simon 'drove' a stuffed goose, a cart and a Jack Russell to London they were 'mapping' both the ground along the old Drovers' Route and the old interrelation of town and country. Their aim was to form what could be described as a 'deep map'. One point of the project was to generate encounters with farmers and 80-90 year-old men who could talk of how their communities and landscape had changed. In the Cotswolds, they found that a farm of 2,500 acres now barely sustained one farmer and a farm worker. To the modern traveller, sealed inside train or car, such places register only as irritants, obstacles in the journey to their destination. If Pete and Simon had been just walking and carrying rucksacks they would have been indistinguishable from hikers, a different, leisure-based group of travellers passing through a landscape without interaction with its residents. But their cart, stuffed goose and dog served as talismans, drawing attention to them and enabling them to interact with the people whose lives they were passing through.

In 2002, the act of walking was affected by mobility restrictions after the Foot and Mouth epidemic. Talking to people over their goose made clear the impact of official rules governing mobility and access on those living in the affected areas. For Pete and Simon, tracing the Drovers' Road was not in any way about nostalgia for a golden vanished past but about understanding the politics of movement and change of the contemporary countryside.

But 2mph was not about politics alone. Retracing the shape of a trade route is not the same as re-enacting a communal experience. Where the drovers walked out of an economic necessity that linked them to their home communities, the artists walked from personal choice. Much of the time they were walking through empty countryside – and exploring themselves as well as the land. The two journeys, into self and into history, entwine.

The bestseller of the ICA bookshop last summer was Rebecca Solnit's endlessly fascinating history of walking, Wanderlust. Her opening analysis could have been made with 2mph in mind: 'to make walking into an investigation, a ritual, a meditation, is a special subset of walking... in some sense about how we invest universal acts with particular meanings.'

Solnit sees such meditative walking as itself creative ('not an analytic but an improvisational act') and contends that the mind works best at 3 miles per hour, when it is unhurried and characterised by 'unstructured, associative thinking.' In her hands, a history of walking becomes a subversive act, a plea for a society based on 'the speed of thought, [which is that of] thoughtfulness.' If the pace of the old drovers was even slower – 2 miles per hour – that was for practical reasons. The physical demands of a journey over rough ground prevent it ever becoming a race to save time: in the past cattle and sheep had to graze on the way; geese could not be hurried over long distances.

Like the drovers whose steps they were following, Pete and Simon concluded their journey by walking through High Wycombe to Smithfield Market. Unlike them, however, they went on to the Royal Festival Hall where ResCen (the Centre for Research into Creation in the Performing Arts), was holding a major artist-led conference, Nightwalking, on the processes of artistic creation. This marked another, complementary, strand to the walk.

ResCen was set up at Middlesex University in 1999 and its conferences replace the conventional academic commentators' analysis-and-illustration with artist presentations and demonstrations, which aim to stimulate debate. The 2002 Nightwalking conference employed multimedia performance, specially constructed installation pieces and web work to celebrate the artist as 'navigator of the unknown' rather than creator of objects. The kind of innovative project the centre promotes is designed, as Christopher Bannerman, Head of ResCen, points out, specifically to challenge 'a view of art as simply artefact or commodity.' While, by offering 'opportunities to draw parallels with the working practices of others from scientists to architects,' it sought to explore artistic expression as a form of thinking, equal to, though different from, that of other disciplines. 2mph was thus perfect for the Nightwalking conference. Pete explained that 'the walk was about revealing the processes behind actions and seeing the reverberations of those actions in a wider context – not the act itself or a single product as the result of the act.'

I have only mentioned the journey part of the project so far, but there were two additional elements, consisting of the walk's documentation and contextualisation, that focused on, respectively, 'the processes behind actions' and 'the reverberations of those actions in a wider context.' Pete and Simon documented the journey as it happened with photographs, video, notes, sketches, and text messages sent to an internet message board connected both to the Nightwalking website and to the SBC Old library in Cardiff. This documentation translated both the unfolding experience into the sketched moment or photograph, and the physical space through which they were walking into cyberspace. The project was also embedded into a broader sense of time. Although both share the ideas about the politics of landscape, the collaboration created a positive dialogue between 'performance', with Simon stating 'the walk is the work', while Pete made ritualised objects to facilitate the project. The handcart that held their camping equipment and mounting for the video camera, also held the goose, creating, in the process, a focus for attention and discussion. Both artists undertook photographic projects, collected retrieved sounds and made drawings, working together to form a truly collaborative body of work. On the journey's completion, they set up an installation at the Festival Hall based on the material that they had made and gathered. Further 'reverberations' of the project have resulted in two more installations and presentations.

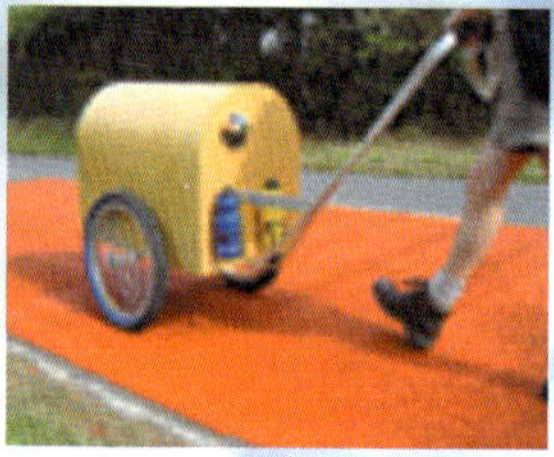

Pete claims 2mph 'shifted [his] perspective and ambition regarding [his] creative practice,' enabling him to extend his work from his earlier, interior installation work to a practice far more concerned with place and with the human relationship with place. He sees two related elements as holding this eclectic work together. The first is conceptual, influenced by thinkers such as Gaston Bachelard or Maurice Merleau-Ponty: 'a phenomenological study in response to landscape, nature and environment.' The second is more personal: a longing to be part of a community – an individual desire that he sees, paradoxically, as the common experience of an alienated modernity. The two elements come together in the journeys he has undertaken since 2mph, which also explore the communal/historical landscape and the personal one of the self. Yet although he continues to engage in exploratory walking projects, Pete still considers himself primarily as a visual artist, one who employs a variety of materials and processes to create images and sculptures and to construct the installations that emerge out of walks and journeys in the broadest sense of the word.

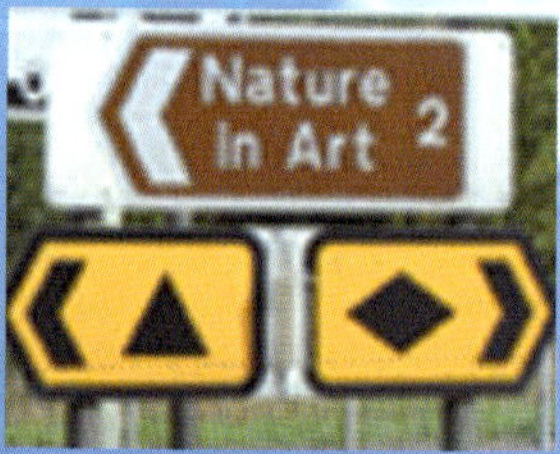

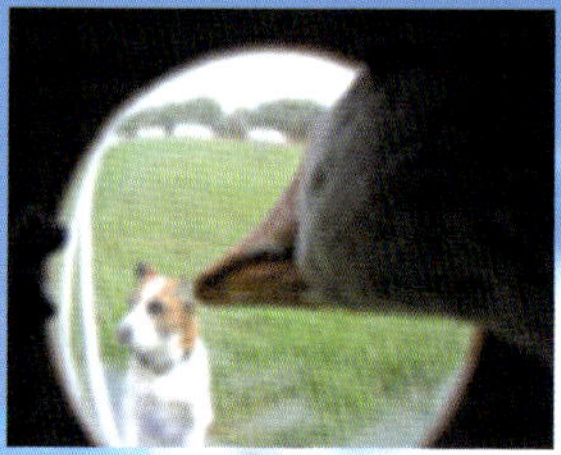

Two of those walking projects took place in 2003. In the spring he participated in another 'Ointment' project: Crwydro/Wander was a series of walks undertaken with itinerant artists from Wales and Quebec. In the autumn of the same year he undertook a solitary secular pilgrimage from St. Dogmaels to St. David's. For Pete the walks themselves were complemented by the collections of sketches, drawings, and carvings he produced in response: material he used to create an installation in Clynfyw Country Park (August, 2003) and an exhibition at St. Clairs (May, 2004).

Crwydro: wandering with itinerant artists

Crwydro: wandering with itinerant artists

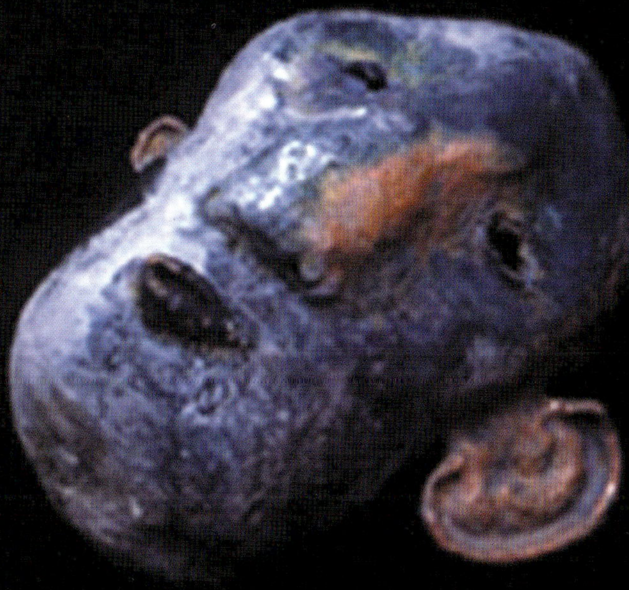

Crwydro/Wander was the first stage of an intercultural project between Wales-based art collective Ointment, to which Pete belongs, and the Boreal Art Nature group from Quebec. A second walk in Quebec is planned for 2005. Both groups define themselves as 'itinerant artists' because their performances or artefacts explore the layered meanings – historical, cultural and environmental – embedded in the landscapes through which they walk.

Crwydro was a sustained if fragmentary series of walks through the Preseli Hills in Pembrokeshire that took place over the whole of May 2003. Each of the participants responded to the landscape in different ways, several contributing to an all day promenade performance at Clynfyw Countryside Park on May 10th. Jennie Savage reviewed it for liveart magazine. She recalled a series of unexplained figures appearing out of nowhere: a swimmer appearing in a pond; a white-clad woman sitting in a tree, singing in Welsh; a gardener dressed in hat and underpants, answering questions about plants. She saw these as embodiments of the memories that haunt a landscape and as testifying to the way that the countryside is 'in a state of flux – residing in the strange space between left over notions of the romantic tradition and a government science project.'

Pete's response to this same in-between space was quite different of course. As a maker rather than a performer, his response to the landscape lies in the objects he makes. He did not – and does not – craft traditional objects in the traditional manner: the kind of work that has

Embedded in

been co-opted into the heritage industry, where single objects like love-spoons are integrated into a reductive, nostalgic vision of the past. For him, the intuitively made objects express connection: they have purposes rather than being decorative. He made a simple wooden box as a rite of preparation for the Crwydro journey, for example. It was made specially to contain the carefully chosen hand tools, including paper and ink pens, that he used throughout. He showed me his sketch books. Every day he had made simple, non-naturalistic sketches – little dome-shaped hills, or small beehive shelters with multiple tiny feet. There was a simplified figure of a naked man, leaning over a two pronged spoon-shaped spade. In each of these sketches, single trees curve over the man, or reach out delicately from the shelter. There are no abrupt, ruler-straight marks and scatters of words trail along the edges of the curving lines. Every day he took branches – some long, some curved, some forked – and carved rudimentary bowls at one of their ends, building up a tangle of crude love-spoons. Some of these were crafted into long gangly ladders with strange spoon-shaped feet.

After the Crwydro journeys had finished he set up an installation with his sketches and carvings in an abandoned grain store, a large, rough plastered space with some natural lighting. In the photographs, apparently random objects are placed carefully in relation to each other. It looks more like a workshop than an art gallery; somehow mysterious because it isn't clear what is being made. The ladders, balanced on their spoon-shaped appendages, leaned at bizarre angles against the walls; the rough love-spoons were either piled on the ground or attached to and curving away from the walls; drawings and automatic writings were strewn on a small table or pinned up by the love-spoons. A paper left on the table sought to demystify the process by offering a written explanation of why and how the artwork was constructed – allowing the objects to be 'seen' more clearly. This was a working art laboratory, even a bigger version of the school 'nature table' which took two days to set up, deliberately placed in a disused rural space.

The Crwydro project builds on 2mph which retraced lost but real connections in the spaces between town and country, but it was also interested in what was missing from the start. One of these missing elements was a tradition of the fine artist and the supportive networks of patrons and galleries without which it is impossible to develop a substantial art presence. The Ointment collective do not only walk through the landscape but address this problem also. They have held four exhibitions/installations in west Wales – usually in disused farm buildings – choosing the site to express their rejection of the metropolitan domination of art and its places of display. In their attempts to build audiences for contemporary art in rural spaces, the group purposely uses spaces that are not dedicated art galleries. The fact that Jennie Savage's assessment of the Crwydro performance piece works perfectly as a description of this installation demonstrates the shared community of purpose that the project established: 'The opening up of genuine cultural dialogue in this area is a vital step towards re-placing ourselves in this context and forging a new relationship with the rural.'

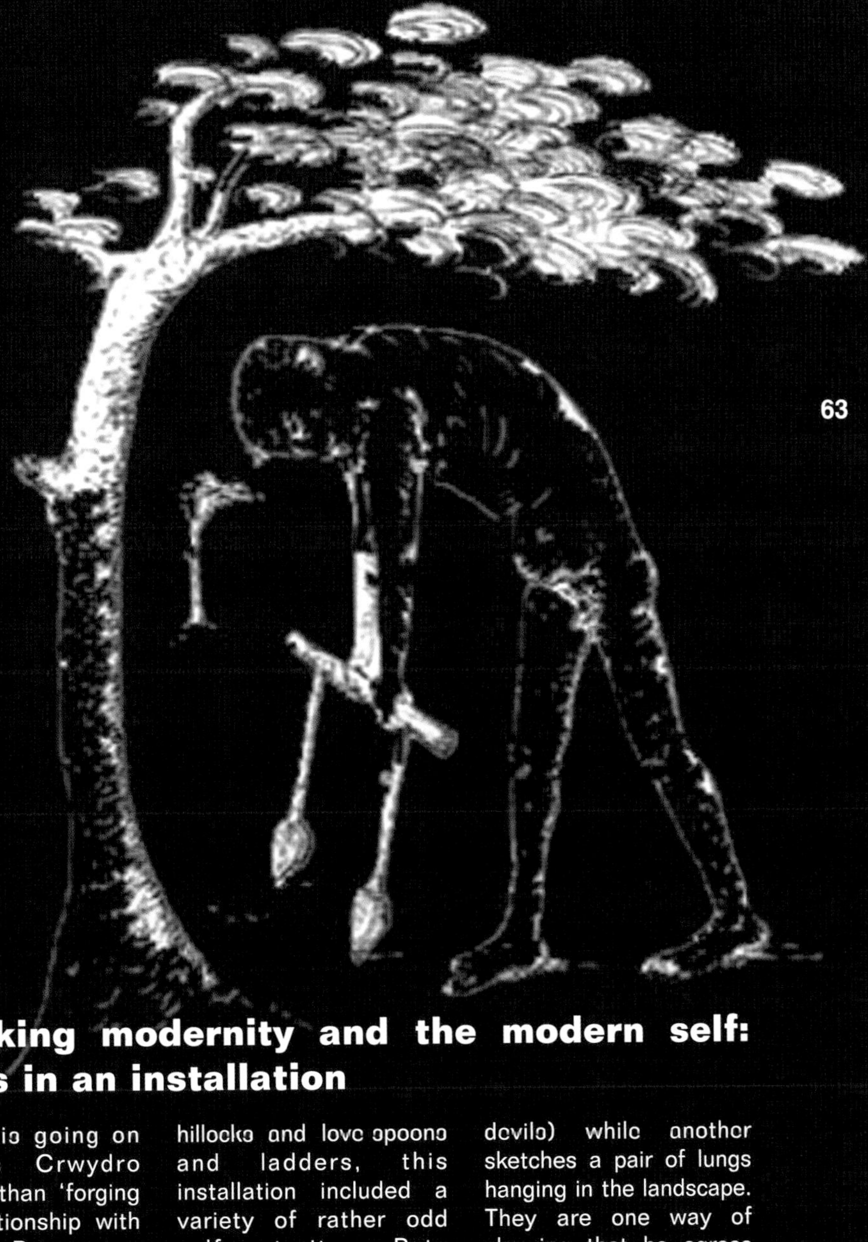

Rethinking modernity and the modern self: objects in an installation

Yet more is going on in Pete's Crwydro installation than 'forging a new relationship with the rural.' Because a laboratory (or a nature table) is expected to convey objective scientific information, it refuses to acknowledge the subjective role of the person who assembled it. But, along with the hillocks and love spoons and ladders, this installation included a variety of rather odd self-portraits. Pete suffered from a chest infection during the walk and his physical illness deeply affected his experience of the journey. One of the drawings shows him in bed (and assailed by hallucinatory devils) while another sketches a pair of lungs hanging in the landscape. They are one way of showing that he agrees with Merleau-Ponty's claim that 'the perceiving mind is an incarnate mind,' that the self cannot be divorced from its perception of its surroundings. His self-portrait as a monkish scribe in a cloister focuses on the curved posture of the body fitting into its curved space rather than on facial characteristics.

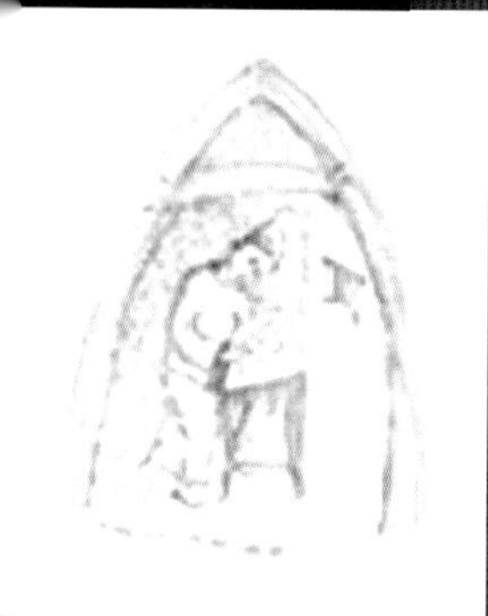

With these images he is not merely reflecting something that happened on the wayside but is establishing new relationships – with what he believes a 'self' to be (not a dislocated individual) and with that self as artist (defined through connections and collaboration). His artefacts do something similar. The rough-hewn quality of his love-spoons are quite different from either the traditional spoon – a personal, individually-crafted love token – or its commercially produced relation, full of standardised, intricate lumps. In his massed half-carved, half-natural spoons, the idea of an individual piece, in either sense, is overwhelmed in the communal expression. He made some of these spoon-ended branches into the resting points for a ladder (in Welsh ysgol means school as well as ladder, a means therefore of moving upwards); conversely, they appear as workmanlike as spades, though they are so small that they could only scratch away surface layers like the tools of an archaeologist.

That a similar image of the crafted spoon appears exactly as a spade in an early sketch, executed soon after leaving college, shows how these sketches build on a repertoire of pre-existing imagery, rather than being individual responses of the moment to the physical landscape around him. In a similar vein, the portrait sketches that depict him in the guise of a cloistered monk, or as lying in bed being tempted by demons, draw on a willowy, non-physical self first seen in the early work. This is a self recognisable from medieval art: ascetic, attuned to thinking rather than consuming, not trusting to the gross physicality of the world. These images of the self, like those of the strange hillocks and mobile houses with their multiple feet and wheels, reflect a preference for the wandering aspect of the journey, and for what may be found on the way, rather than for arrival at the safety of a fixed port. A comparison may be made with the medieval sailors who cast off in their coracles on the sea and gave themselves up to the elements in search of God, some arriving and some being shipwrecked but none attempting to control their fate. Interestingly, one small sketch depicts a coracle with a thin curving mast like a crucifix or a flag bending over it.

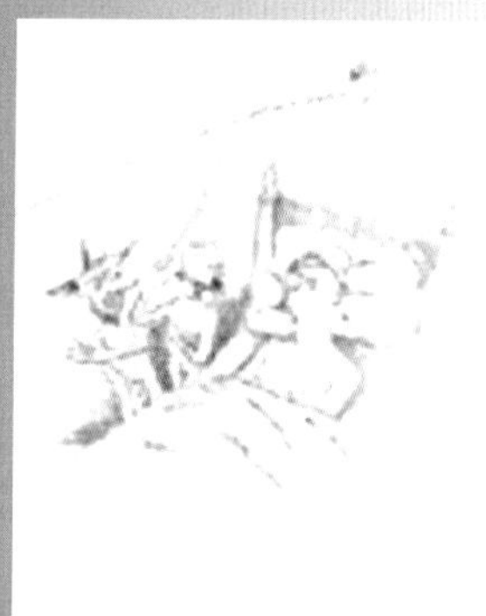

The sketches draw on medieval precursors in other ways. Pete is fascinated by medieval manuscripts and the way that the imagery within them was meant to enrich their viewers' lives. Such images did not merely illustrate either a text or a real life but were meant to be pored over and thought about. They functioned as guides to meditation: attractive precisely because they existed on a different plane to reality. It was because life in the Middle Ages lacked brilliant artificial colour and imagery that the biblical manuscript, or the stained glass window, was filled with it – the contrast emphasising divine power through the artistry of God's human agent, making something out of the natural world. But modern life reverses this contrast. It is cluttered, crammed with constant visual stimulation; everything is 'artificial', so much so that a word that was once a term of praise has now become one of opprobrium. Pete's response is to emphasise simplicity and space to breathe. His notebooks are scattered with delicate spidery drawings, often focusing on a fragment or a vision, usually placed in a small square at the bottom of an empty page. Compared to the luscious solidity of, say, commercial photography they seem thin and insubstantial – but that's the point. He believes that 'the modern eye needs a resting place.'

All of Pete's work turns on this desire for a resting place from which to view and think about the world. This is why his notebooks are laid out as they are: a few words, either thoughts or quotations; some very simple drawings in empty space. On the corner of several pages there are sketches of hills, rounded like a breast or a beehive, each balanced on multiple legs or wheels, seemingly both comfortably solid and impermanent. The range of simplified shapes – from hillocks to houses to a small image of a coracle – has evolved into a complex personal iconography. Each image seems gently crafted; none of them, not even that of the fever-demons attacking him in bed, is actually menacing. It's as if he is continually rejecting fixity and control – even the control of a fixed perspective. This is a kind of landscape art but one quite different to that of the great eighteenth-century practitioners of the art, such as Richard Wilson or Gainsborough.

Landscape art as a significant form in its own right emerged with the rational ideals of the eighteenth century. Artists like Wilson drew on neoclassical dreams of perfect order to paint an ideal reality and lay out their landscapes as perfect, private and privatised worlds, stretching back from the narrow entrances in their foregrounds. Later in the same century, landscape gardeners like Capability Brown transformed the natural 'imperfections' of the actual countryside into versions of that ideal. These kinds of art forms expressed a culture that was just starting to explore, map and colonise large areas of the globe: they express the relation of land to power. It's unsurprising therefore that so many radical artists from the 1960s onwards should choose to have challenged this kind of art by looking at the landscape in different ways –

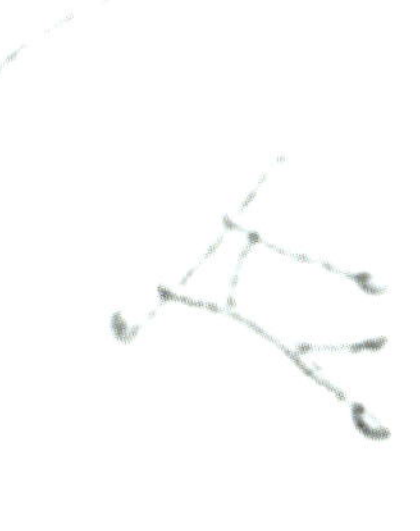

whether as a land artist like Robert Smithson, or as an itinerant artist like Richard Long. Pete fits into this pattern, his art of memory, connection and inclusion rejecting the ideological or aesthetic hierarchies associated with an enlightenment worldview. A snub-nosed wagon in one picture suggests the neo-classical surrealism of de Chirico but without his threatening, city-born shadows there is no predatory subtext. And by sketching swelling horizons rather than the fissured ones of a Wilson landscape, he conveys a sense of openness rather than one of control or ownership.

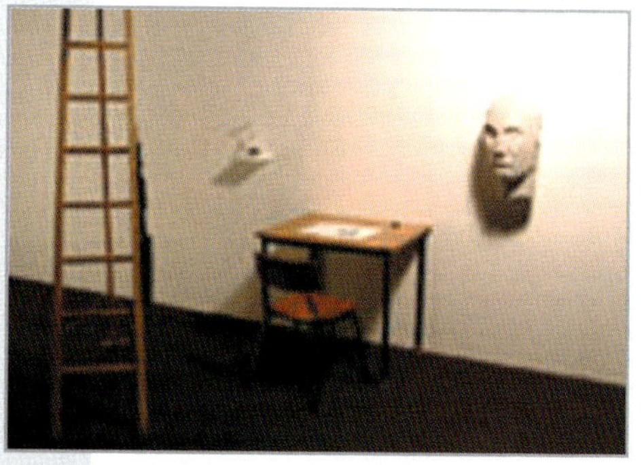

Yet the eighteenth century and its rationalisation of the material world remains a point of reference even as it is rejected. Pete loves eighteenth century art and is fascinated by those other eighteenth-century preoccupations: maps and history. But, as can be seen in 2mph, his interest lies in alternative maps, alternative histories. Conventional maps fix objective realities and facilitate movement, being made for strangers to whom the mapped place is unfamiliar. The maps he constructed during the Crwydro journey are quite different, more like the devotional notes of a pilgrimage than the conventional graph; as concerned with his state of mind, with subjectivity, as with objective information about places and landmarks. He sees these 'maps' as engaging with what conventional cartography leaves out, just as his other images engage with what is left out in conventional representation – in some of his pictures small dots drift amongst the trees to represent invisible sound.

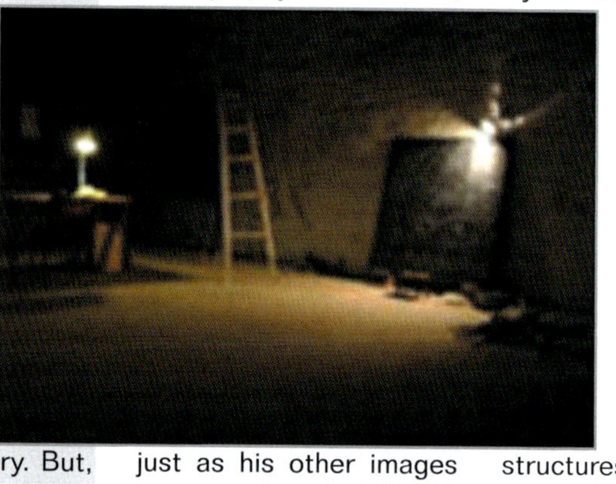

The attraction to the medieval, the refusal of, but fascination with, eighteenth-century codes of representation: both preoccupations point to the way that all of Pete's work is interested in the impact of modernity on contemporary individuals and their relation to the historical landscape in which they live, on how it is seen and the price of that understanding. He says he sees 'everyone caught in the maelstrom of modernity': something he desires either to illustrate or unpick in all his work. It's not surprising therefore that the communal experience of the Crwydro project should be counterpointed by a solitary secular pilgrimage conducted later that year, one that retraced the medieval route from St. Dogmaels to St. David's. After all, as Solnit points out, 'pilgrimage is one of the fundamental structures a journey can take – the quest in search of something, if only one's own transformation, the journey toward a goal.'

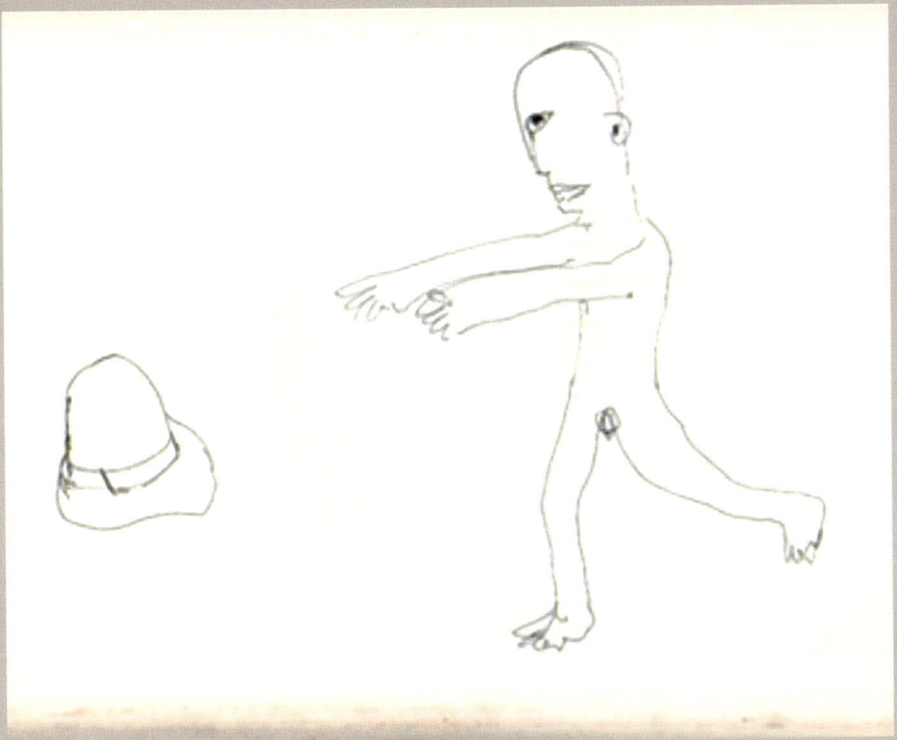

All of Pete's walking projects are careful, thoughtful explorations of place that attempt to respond to the layers of historical changes that affect both the meaning of that place and the way we understand the present through its relation to the past. This is why he is fascinated by the process of recording – mapping – both the actual discovery and the sense of discovery per se. One way he describes his work is that in a range of different ways, he seeks 'to record the patination of experience.'

A note on the wall of Pete's study declares that 'journeys are the midwives of thought.' He put it there as he prepared for the St. David's walk and it marks the quiet and private tenor of that event. The walk is a perfect example of what Solnit calls 'a special subset of walking,' that is, one that transforms the act of walking into 'an investigation, a ritual, a meditation.' This ritual quality was further enhanced by the fact that for most of the journey he walked alone.

He said that both being on his own and walking over familiar ground, had made the walk to St. David's feel very different to his previous walking projects. His mind could wander freely and, encountering neither new people nor new sites, there were no surprises to distract him. As a result – and as befitting the nature of a pilgrimage – the journey became more internal, more meditative.

I talked to him before the walk, as he was preparing for it, and, amongst his sketches and photographs, after its completion. He had initially thought of the journey as a project to be undertaken with his father, desiring not only to explore the relationship of the body to the landscape through which it moves, but to look at the impact of the ageing process through the different bodily experiences of two generations engaged in the same activity. In the end, however, this joint venture did not happen. The project became a personal quest over three days, his father walking with him for part of one of these. This journey, even more than those he had already undertaken, moved simultaneously through two spaces – the physical, topographical and historically determined external world and the spiritual and psychological internal space of the self.

As with the previous projects, Pete made a kind of ritual of the preparation for the journey, crafting objects that he would need. He constructed a light but full-size stepladder which he carried for the entire journey. This was not a symbolic ladder, like those made for Crwydro, but a usable one. The idea

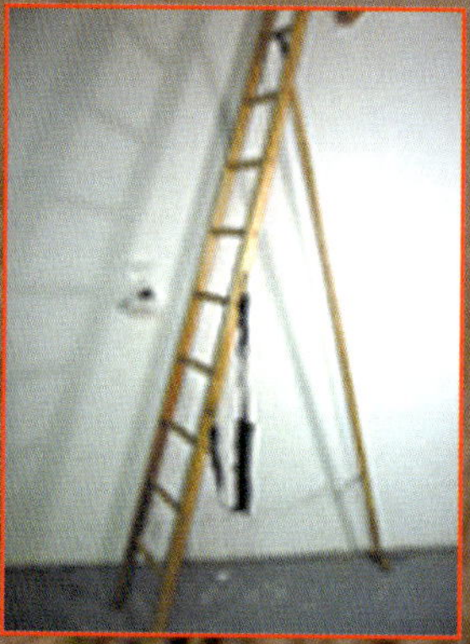

was to be able to climb up it to take panoramic photographs but, in the event, he did not use it much and described it as 'a bit of a hair shirt:' an apt symbol for an object to be taken on a pilgrimage. Solnit points out that, in quest of self-transformation, pilgrims 'often try to make their journey harder, recalling the origin of the word travel in travaill, which also means work, suffering, and the pangs of childbirth.' This more arduous journey produced slower and subtler contemplation, doubling back to and rethinking earlier images rather than producing entirely new ones. The sketchy, abstracted self-portraits became more intensely focused on an internal reflection, on capturing the way his mind was responding to the world outside.

Yet again this focus emphasised the significance of the eye. When he reached Mynydd Carningli he watched his own shadow lengthening and shortening over the grass and was drawn into thinking about the insubstantiality of the self not only in itself but passing through the landscape. He took photographs at different times of the day, images in which the ladder is returned to symbolic meaning, jutting out on either side of his shadow self. On his return he made a small, neat worktable on which he constructed several of the quiet pieces that formed the afterlife of the journey. One of these parodied himself as heroic explorer in the shape of a tiny mountaineer, scaling two stones while carrying a tiny ladder – the miniature installation placed under a small upturned wine glass that he was later to place in his window.

Right from the start of this walk Pete had been reflecting on the nature of pilgrimage, in particular on what it means as a non-Christian to follow a Christian path. In his phenomenological understanding of landscape he believes that the landscape is shaped by human activity, and its meaning for the people who live and work or pass over it is created by and through that activity. Equally however, both human activity and the human self are also shaped by the land. Pete thus rejects the conventional – and standard Christian – oppositions of subject and object, self and world, seeing always the self in the world and the world in the self or the body as 'incarnate mind.' As a non-Christian trying to find a way of thinking about the religious expression, he thinks that 'building a church is significant as a community action, reflecting the community infrastructure [and expressing] a commitment to something beyond self-interest.' This way of understanding churches allies them to the cromlechs that pepper the west Wales countryside: both kinds of structure being defined through social function rather than in terms of architectural design; both produced by the actions of a community and both expressing a desire for something more than an individual self. He sees walking an old spiritual route in similar terms: not as an attempt to

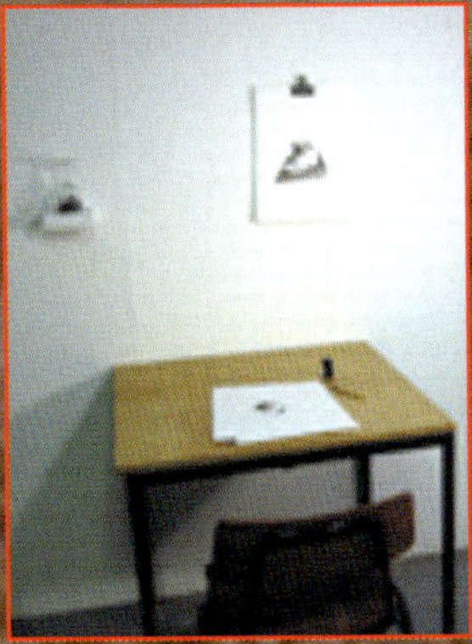

experience what has now long gone but as a recognition of a vanished community and the value of its valid (though now perhaps alien) aspirations.

A non-Christian pilgrimage must therefore be very much to do with an attitude of mind. The earlier walks show Pete's rejection of aspects of eighteenth-century rationalism and his attraction to some elements of medieval art, particularly in the development of his personal iconography. His pilgrimage started here, with a consideration of the meaning of the icon. Before he had even left St. Dogmaels he took photographs of a statue of a Hindu goddess placed by a front gate and a plaque of a pagan Green Man attached to a house wall. He started thinking about religious imagery and about what these images of otherness meant to those who put them there. Did they carry the same meaning? Did the choice of an oriental and an ancient other express an active rejection of modern, Western consumerism? Or were they merely echoes of meaning, images which have lost their function and therefore been relegated to the decorative or the mildly interesting. Still pondering these questions, he took a photograph of a walled garden hung with a heart-shaped mass of ivy at the end of a valley – this time human meaning (the heart) wholly allocated through his perception rather than humanly crafted. These were side issues, however, no matter how they reflected onto the main one of the pilgrimage – the physical movement across the land towards the cathedral at St. David's.

Because Pete responds to the idea of community expressed in the church, seeing it as part of a social infrastructure rather than an expression of hierarchy, he is attracted to the sheltering building rather than the priestly administered crucifix as the site of devotion. This is why, despite the fact that the journey was to a large and imposing cathedral, the church presented in his drawings is always an idea, a shelter as radically simple as a turf house. Some of the sketches further emphasise this symbolic level by placing the church against a rounded, nurturing horizon. The beehive shapes of his sketchbooks represent both hills and churches – natural and man-made elements sliding into each other, just as the physical and the psychological blur on the journey.

The sketchbooks also contain pen and ink sketches created after, and reflecting back on, the journey. One of these shows a self-portrait head looking down in profile inside a dark beehive shape. The image is placed centrally on the page, the eyes are closed and the head appears to be floating up against the darkest part of the dome. Outside that dome all is white. A small coracle is balanced at the top of the dome and on the back of the head in a kind of mirror image, breaking free of the shadowy interior into plain light. Echoing an earlier sketch from Crwydro, a small, thin mast waves above it with a cross bar like a tiny crucifix. Another sketch shows a similar head in profile, also looking down within a dark space, but the setting is less neat, not a beehive shape. This time, what is balanced on the head is a tall, tower-like building with a thin ladder resting against its side and a road sweeping over the head into an entrance at its base. Pete says that the impetus for these images can be found in the statue of St. David that stands, holding a small model of a church, inside the Cathedral. The statue depicts St. David dreaming his religious community into existence. It can be seen simply as an image of the future, but it can also be viewed differently, as an image of a present moment with St. David's thought rendered as a concrete object in his hand. This is what Pete's sketched self-portraits respond to when they show the subjects of his thought (the freedom of the coracle, the shelter of the house) as objects that both balance on his head and counterbalance that head in the patterned imagery within the picture frame. The statue is thus teasingly suggestive. By gazing at it and translating its principles into his self-portraits, he finds a

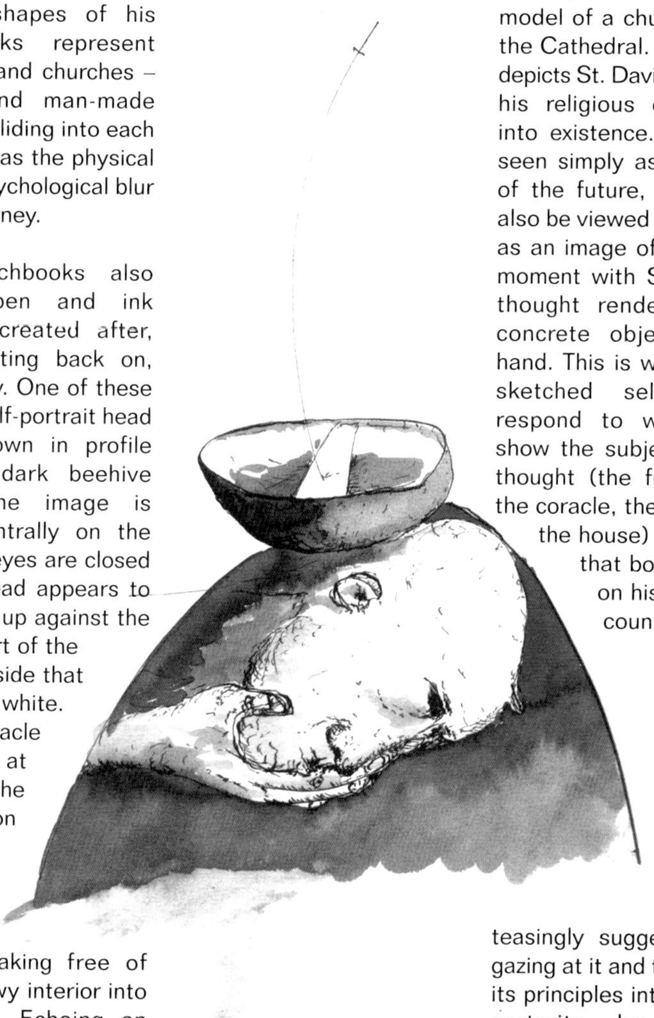

potent image to rethink the relations of physical and non-physical worlds, and to relate his own, twenty-first century interest in phenomenology to the concerns of a vanished Christian community.

There are three important aspects to the site's history: its age, the way that its construction reflects the frequency of early attacks and its symbolic importance as a Christian centre. The first Christian community was established in the sixth century when St. David established the monastery at Menevia though, as Christian missionaries usually chose to build on pre-Christian holy places, as a sacred site it is probably older still. By the twelfth century the monastery had been ransacked several times, an earlier cathedral had almost been swept away by successive Viking attacks throughout the tenth and eleventh centuries and David's shrine had been desecrated. The site's symbolic importance was evident in 1124, 57 years before the present cathedral was built, when Pope Calixtus II canonised St. David and used a devotional arithmetic to calculate that 'two pilgrimages to Menevia were equal to one pilgrimage to Rome' – and that three were equivalent to a journey to Jerusalem.

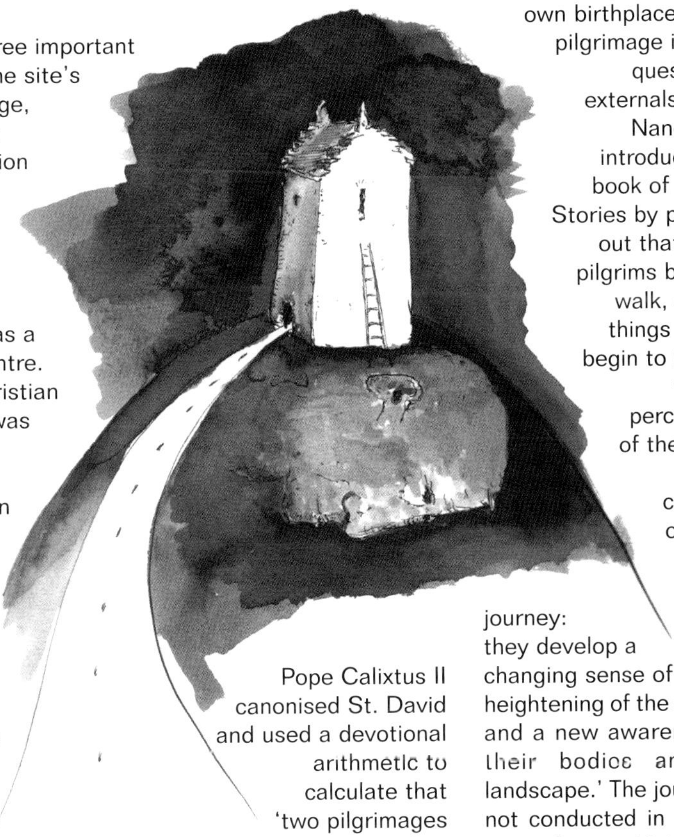

To walk the route from St. Dogmaels to St. David's thus means to retrace the devotional route taken by many thousands of people over the past fourteen centuries. And that process not only recalls a lost community of values but also evokes the historically shifting populace around Pete's own birthplace. But a pilgrimage is not a question of externals alone. Nancy Frey introduces her book of Pilgrim Stories by pointing out that 'when pilgrims begin to walk, several things usually begin to happen to their perceptions of the world, which continue over the course of the journey: they develop a changing sense of time, a heightening of the senses, and a new awareness of their bodies and the landscape.' The journey is not conducted in relation to an abstract history, like following a map on a page, but has an impact on the walker who becomes increasingly attuned to the landscape within which he or she walks.

Foremost amongst these attuned senses is, of course, the eye and the duplicitous terrain around St. David's makes the pilgrimage a wavering, almost unreal experience. At St. Mathri, the road coils round to a magnificent church which was built specifically to be visible from the sea, a false cathedral in full view to decoy marauders away from the real, half-hidden one. The actual cathedral, which is built in a slight hollow, slips into view only briefly and then slips away again. What does this mean for the pilgrim whose senses are fine-tuned to the landscape? Pete is fascinated by a suggestion that the pilgrimage is over once its object is seen, that is when it is no longer held in the imagination but comes into actual view. If this is the case, what happens to the pilgrimage when the cathedral disappears after first being seen? What happens to the journey when its end vanishes? To what extent does it exist only inside the head? If so, what does that mean?

These uncertainties expand to include questions about the nature of (an autonomous) reality: questions with particular resonance for Pete as a non-Christian artist exploring a religious rite such as a pilgrimage. But such confusion does not only relate to a special, spiritual dimension. It feeds into his wider practice as a visual artist as well – not only in these sketched self-portraits but in the more recent dreamscapes, images which also express an uncertainty about being able to separate the act of representation from the reality of the physical world; concerned with what is, and what is not, real. Yet the cathedral is not the only building to appear and disappear from view because of the terrain. Exactly the same thing happens to a rather nice 1940s modernist building in St. David's whose white shape slides into the line of sight of an approaching walker and then vanishes again. Without spiritual content this metaphor of the impermanence of reality slips into bathos – and from thence it is a short step to the flaunted artificiality of kitsch.

The attraction of kitsch is that it's about something that is not there. It is appreciated for what it isn't – it isn't elegant, tasteful, it isn't sensitive – but its garishness and sentimentality needs some idea of taste in order for it to make sense. Yet it's also itself, special because it isn't the tasteful, original thing. Used self-consciously, kitsch is the stuff of much urban-based post-modern art (like Claes Oldenburg or Jeff Koon) and not what I'd expect Pete to be interested in. But, of course, both phenomenological art and kitsch are anti-materialist; they share a rejection of the self-evident; both are about something not being really 'real.' This is the area that Pete was interested in when he made so many love-spoons in Crwydro.

Love-spoons are standardised, mass-produced and sold in craft shops everywhere and yet, because their original purpose has gone, what is bought is a mirage, a nostalgic dream of a real world. Before Crwydro Pete flirted directly with kitsch versions. He showed me an early one he had made, a double love-spoon. This was far more crafted than the rough ones he made during the walk, and in a parody of the craft shop models he had carefully painted the carved real wood to look as if it were plastic, an imitation of imitation, an image that plays ironically with what is and isn't real. Although it isn't typical, it does say something about the essential coherence of his work, which is its focus on the eye, and the trickeries of the eye as an expression of his central concern with the entwined relations of the modern world and the modern subject it produces.

When we had our last conversation about St. David's, I had recently read Frederic Jameson's essay on the 'spatial mutation' of Los Angeles's Bonaventure Hotel and felt this his pilgramage achieved a quiet luminosity through contrast with that tinsel world. Yet the matter and attraction of kitsch felt extraordinarily relevant as a comparison. We talked about Jameson's discussion of the alienated post-modern body, carried in frozen movement on escalators and walkways on a grotesque pilgrimage to the very Mecca of consumerism. Post-modern America, especially Las Vegas, seems built on kitsch – Jameson talks about the numbing effects of moving through a space that pretends to be somewhere else (Vegas imitates Paris, London, Venice), and experiencing a time divorced from mortality and translated into special effects (there are no clocks in Las Vegas; in one building, artificial sunrises and sunsets take place every few hours). Such disorientation blurs the boundaries of what is and isn't real. It's as if the people are just shapes being moved around inside a vast installation – which, in a way, they are. This is why a comparison with the St. David's Pilgrimage, which equally places people inside a constructed frame (here the cultural histories and stories of the landscape), is so interesting. Where the urban environment of Las Vegas reveals the passive isolated consumer created by contemporary American culture, the spaces of the rural landscape (usually unpoliced, except for Foot and Mouth) reveal how they create a quite different self, a wandering active self defined in relation to a community – of either the past, or the present, or both – rather than a market. From this perspective the St. David's pilgrimage develops the preoccupations of the earlier work but seems a stronger statement, perhaps because more meditative. Similarly, in terms of his smaller, crafted objects, a desire to question the heritage industry through his early flirtation with kitsch has been replaced with a subtler critique in which he revisits and remakes the crafted object rather than merely parodying its artificiality.

This focus is important because the heritage industry is not the antithesis of a glittering post-modern city but its complement. It sells a cosy version of tradition, homogenised and mass produced like the love-spoons, to convey a sense of homely authenticity. Instead of chrome, the major material is wood, preferably old and dark, even more preferably oak – or something that looks like oak. Where the post-modern alienation of Las Vegas illuminates Pete's rural spaces, the heritage industry provides the context that explains his whole practice, not just the sparseness of his technique. One of the greatest examples of this artificial authenticity is the pervasive non-specific nature of the 'Celts' and their works (which never, originally, included key rings or biros). Much of this material is highly finished or dense with mechanically-produced detail that now lacks any

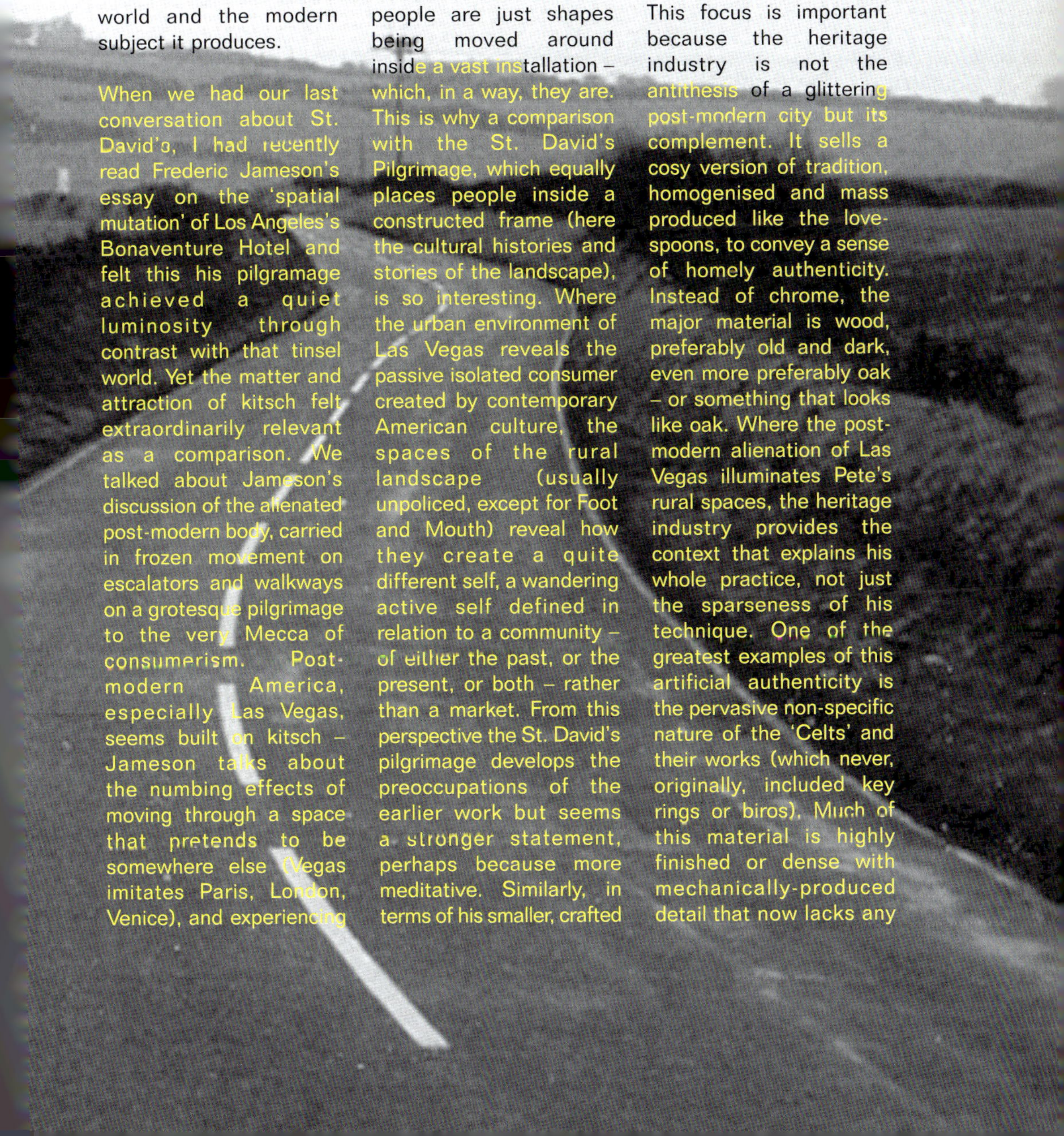

purpose other than decoration. These are objects to be consumed. Pete's drawings are quite different. He sees them not as ends to themselves but as part of a learning process embedded in and developing from his other activities such as the walking projects, the collaborations with others. His dreamscapes and crafted pieces are all unique, made deliberately against the template of the craft shop, rejecting the treadmill of mass reproduction as a Las Vegas walkway where you walk by just standing still.

The problems are the same whether in a commodified city or a commodified countryside. On the one hand, the multiple losses of place and history that lead to a loss of a sense of self, and, on the other, a desire for the art that comments on these losses to change the way its viewers see their worlds. So it's important that Pete says that, even when joined by his father, who has retired, the experience of the walk to St. David's was of moving within a special, fluid space, away from the restrictions created by daily life. A desire to escape from the enforced sterility of the contemporary treadmill: this is the last meaning of the walking projects and their objects. It is the one that qualifies all of them as, in some ways, pilgrimages, as escapes from the physical and psychological structures that, whether at home with family or at work, cramp free thinking.

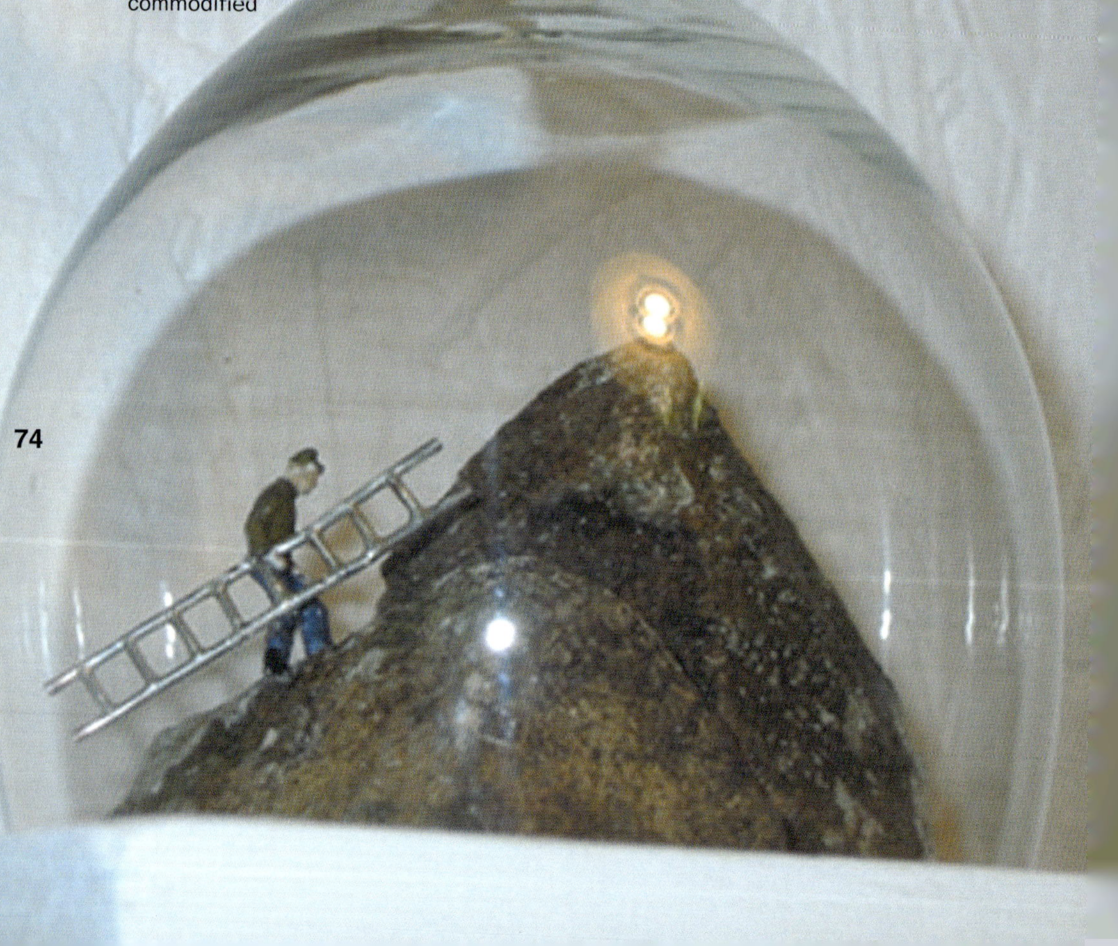

Other worlds; afterlives

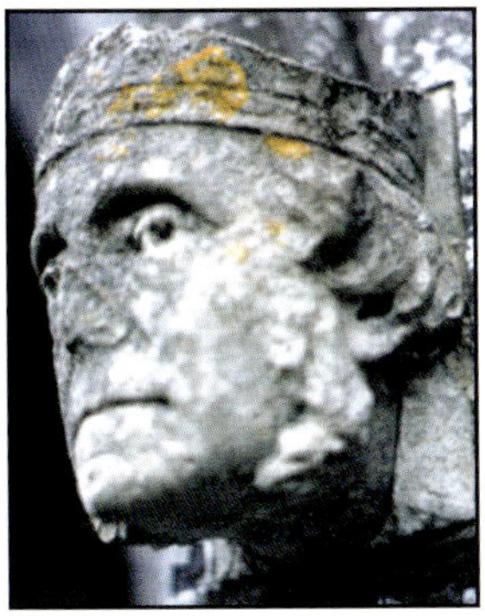

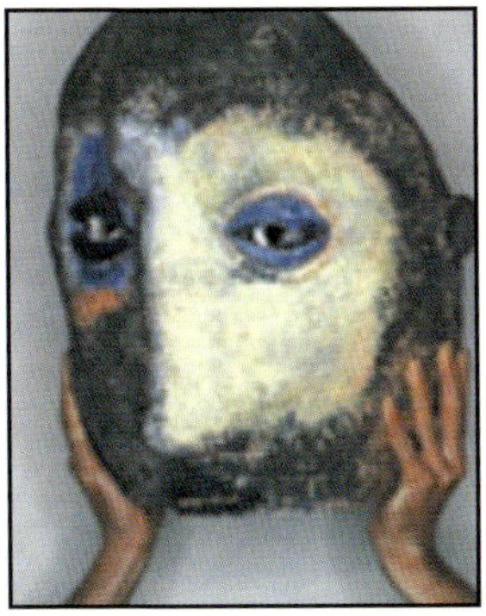

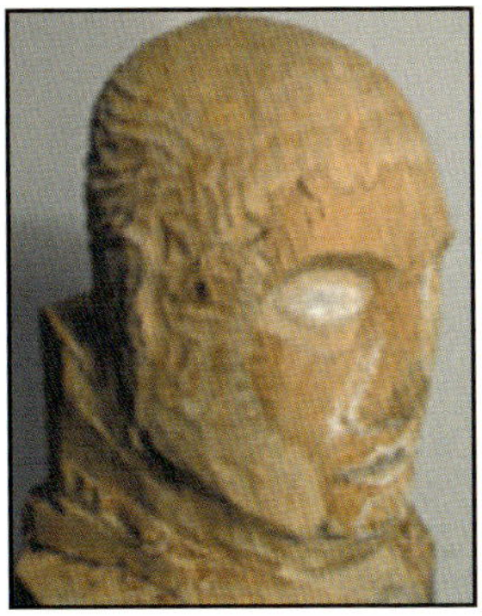

The pilgrimage to St. David's has deeply influenced Pete's work, leading him to reflect on, sift through and refigure earlier preoccupations rather than seek new stimulation. He says that two objects in the cathedral were equally important in this respect – the first, the stature of St. David, has already been mentioned but he was equally drawn to a carved stone head jutting out from the building's exterior, a piece that drew him back to the clay heads and masks he made when first starting his career. These early heads are semi-Expressionist, consisting of depersonalised, rather brutal shapes, with earthy matt colours and an emphasis on simplified rough surfaces. They suggest archaic, unwieldy, psychological drives rather than realism. Yet it is not surprising that Pete abandoned mask making as part of his rejection of art as a kind of Romantic self-exploration, precisely rejecting psychology in the growing interest in histories and landscape that accompanied his return to west Wales. Indeed, when he embarked on the St. David's pilgrimage he had not made any 3-D heads for over 15 years but, after walking through familiar landscape to St. David's, he revisited the earlier motif – with a difference. He turned from clay to wood, chiselling out a wooden head. He explained this shift from one medium to another: 'using clay means the mask is built up by adding layer upon layer of material, constructing something from nothing.' Carving, on the other hand, fascinates him by being 'reductive, removing layers to achieve the end product, revealing what is below the surface.'

Pete continues to be interested in excavating layers of meaning, whether in the material itself, or the forgotten histories and practices of place. The collaborative ventures continue. Cywaith Cymru is supporting Ointment's big project for 2004-5: an exploration of the interrelation of traditional herbalism in west Wales with the biodiversity of the area. Four artists: Simon Whitehead, Maura Hazelden, Stirling Steward and Pete, will learn about the plants and be able, literally as well as metaphorically, 'to make ointment' from them. Yet because they don't want to become herbalists themselves, the act should be seen as performance art rather than acquired skill or scientific practice. They seek to uncover the relation between a diminishing body of knowledge (that of herbalism) and the wider degradation of the local ecology, a learning process that will be documented by film. The project will result in exhibition events – part performance (making ointment) and part installation (objects and film) – to be held in village halls or abandoned agricultural buildings. As always the desire is to produce innovative work that gazes carefully below the surfaces outside the metropolitan boundary.

As a visual artist and maker, Pete is equally interested in exploring layers and surfaces, in challenging comfortable perceptions. He has had two exhibitions in 2004. In May he contributed to a joint exhibition held with Andy Griffiths and Ingrid Murphy in St. Clairs and from July to the end of September he had a solo show in London's GlaxoSmithKlein building. He produced a series of small carved sculptures and paintings, including some of the St. David's work and some dream-scapes, for St. Clairs but the London show was composed exclusively of paintings. These paintings develop out of the earlier dreamscapes and share their fascination with perception. The very latest

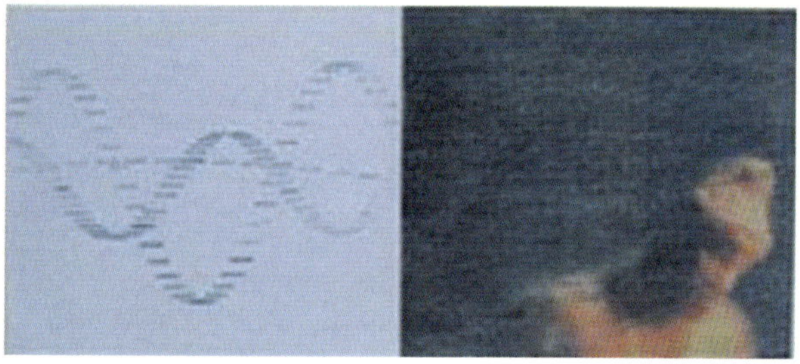

work develops this format on a larger scale. Vague figures float inside a square that takes up precisely half of the 1x2 metres wooden panel; half of the surfaces of wood, as if in a landscape or seascape, counterbalanced by a square of abstract or flat colour, contrasting light and dark.

Two of the recent pieces – Walker and Boy – demonstrate the increasingly delicate, increasingly haunting quality of his visual work. In both, the rectangular landscape is split into equal squares of light and dark, a design that focuses attention on the counterpoint and relationship of two worlds rather than on the single human image placed in each case in the right-hand square. In Walker the image appears in a dark square, a ghostly female head tilted to the right drifting up out of motes of dust, very low in the frame, its gold hues illumined by the large expanse of dark blue above. It is counterpointed by a light blue square with thin, dark blue lines looped into what looks like an infinity sign. In Boy, the hazy image is of a boy, possibly eight or nine years, clad in shorts and set in an unfixed location with only clouds behind his half-defined figure. In this piece the left hand block is black. Both pictures suggest unspoken narratives through his juxtaposition, giving us human figures and non-human contexts equally balanced. The simple titles intrigue: Walker evokes endless – perhaps eternal – journeys; Boy, by setting the youth in light against a featureless black void, hints, dreamlike, at innocence and its corruption, at death. For a man who gave up a successful academic career at 37 because he believes that 'the modern eye needs a resting place', these quiet images seem a good place to stop. They are as much about looking as about content, as much about questioning the norms and expectations as about constructing new ones. Like all of his work they draw the eye to the slow pace of thoughtfulness.

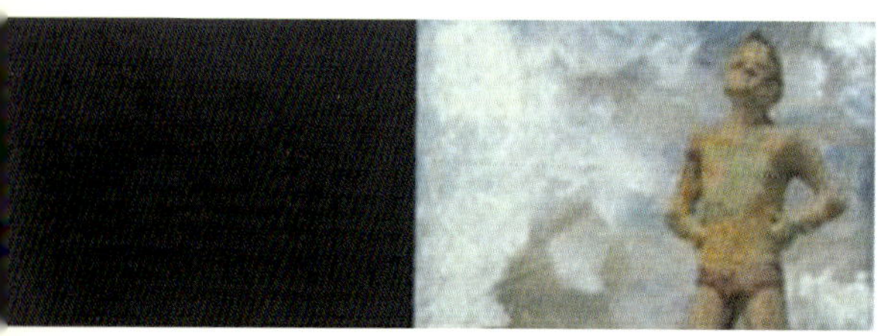

shapeshifting: the story of megan lloyd

maria donovan

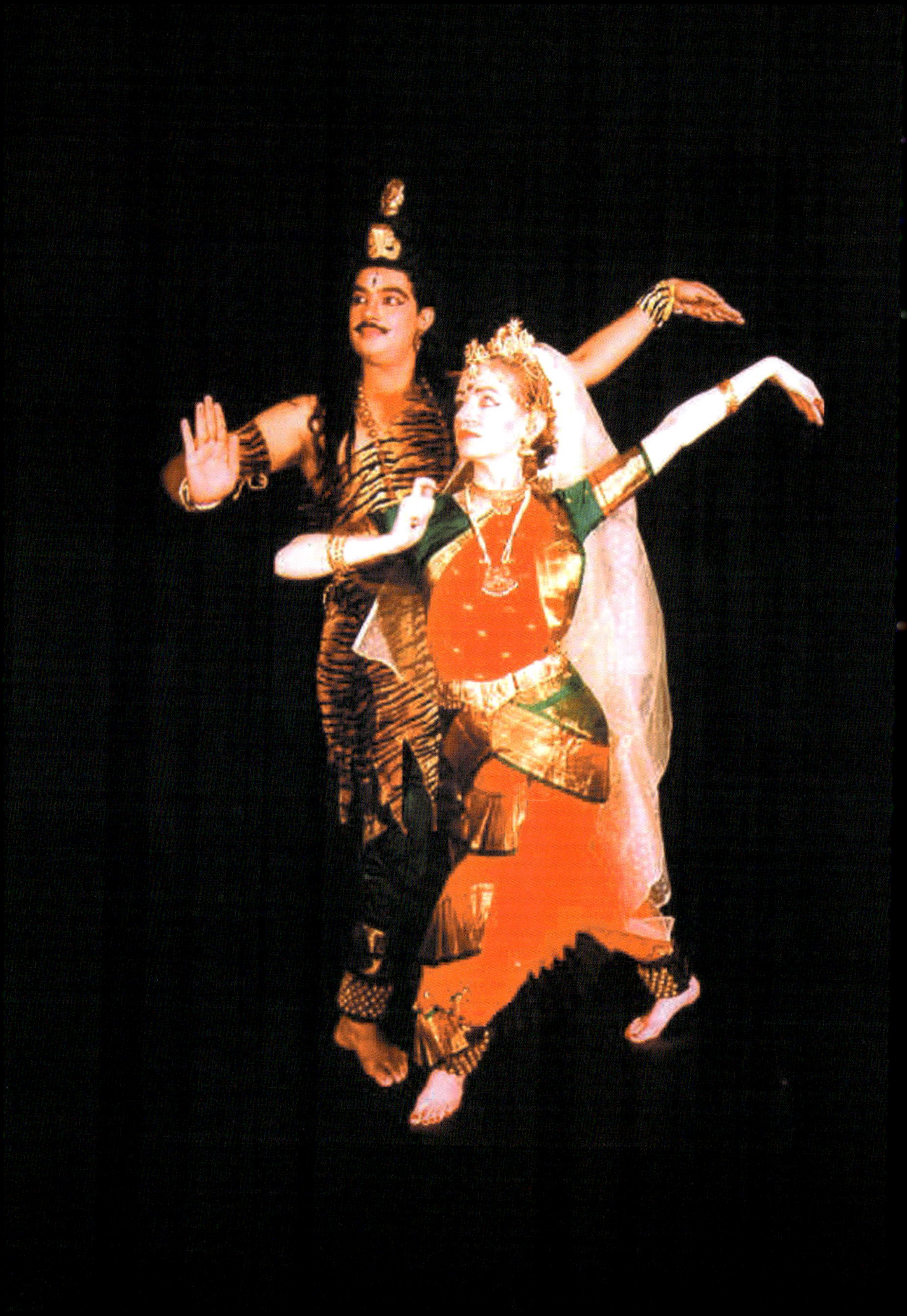

THE WELSH-ASIAN EXTRAVAGANZA – SHAPESHIFTING: August, a dark field, west Wales. Inside a warmly-lit marquee the women of WIT are gathered. This is a night of Welsh and Asian culture: we have seen the Shawl dance, heard Roma Choudhury singing ragas of boatmen and Lynn Denman calling home the Welsh cattle. Now comes Megan Lloyd. She steps on to the stage, the Indian dancer, in her 'patriotic sari' of red and green, her hair dressed with ornaments, exquisite as a picture in a story-book. The make-up that looked so dramatic and overloaded backstage, softens under the lights, leaving her beautiful. Before she begins she leans forward, hands on hips and looks at us. When she speaks, *in* English, her voice is sprightly. 'I think,' she says, and the idea seems to amuse her, 'I must be the Welsh-Asian connection!'

This is the Festival of Women in Tune: Cytgord y Merched. The atmosphere is intimate, supportive, expectant. We're not far now from where Megan grew up in Carmarthen, the grand-daughter of a minister. With her *guru*, her teacher, Kiran Ratna, of India Dance Wales, who has taught her *Bharat Natyam* – perhaps the most renowned of the classical dances of India – the joke is that this makes her priest class, Brahmin caste. There isn't supposed to be a caste system in India anymore, but if there was, Megan says she would, in fact, be very low ('shit class'), because she's not even Indian.

The theme for the night was chosen, says Esyllt Harker, organiser and storyteller, because Indian and Welsh cultures both involve a belief in shape-shifting: this makes Megan a perfect link in a running order that also has harpists and a Bollywood dancer.

Megan is working alone tonight, telling a story of transformations – the story of the Cauldron of Inspiration, brewed by Ceridwen the witch – from the Mabinogion. The telling is partly in English, partly in Welsh, with gestures; then she dances the story, with the form of Bharat Natyam that gives expression to narrative. The music Megan has chosen begins with a Welsh hurdy-gurdy and changes to Indian music. Stamping her feet to the rhythm, Megan's movements are dramatic and sure, telling the story through movement, gesture and expression. Her hands make *mudras*, pictures of things – a fleeing fish or bird – while her face (especially the eyes) offers emotion.

For the storytelling, Esyllt turns Megan's words into Welsh or English, so that language flows between them; a signer to the left of the stage interprets both spoken languages with equal facility. Sometimes, her movements and Megan's are alike: comically, they stir the cauldron together.

The performance has been prepared just for this event and Megan has chosen a story the women will like. So, not the story of how the festival of

Holi came into being (for *Holika*, the auntie who was burnt to ashes in an act of self-sacrifice and love), or a folk tale in which the heroine is well-behaved and wins herself a husband, by bearing gracefully and silently with her troubles, but the story of a woman who wants to improve the lot of her 'stupid boy' by brewing him a magic potion.

Another boy, Megan tells us, brought in to stir the cauldron for a year and a day, becomes bored at the very last, stops stirring and allows a great bubble to form. When it bursts, the first three magical drops fall scalding hot onto the boy's thumb. Quickly, he licks them off, and so acquires the power of transformation, and the wit to know that Ceridwen will be after him. He flees her, diving into a river and becoming a fish. She turns into an otter and the chase goes on. They continue to change shapes, until at last he disguises himself as a grain of wheat, and she pecks him up. 'That would be the end of the story,' says Megan, 'but nine months later....'

Her audience bursts out laughing and into applause. In nine months will be born Taliesin, the first bard of Wales.

It's an impressive performance. The movements of the dance are precise and dramatic, fluid and expressive; there is a sense of completeness. The modern forms of Bharat Natyam are derived from temple dances, sacramental and artistic in intention. Sometimes it is pure dance, movement in space and time. Sometimes there are mythic stories: of gods and heroes. Megan's costume is vibrant and exotic, made in the traditional way by an Indian tailor from a sari length of silk, into trousers with a kind of pleated skirt and the *dallu*, as they call it in Tamil, the end of the sari (sometimes decorated), coming over the shoulder, over a silk or cotton blouse. Her reddish hair looks darker when gelled down under the headpiece of her costume. Such an image as she presents might be found on the fourteenth century Temple of Chidambaram, which Megan says is, 'encrusted with carvings of dancers'. She's been there on one of her trips to India; it's an important place to visit: 'This is where Shiva danced.'

Shiva is the Lord of the Dance. 'There was that song in school assemblies: "Dance then wherever you may be!"' We remember later, and laugh about it; as if there ought to be a connection.

It is important to note Bharat Natyam is a classical dance. There are folk dances in India too and Megan has tried Kuchipudi, which comes out of folk traditions blended with Bharat Natyam. 'You stand on a plate and dance with a pot on your head.'

Why?

'Why not?'she says. But the origin of the dance has a story attached, and she tells it to me: 'There was a little boy who loved Krishna, who was taken in by the Temple; they could see he had talent so they taught him dance. But he always remembered the folk tradition from the streets where he grew up, so he put a little bit of that into it.'

Some authorities dispute the age of Bharat Natyam as an art form, perhaps because it is continually evolving. Certainly its influences and origins go back hundreds of years. India classical dance has its origin in the *Natya Shastra*, the fifth *Veda*, which drew on elements from the other *Vedas*, but, unlike them, was intended to be open to all castes and creeds.

Bharat Natyam is still thriving as a dance of worship in India. But alongside that it has always been considered an art form, therefore it is not supposed to remain static, but to evolve. Traditions are preserved but over time there has been a proliferation of styles and Bharat Natyam has spread from Tamil Nadu in the south of India, to be taught and performed in many countries around the world. Though Megan is Welsh, there is no doubt that she is skilled in her practice of the art, and the stories associated with the dance are as much a part of her life as the Mabinogion.

So Megan is a perfect choice as the lynch-pin of the evening's programme. She brings together Asia and Wales in her performance, and exemplifies the idea of shape-shifting in her life and person. She happily inhabits several lives: as performer and teacher; visual artist, storyteller and dancer.

UP AND DOWN THE A470 AND OFF TO OTHER PLACES: Things are 'hectic, manic' with Megan Lloyd; she has to talk fast to keep up with a review of her schedule: art projects, art classes, educational projects, storytelling, dance performances. Bharat Natyam seems to be her main focus; it brings together all three of her capabilities: dance, storytelling, visual art. 'It's everything.'

Her work with India Dance Wales involves education and performance. So, on the teaching side, she's kept busy running schools' projects as well as her own regular classes in batik, drawing and painting, at Llanover Hall. Megan also regularly attends the workshop run by Kiran Ratna at the Rubicon Dance Centre, joining in with whatever the group is learning.

Kiran is the artistic director and founder of India Dance Wales (formerly the Kiran Ratna Company) where Megan works as dancer, artist, storyteller and educator and plays her part in devising projects. Ingrid Wilson, then a director of India Dance Wales, called Megan their 'chief education, outreach person', though she is quick to point out 'Everything Megan does has Kiran in the background, because Kiran is her guru.'

Sometimes Megan and Kiran work together on a project, with Megan helping the children to produce art works and Kiran organising the dance. But at Maindy Primary School, in July 2003, Megan worked alone with the children for ten days on devising a performance of the story of Rama, Sita and the ten-headed demon. This is from the epic *Ramayana* and leads the children to an understanding of the origins of the Hindu festival of Diwali, so fitting nicely into the requirements of Key Stage 1 and 2 (R.E.) for the Year Threes. As well as learning the dance, the children make shadow puppets and batik flags, and those who have speaking parts make a recording.

Megan works all hours. After our morning at the school, she spends the afternoon showing me videos of her *Arangetram* (a solo performance consisting of nine or ten dances, before an invited audience, to demonstrate the high level the dancer has reached in Bharat Natyam) and pictures of her art work and photos of past projects. Then it's off to Kiran's workshop, at the Rubicon Dance Centre, where Megan did her foundation dance training, and first became Kiran's pupil.

Next time I see her is at Llanover Hall, where for several years she has run an art class for a special needs' group. Megan arrives in her practice sari from a morning's work at a school in Abertillery. After the workshop she returns there: the children are giving their performance that evening.

Later, we meet at the Beyond the Borders International Storytelling Festival at St. Donats. In the afternoon she tells stories alongside the traditional storyteller and musician, Francis Maxey, before transforming at night into the Bharat Natyam dancer again, to help interpret for the audience (who require a translation), the stories of great power from the epic Mahabharat, sung by Ritu Verma and her Pandvani Party. Then there's WIT, where she works solo, bringing together storytelling, dance, Welsh and English in a fine performance.

Megan is a hard worker. She takes things on, but does not seem to give anything up. Despite her success as an educator and performer, she still does the cleaning job she started doing years ago, to be sure of £20 a week coming in. It's not a big deal, she says, and finds it odd that, if she tells people about it, they look sorry for her. To Megan it is work, with its own value: in this case (apart from the twenty quid) the thing is that it's not a particularly dirty office, and she doesn't have to use her brain for a change. Occasionally, when her picture appears in the paper, people became aware that she has another life,

People know Megan. One day I bump into Peggy Holder who works for the BBC. When I tell her what I'm doing these days ('following Megan around') she nods at once: they're working together on a project at St. David's Hall. 'She's a very talented lady,' says Peggy. I look at my list of things that Megan is doing. This project is not on it. What else have I missed?

A talented lady: that's the opinion of a woman I meet at Beyond the Borders. While waiting to get into the marquee we fall into conversation. She's such a fan and she's brought her shiny-eyed grandchildren along to meet Megan and ask her to sign some story-books, a link to the Haiti Fund project she had been working on. Haiti? I rack my brain; again I check my notes. We've been talking for what seems like days now and I don't remember Haiti coming into the conversation. What else is there to discover? That she also sings and plays the violin, has told stories for Father Christmas in Lapland, appeared on Sky History's 'Celtic Myths', and made a giant lino print with the aid of a vintage steam roller at the Royal Welsh Show.

'I WAS HERE FIRST!': The boy was so excited about it, he had to tell all the other Year Threes as they arrived.

The school hall at Maindy Primary in Cwmbran is decorated with fantastic birds; there are two elephants walking out of one of the walls. The school has had an artist-in-residence working with the children for some weeks. Megan's is a ten-day project for India Dance Wales, the last in a two-year run, funded by a Lottery Arts for All grant. Near the centre of the hall is a calico screen, decorated around with batiked flags. This is the stage for the shadow puppets the children have made with Megan.

There will be two performances: Year Three teacher, Leigh Beddow, is setting out small chairs, on which parents and guests will sit for the first show. The second will be for the other pupils. Two weeks ago the whole school watched Megan's performance and heard the story of Rama and Sita and the 10-headed demon, so the tale and the dance will have some familiarity. In order to win the project, the school had to bid against others, to show how it would benefit them. The commitment of the staff and their appreciation of the project's educational and artistic merit, is as apparent as the children's excitement at putting on the show. All of the children are white and local to Cwmbran and they seem to be enlivened by this involvement with, and understanding of something they knew little about two weeks ago.

Already, parents are waiting to be let in. As soon as Megan arrives – dressed in her red practice sari and green blouse, eyes rimmed with kohl, reddish hair pulled back in an unfeasibly long plait (it's false but matches her hair colour perfectly; it's even a bit fluffed out) – the children cluster round her: they want her to tell them what to do.

'Costumes go on *over* your P.E. kit. Don't forget, boys, wear your trousers round your waists. That's where your belly-button is. Your skirts must be *tight*, girls.'

The children help each other with unfamiliar ties and gradually the colour-scape of the room changes, as monochrome gym kit disappears and bright red, blue, brown, and purple costumes blossom. Megan pins the girls'

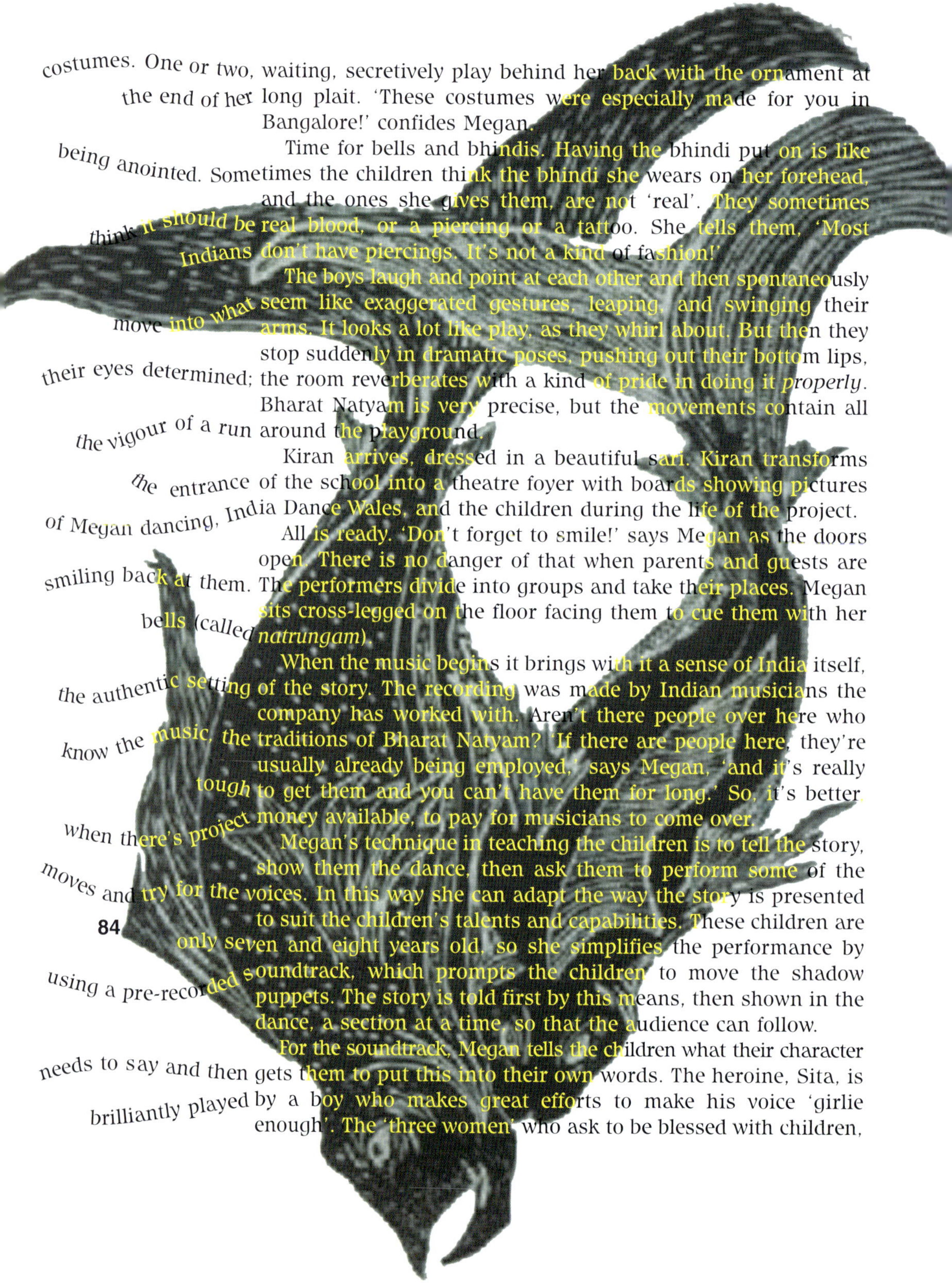

costumes. One or two, waiting, secretively play behind her back with the ornament at the end of her long plait. 'These costumes were especially made for you in Bangalore!' confides Megan.

Time for bells and bhindis. Having the bhindi put on is like being anointed. Sometimes the children think the bhindi she wears on her forehead, and the ones she gives them, are not 'real'. They sometimes think it should be real blood, or a piercing or a tattoo. She tells them, 'Most Indians don't have piercings. It's not a kind of fashion!'

The boys laugh and point at each other and then spontaneously move into what seem like exaggerated gestures, leaping, and swinging their arms. It looks a lot like play, as they whirl about. But then they stop suddenly in dramatic poses, pushing out their bottom lips, their eyes determined; the room reverberates with a kind of pride in doing it *properly*. Bharat Natyam is very precise, but the movements contain all the vigour of a run around the playground.

Kiran arrives, dressed in a beautiful sari. Kiran transforms the entrance of the school into a theatre foyer with boards showing pictures of Megan dancing, India Dance Wales, and the children during the life of the project.

All is ready. 'Don't forget to smile!' says Megan as the doors open. There is no danger of that when parents and guests are smiling back at them. The performers divide into groups and take their places. Megan sits cross-legged on the floor facing them to cue them with her bells (called *natrungam*).

When the music begins it brings with it a sense of India itself, the authentic setting of the story. The recording was made by Indian musicians the company has worked with. Aren't there people over here who know the music, the traditions of Bharat Natyam? 'If there are people here, they're usually already being employed,' says Megan, 'and it's really tough to get them and you can't have them for long.' So, it's better when there's project money available, to pay for musicians to come over.

Megan's technique in teaching the children is to tell the story, show them the dance, then ask them to perform some of the moves and try for the voices. In this way she can adapt the way the story is presented to suit the children's talents and capabilities. These children are only seven and eight years old, so she simplifies the performance by using a pre-recorded soundtrack, which prompts the children to move the shadow puppets. The story is told first by this means, then shown in the dance, a section at a time, so that the audience can follow.

For the soundtrack, Megan tells the children what their character needs to say and then gets them to put this into their own words. The heroine, Sita, is brilliantly played by a boy who makes great efforts to make his voice 'girlie enough'. The 'three women' who ask to be blessed with children, do so with muffled giggles. When the hero introduces himself, he is polite, but informal: 'Hi. I'm Rama.' The Creator, Brahma, has made up his own solemn warning: 'I'm watching you, 'cause I created you.' When the big bird Jatayu comes to help Rama, the ten-headed demon shakes with anger and shouts, 'You pesky bird!' Poor Jatayu is defeated, flutters down and dies. The children, bypassing any issues of mythological relevance, comment with dismissive finality on the bird's effectiveness in a fight: 'He wasn't much good, was he?'

Eventually the hero and the demon fight it out. The dance that follows is one the children thoroughly enjoy. There happen to be ten children representing the ten-headed demon; these are encircled by others and defeated. But because it's no fun to only play the vanquished, this part of the dance is repeated so the children can take it in turns to be on the winning side.

Many of the parents stay to congratulate and thank Megan, telling her how the children in the play have been practising at home. 'It was beautiful,' says one. 'The children's eyes were sparkling; and the costumes.'

Ingrid Wilson sums up her feelings about the value of the experience: 'These children will never see Indians in the same way again.'

At the end, when it's all over, so is the project. One girl is sad and keeps returning for a 'last' hug, because Megan won't be back tomorrow.

CAN A WHITE WELSH GIRL DANCE BHARAT NATYAM?: Into a school such as this, Megan breathes the air of another world; small children sometimes assume that she has just come from India. 'How did you get here today?' they ask. 'By car,' says Megan. And, if they look puzzled, she might add, 'Well, I didn't come on a magic carpet!'

Sometimes the children won't believe that Megan is Welsh, saying, 'No she's not; she's Indian.' And that Kiran and Megan 'are sisters'. Obviously. But more than once people say they are 'like mirrors' of each other. This gives them an advantage in their performances: as Kiran's pupil, Megan has learned, largely by being shown, those styles of Bharat Natyam that Kiran knows.

In some of the schools Megan visits, the cultural range and mix is greater; if they know something of the stories, or elements of traditional performance, Megan can incorporate that. At the Kitchener Road School she remembers a Sikh boy who knew how to make 'the horse', which involves acrobalance in motion. He was one of those 'stroppy' characters that Megan recollects with a kind of affection, the sense of achievement of having got good work from them. She said to him, 'You know how to do the horse: get your friends, teach 'em.' And at the end of that show, the boy made the horse and rode it off.

As Ingrid Wilson says, 'The children's experiences affect the way the art is produced and the art affects the children's experience.'

It is certain that, for some people, seeing a white Welsh person able to perform the traditional Indian art of Bharat Natyam to such a high level makes them realise that it is possible that those who are also 'not Indian' might be capable of engaging with it. Inevitably, the question of authenticity comes up. Though it is not something that Megan needs to think about much from her own standpoint (this is an art form, like any other, and if she can dance flamenco why not Bharat Natyam?) sometimes other people come with their own expectations and are less accepting than the children.

At the WIT festival, backstage, I talked to Noni Jenkyn Jones, a white girl who dances Kathak which is, traditionally, the classical dance of northern India. Noni and I had been chatting happily, but her expression became weary as I broached the subject of cultural expectations – 'That age-old chestnut,' she called it – whether a white girl would be accepted as an exponent of a form of classical Indian dance. As with Bharat Natyam, the practice of Kathak has been subjected to misreadings and misinterpretations; for instance, because these dances were performed by unmarried women who sometimes had children (women who devoted their lives to the temple and the practice of their art) it was seen, under the British Raj, as being somehow salacious. Now that the dances are performed around the world, inevitably some members of the audience question whether what they are seeing is 'the real thing'.

Watching a Bharat Natyam performance by India Dance Wales, it is sometimes easier for certain members of the audience to accept Kiran Ratna's 'right' to practise the art form, because she 'looks Indian'. Yet Kiran is no more from Tamil Nadu than Megan. Kiran was born in Kenya, and spent her early years in the Punjab, where she learned to dance Kathak. As a young girl in Britain, Kiran went to ballet classes. When her guru (Chitraleka Bolar, herself from Kerala) moved to Birmingham where Kiran lived with her family, it was an opportunity to do Indian dance of some kind. So, says Megan, Kiran 'switched to Bharat Natyam because of who was there and the opportunity at the time.'

When the songs that accompany the dance are in Sanskrit, Kiran, as a Hindi-speaker, has an advantage in understanding. But, many are sung in Tamil, and in such cases all the dancers are in a position of needing to achieve familiarity with the story in English, and learn key words to listen out for.

On the subject of 'right to perform', Megan mentions the case of a white practitioner of Bharat Natyam, called Madeleine, who was brought up in Tamil Nadu, and speaks Tamil. Even her teacher, her guru, sometimes says to her. 'When are you going to dye your hair then? You've got to dye your hair.' Because Madeleine is blonde. Though Megan says it was fashionable for dancers to make themselves fair-skinned, the blonde hair is a sure marker of a different ethnicity from the one audiences expect to be associated with an 'authentic' practitioner of the dance.

The way Kiran sees it, according to Megan, is this: 'She's teaching an art form. It's like, you don't have to be French to do ballet, or you don't have to be Spanish to do flamenco.'

Generally there is acceptance; when there is not, neither Megan nor the company allow this to affect the way they feel about their work. They cope, with characteristic humour. Sometimes, Megan tells me, white members of the audience say the oddest things. 'We did this show once (in Llandrindod Wells) where I was the storyteller as well. This woman said afterwards, "Oh yes, I really enjoyed the show. But it was a pity that the first person we saw was white. Couldn't she wear a mask or something?"

'Get a mask on' has been a running joke in the company ever since.

When the company did *The Tempest*, Megan did wear a mask. 'But that was just coincidence,' she says.

In fact, there is no large community of people from Tamil Nadu in south Wales and India Dance Wales is the only professional dance company bringing Bharat Natyam to Welsh audiences. Part of what Megan does is to act as a bridge between cultures.

Megan tells another story: she and Kiran had done a big show in Manchester. An Indian lady saw them off-stage and said, '"Oh, the dance was really good." You could see the look of confusion on her face, when she saw me close up,' says Megan, 'that I was white.' She bursts out laughing as she recalls what Kiran said, voicing what the woman was clearly thinking: '"She danced really well for a white person, didn't she?" The poor woman was looking for a PC way to say it.'

Well, you might be able to change nationality, but trying to deny either your culture or colour would be to become *more* false. Megan says Kiran's attitude is: 'It's art. You do art, whatever you are.'

Sometimes Kiran is asked of Megan's performance, 'But is it Bharat Natyam?' and Kiran will say, 'Well, what else have I taught her?'

ALL GURUS TOGETHER - HOW MEGAN BE CAME A DANCER: Every guru has a guru of their own. Megan teaches the children and her guru is Kiran. Kiran learned from Chitraleka Bolar and Chitraleka had her guru. Through Chitraleka came the connection to Master Ji, who made much of the music still used by India Dance Wales. Master Ji, Sreedharan Mundanghat, was a greatly respected figure and versatile composer of verses. He was Chitraleka's guru's musician (he died of cancer in 2000). 'We haven't found anybody like him,' says Megan, 'who could just...' she snaps her fingers, 'wander off into a corner and come back with the next verse.'

Having herself reached the high standard in Bharat Natyam necessary to perform her Arangetram, Kiran decided she would like to teach someone else to that level. For the Arangetram, the dancer demonstrates familiarity with and skill in dancing the classical repertoire, performing solo nine or ten dances in a traditional sequence – including an invocation, and examples of both pure and narrative dance – before an audience of invited guests and well-wishers. Kiran asked Megan if she was willing to try, and Megan agreed, 'Not thinking anything would really happen; it would take three hundred years.' But in 1994, at Chapter Arts Centre, Megan's Arangetram took place. It was the first time Kiran did this for a pupil, so it was a big occasion for both of them. Her own guru Chitraleka, was present, along with Megan's friends and family, and special guests.

Megan's Arangetram was timed to coincide with one of those periods when musicians were brought over from India. So, Master Ji himself was there to provide the music.

'It was pretty scary,' says Megan, 'there he is, this guy whose voice we hear all the time; and he knows everything about dance.'

What did he think about a Welsh girl wanting to do Indian Dance? 'They don't seem to mind because they think, "Yes, of course, everybody wants to do Indian Dance. Don't be stupid!"' But she adds, 'They will always think that you will be second rate. They will think that. But you can still do it. And they will also be impressed.'

'There was a lovely song, a special Master Ji's done, to the goddess Parvati. And every time we rehearsed it, he used to get up and walk out. I thought, "Oh God. What have I done wrong? It must be so bad he can't bear it." But what it was, the song upset him. So he would go out because he was a bit "done in". And it is beautiful; we've got a recording of him just singing it. When we did my Arangetram, I loved that piece, and I ran off-stage and burst into tears. And that was really good, because I was scared I wouldn't enjoy it – but to cry your eyes out on your Arangetram is quite good really.'

Teaching methods are on the change, as there are now formal exams that can be taken in Bharat Natyam. Some of the dance steps Megan learned by being shown and by doing, have been given standardised names. The way that Megan learned was a follow-on from the way Kiran was taught, and Kiran's teacher before her. 'Chitral learnt as a little child and she just did whatever she was told (her dance teacher's really good. Kiran's been out to him); and she said she never questioned; just did it all the time, all the time. And she taught a little bit like that and that's how Kiran first started teaching. She taught us all the steps as we went along.'

I wondered if learning Bharat Natyam was a case of 'just doing hands' for a year. But at Kiran Ratna's workshop at the Rubicon, I find myself involved in whole dance sequences.

Some of the students are tiny children, others women older than I am. The workshop mantra 'all ages and abilities' runs through my head. Though I stand, instinctively, with the grown-ups, Kiran sends me to be with the small children and newest recruits, who are kind to me, when the dances become more complicated.

Each sequence is performed at three or four speeds. In the simpler movements I can keep up, but when several things have to be thought of at once, hands, feet, arms, I struggle at second speed, am lost at third. It's hard work, but hugely enjoyable and I can see how easy it would be to become hooked on trying to do this well.

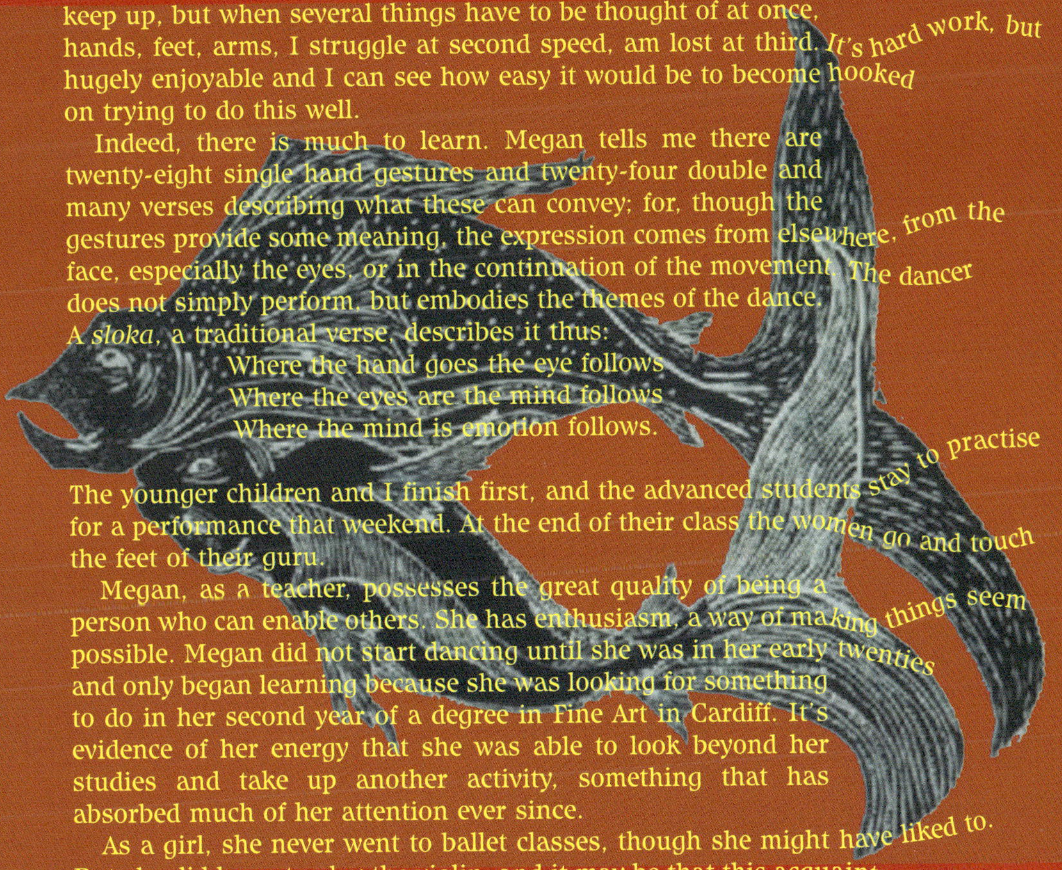

Indeed, there is much to learn. Megan tells me there are twenty-eight single hand gestures and twenty-four double and many verses describing what these can convey; for, though the gestures provide some meaning, the expression comes from elsewhere, from the face, especially the eyes, or in the continuation of the movement. The dancer does not simply perform, but embodies the themes of the dance. A *sloka*, a traditional verse, describes it thus:

Where the hand goes the eye follows
Where the eyes are the mind follows
Where the mind is emotion follows.

The younger children and I finish first, and the advanced students stay to practise for a performance that weekend. At the end of their class the women go and touch the feet of their guru.

Megan, as a teacher, possesses the great quality of being a person who can enable others. She has enthusiasm, a way of making things seem possible. Megan did not start dancing until she was in her early twenties and only began learning because she was looking for something to do in her second year of a degree in Fine Art in Cardiff. It's evidence of her energy that she was able to look beyond her studies and take up another activity, something that has absorbed much of her attention ever since.

As a girl, she never went to ballet classes, though she might have liked to. But she did learn to play the violin, and it may be that this acquaintance with melody and rhythm, and her feeling for line and colour from her work as an artist, helped her to catch up. Undoubtedly she drew upon innate, unpractised ability as a dancer.

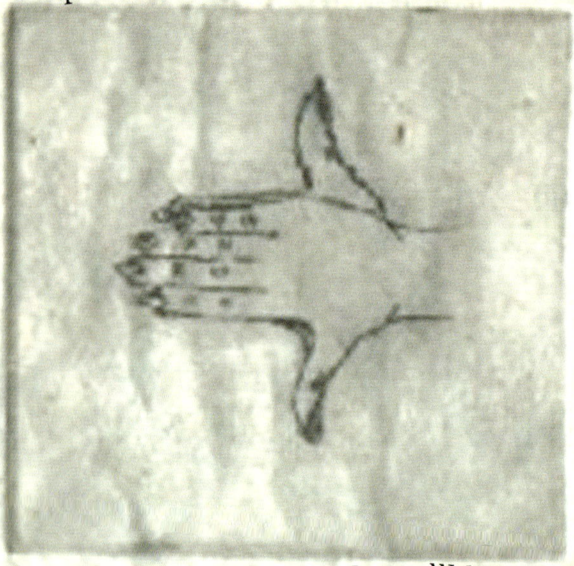

Megan started very late, but the fact that she has come so far since then is evidence of her way of thinking 'I can do that', which is carried over into her educational work. She gets the best out of people, and so helps them see the best in themselves. Though she readily admits that she would like to be a performer all the time, and that educational work is the bread and butter to the jam of performance, she does a great job as a teacher. Somehow, I think she likes to encourage those who don't usually have much of a chance.

Though Megan is involved in all aspects of outreach work for India Dance Wales, when they work together on such projects it is usually Kiran who directs the dance side, while Megan takes care of the art work. And this is appropriate, because, as a teacher, Megan has previous experience: she's been running art workshops for years.

ART – LLANOVER HALL: Richard Manners, then the Art Therapist at Ely Hospital, brought a group to Megan, as their first step towards a life outside the hospital, and in the community. That group, her first at Llanover Hall Arts Centre, is still running, with some of the original members in attendance.

Apart from her special needs class, Megan also runs Saturday morning junior arts, a class in batik, and a painting and drawing class. The work at Llanover Hall has led to commissions. She's run summer schools and various art projects. From Bargoed to Barry there are works on show that Megan has had a hand in producing: exhibitions, murals, prints.

'Print-making, etchings and photography, silk screen…' these are things she 'just did', learning 'along the way', and producing her first works at the Cardiff Print Workshop. One thing informs another: from there she moved into textiles; batik, she says, is similar to printmaking in its process.

On the day I meet her at Llanover Hall she turns up in her dance sari to work towards an exhibition with her special needs group, making pottery and batik with a Japanese theme. The results will go on show in Cardiff Central Library.

They are making batik banners and Megan demonstrates three different design motifs they might use, and guides them through each stage, showing, for example, how to create the outline of a bird by drawing around their hands. There is a moment when it seems as if nothing will happen, when all there is, is blank paper; but magically, with encouragement from Megan, and various support workers, a wealth of different pictures takes shape. And Megan is happy to go along with the variations and changes produced. The students do as much of the process as they can complete themselves, including the application of the hot wax.

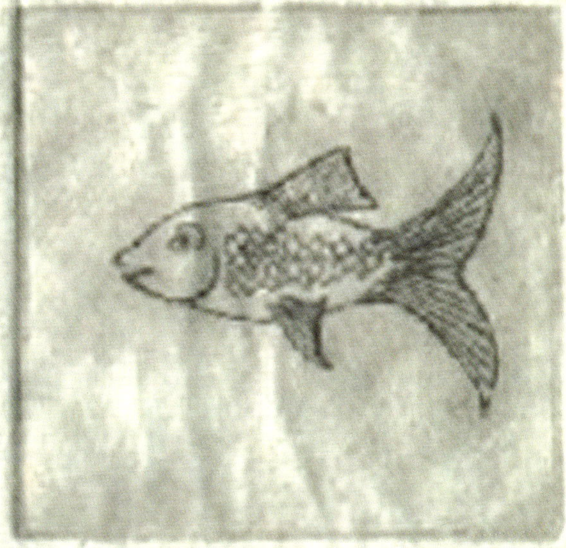

Earlier Megan showed me photographs of murals she's helped to produce. Often these have an educational intention, though they also function to transform drab walls into vivid, energising backdrops to play.

She remembers these projects with pride and affection. In one school in Llanrumney, the older children were asked to make a Welsh alphabet for the infants. 'It went on for ages; all those double letters! What we did was a letter with a little picture, so it was huge in the end; it probably covered the hall.'

At St. Helen's School, Barry, they were wondering what to take as their theme. Megan suggested a journey: from the Valleys to the sea. The children were asked to draw their impressions. Castell Coch featured in everybody's pictures, that being, 'As far up the valley as they could think from Barry.' In her own way, Megan is engaged in making children aware of their place within south Wales, their links to those near to them, yet out of sight. The mural showed, in the end, 'Castell Coch, the train, houses getting closer and closer and closer, Barry Island, round the corner, then we went underneath the sea and had a shipwreck.'

Some children have achieved junior immortality through Megan's work. At Moorlands she had led a project to create a Millennium Line and was then invited back to help make a wall that reflected school trips to a farm which was visited by a group of pupils every year. 'They brought in photographs of the things they liked on the farm, like milking

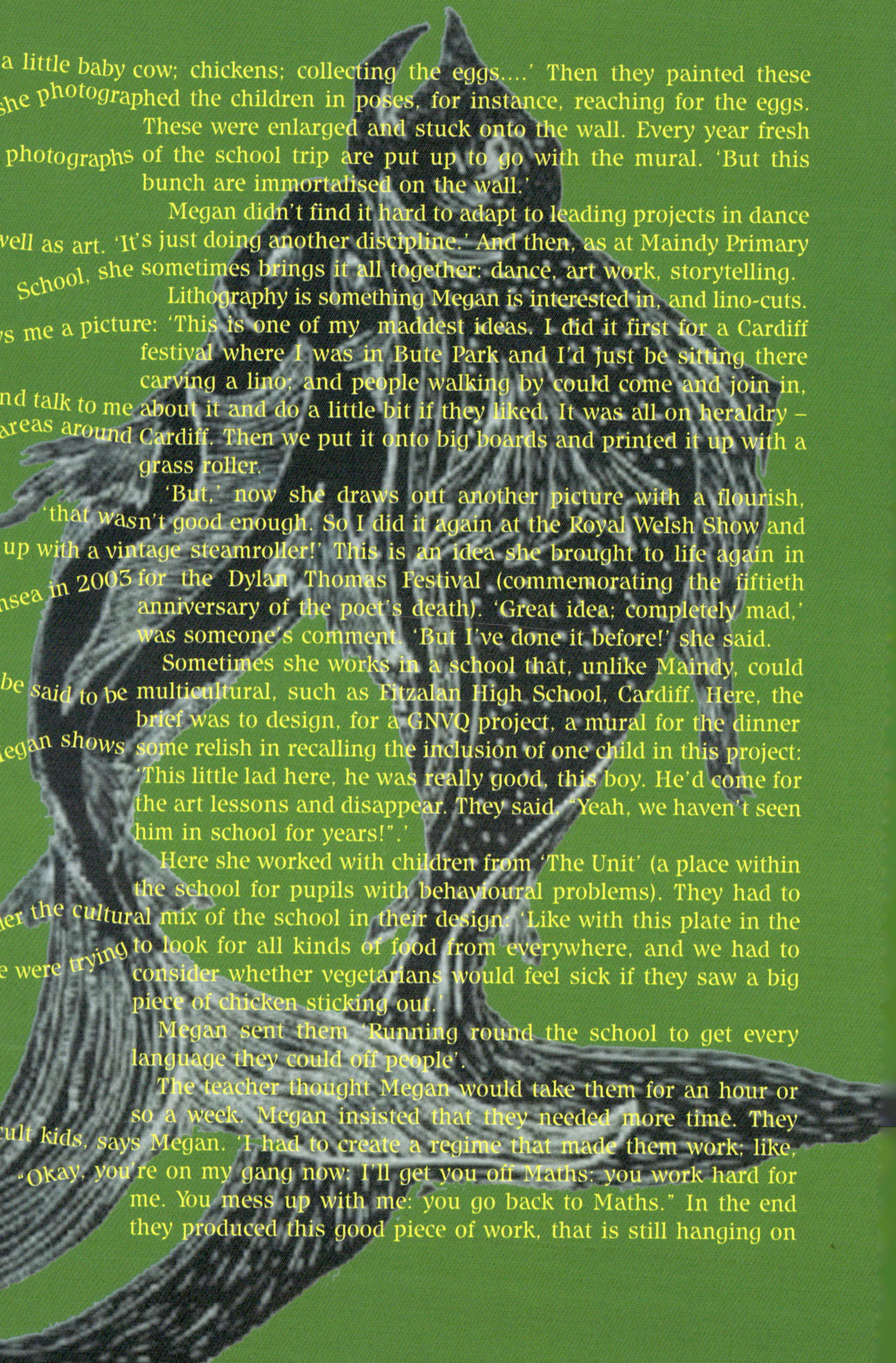

the goats; a little baby cow; chickens; collecting the eggs....' Then they painted these and she photographed the children in poses, for instance, reaching for the eggs. These were enlarged and stuck onto the wall. Every year fresh photographs of the school trip are put up to go with the mural. 'But this bunch are immortalised on the wall.'

Megan didn't find it hard to adapt to leading projects in dance as well as art. 'It's just doing another discipline.' And then, as at Maindy Primary School, she sometimes brings it all together: dance, art work, storytelling.

Lithography is something Megan is interested in, and lino-cuts. She shows me a picture: 'This is one of my maddest ideas. I did it first for a Cardiff festival where I was in Bute Park and I'd just be sitting there carving a lino; and people walking by could come and join in, sit down and talk to me about it and do a little bit if they liked. It was all on heraldry – on the areas around Cardiff. Then we put it onto big boards and printed it up with a grass roller.

'But,' now she draws out another picture with a flourish, 'that wasn't good enough. So I did it again at the Royal Welsh Show and printed it up with a vintage steamroller!' This is an idea she brought to life again in Swansea in 2003 for the Dylan Thomas Festival (commemorating the fiftieth anniversary of the poet's death). 'Great idea; completely mad,' was someone's comment. 'But I've done it before!' she said.

Sometimes she works in a school that, unlike Maindy, could be said to be multicultural, such as Fitzalan High School, Cardiff. Here, the brief was to design, for a GNVQ project, a mural for the dinner hall. Megan shows some relish in recalling the inclusion of one child in this project: 'This little lad here, he was really good, this boy. He'd come for the art lessons and disappear. They said, "Yeah, we haven't seen him in school for years!".'

Here she worked with children from 'The Unit' (a place within the school for pupils with behavioural problems). They had to consider the cultural mix of the school in their design: 'Like with this plate in the middle, we were trying to look for all kinds of food from everywhere, and we had to consider whether vegetarians would feel sick if they saw a big piece of chicken sticking out.'

Megan sent them 'Running round the school to get every language they could off people'.

The teacher thought Megan would take them for an hour or so a week. Megan insisted that they needed more time. They were difficult kids, says Megan. 'I had to create a regime that made them work; like, "Okay, you're on my gang now; I'll get you off Maths; you work hard for me. You mess up with me; you go back to Maths." In the end they produced this good piece of work, that is still hanging on the wall, apparently.'

Her careers overlap: while she was learning dance she was running art classes and developing her interests in print-making. Having taken classes in Bharat Natyam with Kiran, at the Rubicon Community Dance Centre, which she had picked 'by pure chance of curiosity', she was 'hooked on dance.' She wanted to do more. In 1986-87 she attended the Rubicon's pilot scheme for Primary Dance Training. 'I went to everything,' she says. As well as Bharat Natyam she tried flamenco and Egyptian belly dancing. Her first professional performances as a dancer were for Consort de Dance Baroque, with Phillipa Waite, doing original early dance works.

Her own early, independent art works were strongly influenced by dance. She says she's had little time for her own work lately, because of her involvement in 'bigger things'. But among her past works, she shows me an etching, depicting a fish and a line drawing of two hands, with the word *matsya*, the name for the two-handed *mudras* meaning fish, written in Sanskrit between them; and a colour lithograph of a pose, showing the feet and hands of a dancer, performing *namaskar*, which is, in this case, a reverent salutation where the dancer touches the floor and asks pardon for the act of stamping on the earth that will follow. Megan used to wear socks with parrots on them, and fancied how it would be if they made her as light and agile as she could wish. The caption reads: 'If my feet became birds.'

BROWNIES (AND BEYOND): When Megan was eight, the Brownies had a Thinking Day. They were asked to think about the Commonwealth. Each Brownie put her hand into a bag and pulled out the name of a country. Megan brought out 'India' and that was the subject for her project. This was Carmarthen in the early Seventies. She didn't know any Indian people. But her father, a dentist, did. In particular he knew doctors in the hospital. There was one, Dr Sinharoy who was his friend. Her father would often talk about him, admiringly, how, when he was speaking his own language (she thinks it was Gujarati) on the phone, he would turn and say, 'Oh yes, that was my wife. I was talking to her in Welsh, fluently.'

Then there is the family mythology. Megan's Uncle Ambrose was in India at the end of the Second World War and asked to be there for Independence. 'Uncle Ambrose knew a lot about India, and I think Dad had a yearning, he would have liked to have gone, but he never did.' If an Indian lady came into her father's surgery he would tell Megan about it later, with a kind of wonder: '"The perfume!" he would say; and once, "she had rings on her toes!"'

Megan drew a map of India and put that in her scrapbook, together with, 'Whatever you do when you're eight and you do a project on something.' Her Auntie, Gwenda, a primary school teacher, had items on 'tea' from Tetley's. Great Aunt Ethel gave Megan a little brass bell and a printed piece of fabric which was thought to have come from India, brought back by Great Uncle Iram after the First World War. From her Dad's friend, Dr Sinharoy, came two cards, 'One of red velvet, with little white silhouettes cut on it, of little people, a little Indian scene. I thought these cards were the best thing ever. They were like magic.'

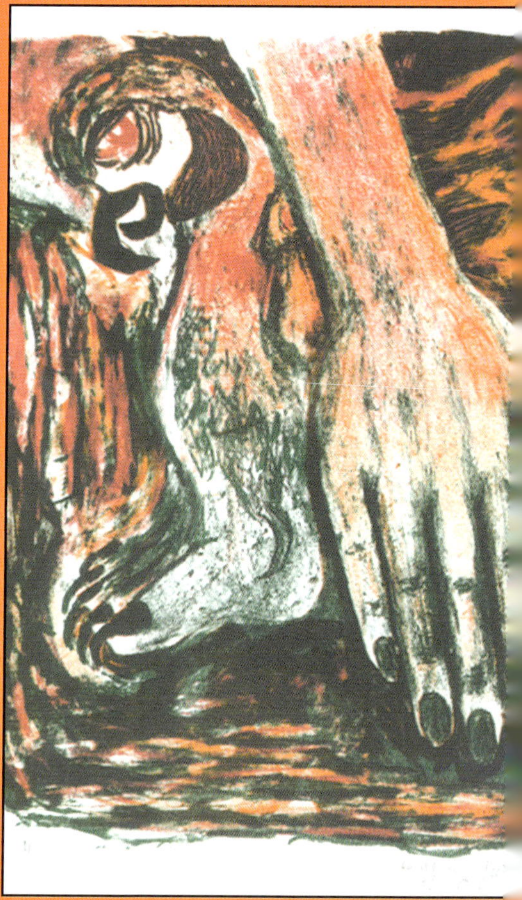

VISITING INDIA: Megan's experiences in Tamil Nadu (she's been out there twice) helped her decide to favour Bharat Natyam over the other forms of dance she'd been learning at the Rubicon.

The first visit was before her Arangetram. She went on a dance course. 'It was for people from all over the world, to do south Asian arts. A lot of Australians, some people from India, like designers, an actor, musicians. There were some British Indians there. We were taught by really good people. We did Bharat Natyam, and Kathakali, and Kalari, which is a martial arts form. I reckon I got my stamina from that course.' We'd talked about how she would love to dance every day, and that was the time when she could do just that. It was then that Megan decided that she should choose to concentrate on one dance form: Bharat Natyam. Why choose this? It has visual colour, linear correctness, expression through hand movements, dance, and song. It's the ultimate performance. 'This is opera,' says Megan. 'This is telling a story. It's everything.'

A dancer wishing to study Bharat Natyam would think themselves well-placed in Tamil Nadu. But here there have been changes. When Megan did her course there was a contemporary-type class.' She tried that but did not get on with it, though certainly it seems to be a fashionable and developing form in India. At first, when Megan saw performances of contemporary dance, she thought they were not getting it right, and it seemed a waste of the talents of the Bharat Natyam dancers, when they could do that 'so beautifully'. But now companies are using contemporary dancers and incorporating Bharat Natyam styles and influences and something new is happening, a contemporary Indian style.

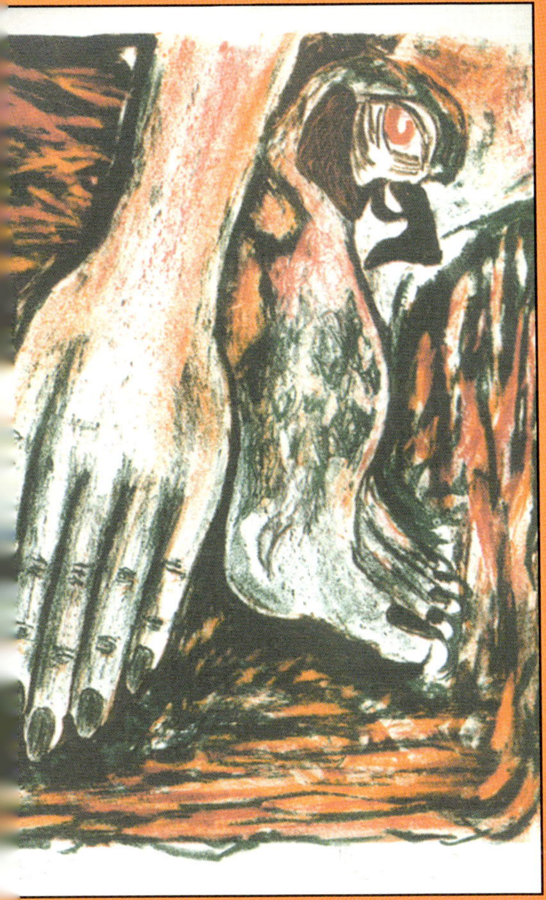

When Kiran went out some years later, the same course no longer offered Bharat Natyam. And this was a matter of regret for someone wishing to tap into the dance form at what is regarded as its source, even though, in Wales, the company produces work that goes beyond tradition. With India Dance Wales, Megan has been involved in productions that tell stories from the Mabinogion, as well as the Mahabharat and the Ramayana, the epic tales of India. Some productions are large-scale, others focus on Kiran and Megan as dancers, as with the *Navarasas*, the nine emotions of Shiva. Adventurously, there have been shows such as *Puranic Visions* which used ultraviolet light and effects, and *The Tempest*. Here for once, Megan, playing Ariel, was able to understand all the words of the song (as it was in English) played for her freedom dance, and improvise her moves in rehearsals. It made her realise that, if she spoke Tamil, 'This is how easy it would be'. Even so, she's happy it's not all in English. It would be easier, but, she says, 'I like the idea of doing mixtures.'

Hoping for a tour that reflected a two-way spread of ideas, the company wanted to take *The Tempest*, in which Kiran and Megan worked with dancers and musicians from Bangalore and Mysore, to India. But no funding was forthcoming for a tour. Apparently, even if you're bringing an Indian dance version of Shakespeare, that's not 'new enough'. Yet it seems that India Dance Wales excels in finding ways to make Bharat Natyam relevant to its Welsh audience.

Megan and Kiran's costumes were made for them in India. On her last trip, Megan found herself putting her artistic skills to use, sketching for their tailor the costumes they would like to wear, a mix of Indian dance-sari style and something resembling Welsh flannel, for their production of the Mahabharat-Mabinogion.

The Mahabharat-Mabinogion production came about because Megan and Kiran told each other stories from their own traditions. The Mahabharat, one of the epics of India is as well-known there, as the Mabinogion is here. That is, even if some children these days haven't heard the stories, the older generation knows them. In India the stories are adapted for children and sometimes told in comic books. In her own way, Megan is involved in keeping those Welsh storytelling traditions in the eye and mind of the audiences of today as well as bringing them an understanding of how similar the underlying myths and legends of different cultures can be.

Kiran and Megan would tell each other stories and found there were similar themes. 'And similar outrageous things. In the Mahabharat there's a guy called Bishma who has a charmed life and can't die'; in the Mabinogion his equivalent would be Lleu Llaw Gyffes.

So they came up with a production that incorporated stories from both traditions. All were in Welsh, and used storytelling and Bharat Natyam.

In Bangor they threw sweets!

NOT WELSH ENOUGH?: In some ways Megan has been a bridge, drawing Welsh people, not least her own family, friends and connections, to an appreciation of the art and myth of Indian culture. But, she has sometimes found herself in a cultural no-man's land when it comes to representing the company in interviews. For, though Megan's father speaks Welsh, she did not grow up bilingual. Here is a source of certain regrets – such as being unable to represent the company in the Welsh-speaking media. It seems that for Kiran not to be able to speak in English on a Welsh-language arts programme would be acceptable. But for Megan, a white girl with a Welsh accent, it is not. 'They would dub Kiran,' she says, 'whereas they wouldn't dub me.' Thinking back to the way she is sometimes treated for being white and daring to want to do Indian dance she says, 'So, I'm still the underdog.'

That is changing. Megan is attending classes in Welsh, and is learning to speak her father's language. Following a course at summer school, she is having regular lessons and is already leading an art class for Welsh-speaking children at Llanover Hall. The lessons are conducted all in Welsh: 'Unless I'm desperate,' she says, in which case she can call on the help of her two assistants, who know her, one through attending a painting and drawing class, and both from batik classes.

BEING DANIEL MORDEN: This is how Megan's storytelling career began: in 1992 she joined the Kiran Ratna company. Daniel Morden was their storyteller – the use of a narrator helped to open up the dance to a wider audience – but he couldn't always be there. So Megan became his understudy. Though she loves stories, she didn't know before then what it was to be a storyteller. Characteristically, she said, 'Okay, what is it? I'll do it.'

Daniel was asked if he would have an apprentice, 'And he didn't mind and so,' says Megan, 'I had a little session with him, where he said, "Right, come back tomorrow and tell me a story."' She passed that test. Then he said she should go on a course at St. Donats with Abbi Patrix, who had been in Peter Brook's *Mahabharat*, 'Which was scary'. This led to her getting together with other people from that course: David Ambrose, who now organises Beyond the Borders; Daniel; Francis Maxey; and Peter Stacey, the musician. Peter provided traditional sounds for their Welsh tales, and coaxed them into playing. 'We were like an advert for the storytelling festival,' says Megan, 'and we'd go round telling people about it; telling people what stories were and doing shows all over the place.'

So now Megan performs as a storyteller, independently of her dance work. Sometimes it is 'pure storytelling', that is, the storytelling is the main feature. But still it is influenced by her knowledge of gesture and expression. With India Dance Wales, she says at first, 'The storytelling was just to "be Daniel" really. To say what he said. And from then it developed.' It was soon clear that Megan would look the part, dressed in her dance sari, and could easily add the gestures and expressions of the dance to illustrate the story. This also helped the audience to associate elements of the dance with the narrative thread, characterisation, and emotion of the tale. It was fitting that Daniel Morden came to Megan's Arangetram and performed the Introduction.

Megan's first storytelling experience with India Dance Wales was for their production of *Shakuntalah*, in which the company also used her art work for the first time (for the poster and backdrop). In this story a significant ring is dropped overboard and swallowed by a fish.

One of the first stories Megan told, working on her own as a storyteller, and one that people remember her for is 'The Salmon Cariad', which appears in Alan Garner's collection, *A Bag of Moonshine*. Here is a story where a fish becomes a woman and lives happily with her fisherman husband.

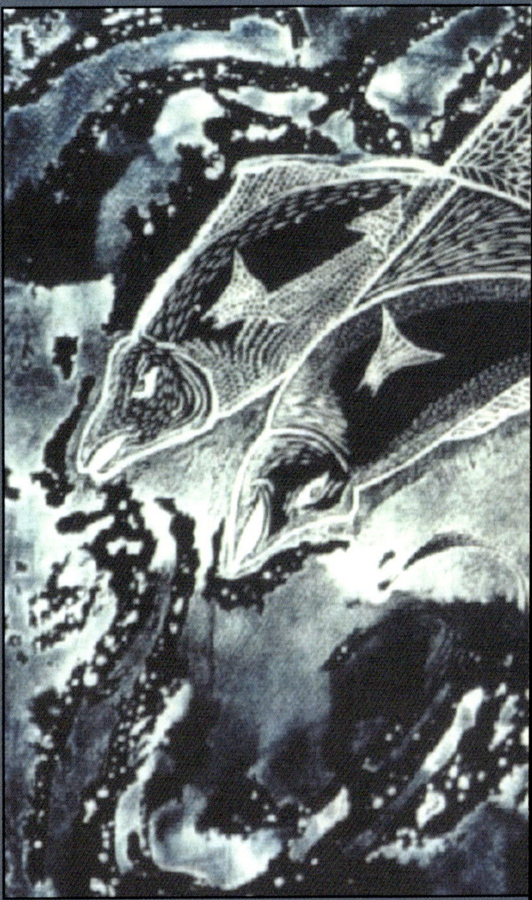

It's a story she loves. And that, says Megan, is part of the secret of being a good teller of tales: 'You have to love the story.'

THE TRANSCENDENTAL FISH: Megan seems to have an affinity with fish: fishy stories, pictures of fish, the flapping, swimming fish illustrated by the hands in Bharat Natyam; they swim in and out of her work, as storyteller, artist and dancer, surfacing in all that she does.

Maybe we like fishy stories because they speak to us of our evolutionary origins; because inside us we carry the salt water that surrounded our ancestors. How many legends have something to do with fish? The fish that swallows a ring, the fish that becomes a woman, or a man. Mostly the tendency is towards the fish becoming more human. Even Anderson's Little Mermaid makes the transition from water to land.

But one story of a fish, collected by Daniel Morden in Haiti and told by Megan at the tenth anniversary of Beyond the Borders, is a little different.

St. Donats; the Storytelling Pavilion. In this afternoon performance, Megan takes turns with Francis Maxey, the one providing musical sounds for the story the other is telling. Megan looks very different today: her long hair loose, her skirt full and candy-striped, a black gypsy blouse; she's like a miniature Rita Heyworth – with a fiddle.

Francis plays the dulcimer, and the music bubbles into silence. 'There is a hill in Haiti,' begins Megan.

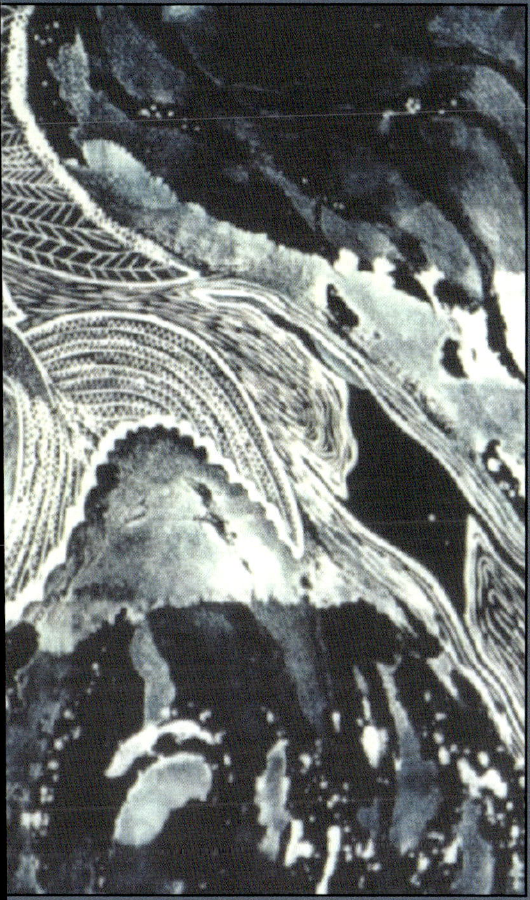

This is a family story. There is a son, and a daughter. 'But the girl was not prized, as the boy was.' However, 'There was no task they could put upon her shoulders that she wouldn't be able to do.' When she draws water from the stream it is clean and fresh. When the boy, on a day when the girl is sent elsewhere, tries it the water comes out murky.

Megan has great presence and a clear voice. She makes eye contact with her audience, including us in her story, and is not afraid of a joke, of being herself, sometimes straying from the set language of the tale, to bring it closer to the people here today.

When the girl goes to collect water, she sings (through Megan), 'César, my friend, César, my friend. How are you?' And out of the water comes a great big beautiful golden fish. Here Megan makes the double-handed movement from Bharat Natyam, as of a fish swimming.

The jealous family find out and decide to kill the wondrous fish and eat it. Megan stamps her feet as she goes, 'Chop, chop, chop: the fish fell into four pieces.' The girl is called to the meal, but she will not eat the fish. 'She cannot bring herself to put one piece of it into her mouth. Afterwards she gathers up every piece of skin and bone that's left, takes them to the water and throws them in, upon which the fish is miraculously restored.

The best part, for me, is that instead of the fish being transformed into a man (the old frog-into-prince scenario), the girl is released from her human body and she turns into a beautiful silver and gold fish and escapes with her friend, César, from her life. It seems a fitting story for Megan, because it holds a surprise and is about transcending limitations.

Her second story is of a silver-tongued gypsy girl, and the power of words. 'She would begin with a dance.' Here Megan strikes a pose; there's more of an Arabian feel to it this time, and she looks the part she's telling.

At the end of each story she makes the Indian gesture of thanks. It seems a natural thing for her to do.

WHAT MEGAN DID IN HAITI: Daniel went first and collected the stories. Megan's part of the education project for The Haiti Fund, a trust between Wales and Haiti, was to run a painted and printed fabric project, using her skills as an artist and innovative batik printer to create works related to folk tales. When she came back there was an exhibition of the work in Llanover Hall, 'Children of Wales, Children of Haiti.'

She offered them Welsh and Haitian tales to illustrate, but in the end they reverted to things they knew, things they saw, like cruise ships. Out of that visit also came a book called *A Handful of Fish*, about fishermen in Haiti. She went out one day and took photographs and wrote about the day in a life of fisherman. The text Megan wrote in English also appears on the page translated into Welsh, French and French Creole.

A BRIDGE BETWEEN CULTURES: At Beyond the Borders there was an uncomfortable moment. Megan had been asked if she would, through gesture, interpret the words spoken by storyteller, Ben Haggarty, who in turn was translating (the original being in a dialect of Hindi), an epic song from the Mahabharata, which the audience was waiting to hear from Ritu Verma and her Pandvani Party. Pandvani is an epic singing tradition, with musical accompaniment.

This method of telling the story first in English was much used during the festival to make the stories accessible. Ritu's presence is tremendous, her song powerful, the tradition and the stories are in her blood. Inevitably the translation, even with Megan's gestures, which usefully incorporated some of those Ritu would use at key moments, but only rehearsed that day, seemed distant from the centre of this power. In a sense it did not matter. It was a medium to help us better understand what

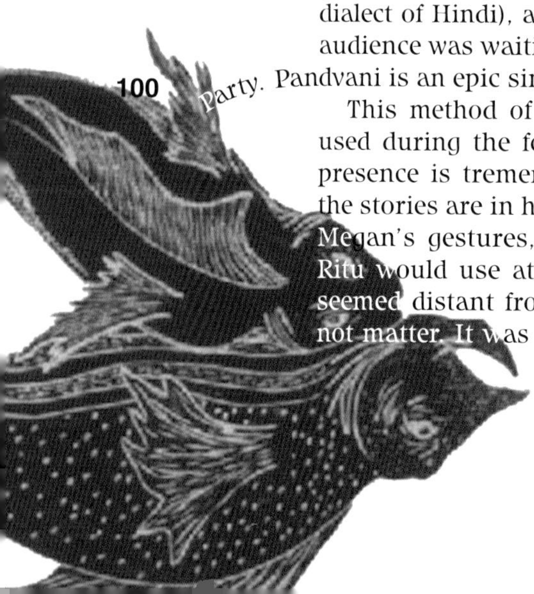

was to follow.

But the audience tended to look towards the speaker and this visually put Megan on the sidelines. Then we wanted to look at Megan. Ben sometimes moved too. Our eyes flickered between them, and, as we were not watching a slow rally at tennis, this was distracting. In the next performance they stood together. Much better.

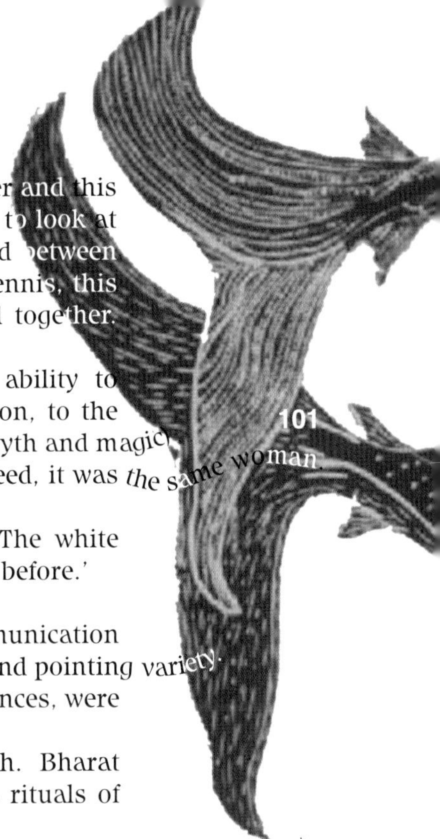

I wondered if people appreciated that Megan's ability to transform herself from the Storyteller of the afternoon, to the Indian Dancer (both figures equally associated with myth and magic) was not simply a matter of changing her clothes. Indeed, it was the same woman. But who would expect that she could do both?

Behind me, a woman whispered to her friend, 'The white woman in the sari; she's the one who told us stories before.'

'I BELIEVE IN THE MABINOGION': Megan's direct communication with Ritu was of the 'nice bangle', nodding, smiling and pointing variety. But they all seemed happy with each other's performances, were complimentary, and respectful of each other.

These stories are linked with religion and myth. Bharat Natyam, originally a temple dance, involves various rituals of Hindu belief. Does Megan believe?

'I was brought up going to Chapel. Welsh Independent Congregationalist, but the Chapel I went to was all in Welsh, so I sat there, quite happily, not really understanding what was going on. So you can do it in another language and I'll sit there, quite happily, not really understanding what's going on.'

She doesn't practise religion every day, but says that she observes those rites that are contextual to the dance, for instance asking pardon for stamping on the earth.

'But no,' says Megan, 'it's not that I'm dedicated completely to any faith. But I believe in the Mabinogion. I believe in folk tales and things like that. I believe the Lady of the Lake really existed. What I say to kids is "If it's fantastic enough, I'll believe in it!"'

WORKING FOR FATHER CHRISTMAS: And so it came about that Megan was storytelling in the Green Field at Glastonbury one year, when another storyteller, known for setting things up, said, 'I can't do Lapland next year? Anyone want it?'

Megan intended to do it as a job share, but ended up going it alone. She was there on the eve of the Millennium. She didn't have to dress as an elf, though other people did. Her main job was telling stories, but she'd told them she could dance too, classical Indian and early

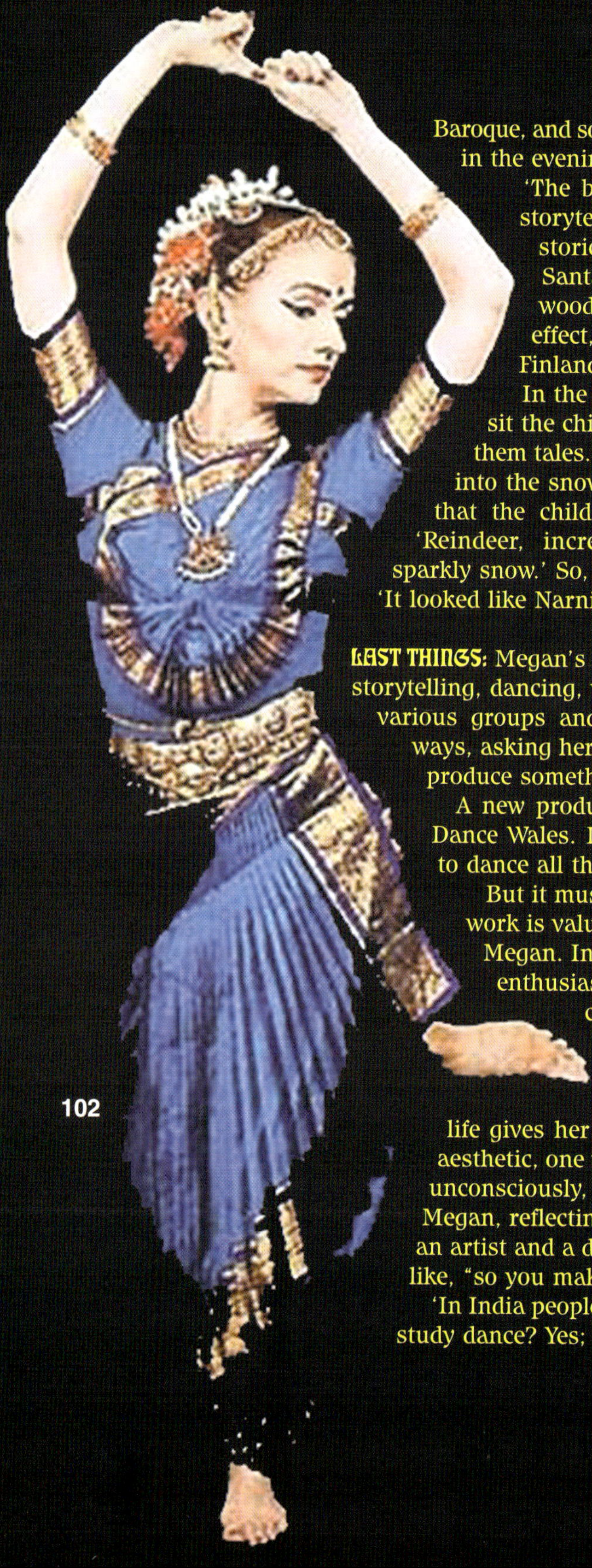

Baroque, and so joined the children's entertainers in the evening and picked up some S Club 7 steps. 'The best part of the job was a fairy storytelling session and the bedtime stories.' There was a 'search for Santa' leading children through the woods. It was all done in English. In effect, 'Britain takes over an area of Finland.' The locals put up with it.

In the evenings, the storytellers would sit the children round in a big log cabin and give them tales. Nordic tales, in keeping with going out into the snow. And they would put in things that the children had seen during the day: 'Reindeer, incredible landscapes, trees with sparkly snow.' So, some of the magic was real. 'It looked like Narnia,' says Megan.

LAST THINGS: Megan's still at work, teaching art classes, storytelling, dancing, working in and for the community. The various groups and schools support her in their ways, asking her to enrich their walls, or help them produce something they can call their own.

A new production is in rehearsal for India Dance Wales. It would be lovely, says Megan, to dance all the time.

But it must also be fine to know how much your work is valued. Everyone I met was pleased with Megan. In the schools they were happy with her enthusiasm for getting the best out of the children, and doing the best for them. S engaged with everything she does as if it really *matters*.

The Indian influence on her life gives her some connection to a different aesthetic, one that suits her, one that consciously or unconsciously, she is passing on to others. 'Here,' say Megan, reflecting on how the very idea of being an artist and a dancer is commonly viewed in Wales, 'it like, "so you make a living out of it?"'

'In India people would say, "You do art and you study dance? Yes; good. So you should."'

ow are ewe?: neale howells seen from the edge

rachel trezise

Owe Are Ewe?

I recently described myself to a rock star who had e-mailed to compliment me on my debut novel, as 'a humble poet girl'. But I usually like to think of myself as a rock star. I might have been if I'd persevered with my violin or guitar lessons. Instead I'm a writer, but a novelist and a journalist, not a poet, though I also like to think there is poetry in my work. Maybe because poetry sounds more philosophical and beautiful, more meaningful than prose and art is about trying to interpret life into digestible chunks. Nobody wants to eat beefburgers when there's steak on the menu so I write literature and not science fiction. But I grew up throughout the 1980s, in the poverty-stricken Rhondda Valley, amongst a street full of unemployed miners. In the midst of Thatcherism I couldn't remember a Labour government. Socialism was dead and capitalism wasn't taking off, not in the Rhondda anyway. To the adults around me, any early interests in art or literature or music I let slip were cute, but the most I could really expect out of life was full-time employment, money to bring up my own children. To say I came from a working-class background isn't true. I came from an unemployed one. For me, throughout my school years, it seemed

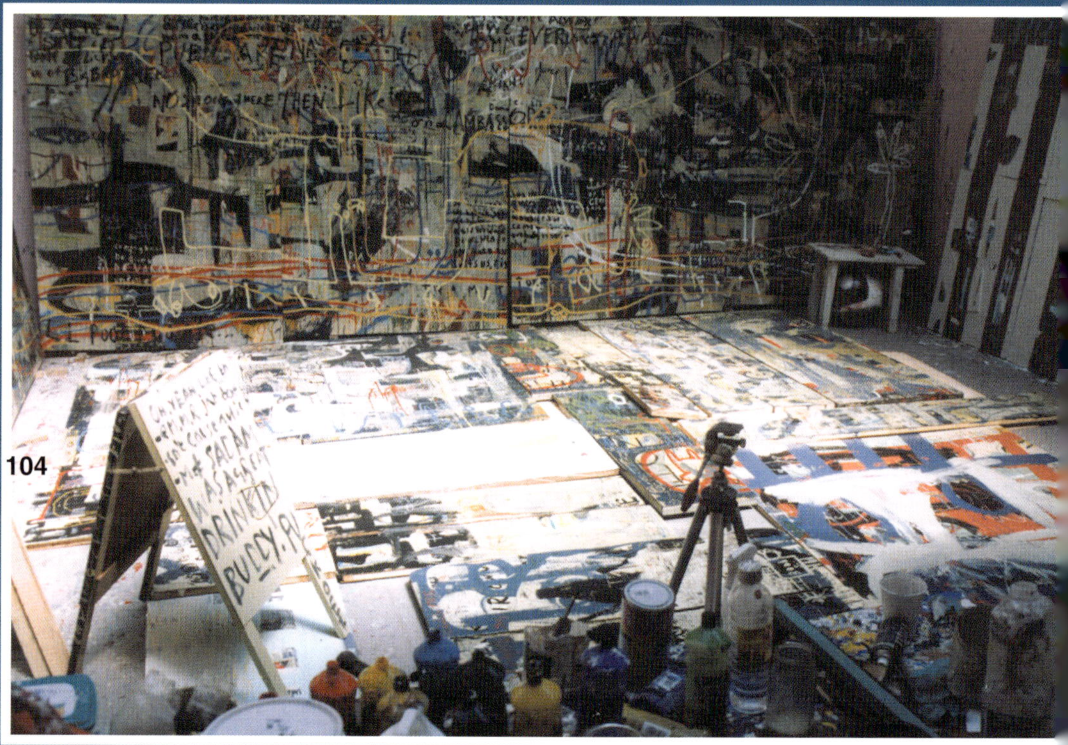

s though the nly way I ould escape his pre-set rudgery was ith some sort DIY miracle, y setting up ome sort of latinum-selling and or painting ome masterpiece, riting some best eller.

was fixing to ecome a fine artist. I asn't sure how it as all going to fall nto place. There was o college fund to go to t school in London. here was no art work n the walls in my house. n fact, the only real piece f art work I had seen was tatty, old Constable print a chipped wooden frame my great grandmother's. had never put foot into a useum or a gallery. The nly days out my family ould afford were afternoons ating chips on Porthcawl each and if there was a oliday it was before I can emember, probably in Butlin's Barry Island. Cities were enerally expensive places to e, and therefore boldly avoided. ut art was my favourite subject school. Constantly, I was etching, if not for course work, en for myself. I liked pop art and photocopied Warhol's soup cans nd Marilyn Monroe portraits and asper Johns' flags from library ooks and stuck them to my walls. or my GCSE I built a portfolio of brightly-coloured charcoal hairspray-set sketches of electric guitars and Madonnas in conical bras. It was the only exam I passed above a C grade. Then very suddenly, as I turned from a teenager into a young adult that summer, as lust and alcohol became features in my life, I decided I'd rather become a music journalist so I could bag myself a rock star boyfriend. Art fell easily from my life, and my focus landed on words. It only ever reappeared in glimpses, inside the graphic design of album covers and the logos I saw painted on the back of leather biker jackets.

When I left school at sixteen, after a few years of listening to my older brother's Sex Pistols records and smoking out of the window sash in my bedroom, I read Maya Angelou's I Know Why The Caged Bird Sings, and then decided to write my own novel based on my own experiences of poverty and rape. It was five years in the making while I ploughed through the local college and university, just barely hitting my grades, and the year I graduated, it was published. It won an Orange Prize. My DIY miracle had transpired. In a review, Lisa Gee, editor for the Orange Prize for Fiction web site called it, 'A jagged, imperfect piece of writing – occasionally the syntax seems jumbled, the imagery confused or confusing, but somehow this all adds to the credibility. A careful, considered writing style simply couldn't do justice to so much suffering, action, partying and achievement.' I'm no William Shakespeare, but I am a writer. I've never read Dante or the Brontë's or Dickens, or anything considered highbrow, and actually completely enjoyed it. My influences are lyrics from rock songs, not even classic rock songs, but run of the mill chart radio songs. And I pulled it off, so I am humble. But in my own way, I am a rock star too. I write lyrics, I just process them through a computer instead of a microphone. I still call readings `gigs' and more than one reading in a week 'a tour'.

At 26, I am part of the MTV generation, a girl who grew up watching cartoons and music videos, and it probably shows in my work. I write about the thoughts, feelings and experiences of people close to my age, status and area. I write about youth, hopelessness, decadence; sex and drugs and rock 'n' roll. Much of my work deals in human misery. I don't think I'm a miserable person but I see misery around me and I'm drawn to document it. The first war I encountered, politically aware of its savageness and implications, was televised on the evening news. Media Studies had become an A level subject on the National Curriculum before I had left school, so I have been bombarded with all sorts of images mostly all of my life, but I hadn't touched a broadsheet newspaper until my second year of university, and rarely touch one now unless I'm looking for a job, or reading one of my own reviews. I would still rather read the NME than the Observer and I'm still not drawn to art galleries. On a recent trip to New York, I forfeited visiting the Guggenheim to see the CBGB stage where Blondie had played. At the Edinburgh Festival, I preferred to watch comedian Charlie Chuck act in a ridiculous adaptation of Scrooge than a piece of theatre that required any serious concentration. I'd still rather spend a weekend at the Reading or Glastonbury Festivals than the corridors of Parisian galleries. Having said that, I do appreciate art, but it's the type of well-publicised art daytime television programmes feature, along with a debate on whether it actually is art. The essay that you are about to read is definitely a view from the edge; a glance at Neale Howells' work through my art gallery-virgin eyes.

I see myself in Neale Howells' paintings, so I'm easily attracted to them, like a narcissist to a mirror. What I have just explained about my own work, I see in Neale's; hopelessness, misery, decadence and youth. Ramming Home (right), from 1996, is mixed media on polystyrene. It's disturbing. Its sheer messiness is frightening. A moment's glance at the work will tell you that everything is not right in the world. And of course, it's not. There are three figures in the painting, faceless stick figures and only one bears a head. The other two have been cut out of the picture, as though they are nobodies, numbers not names, and two of them are sat rigid in stick chairs as though tied there, powerless. The remainder of the work is a mishmash of blurred and childlike writing and scratchy, nonsensical daubs of pale, lifeless blue, black, white and red paint. It doesn't tell me a comprehensible story but it does provide me with a glimpse of a confused, rushed and war-torn world. It's raw, and it's life as I know it. It isn't a street made up of detached and water-coloured houses, a lazy cat stretching itself in the sunshine on the path, a rose bush in the garden. Life is messy. Life is frightening. In life, the punctuation isn't always in the right places. What I like too, is that there are no conclusions in Neale's work. Like the lyrics to a rock song, you interpret them as you choose.

Plus, there were plenty of rumours flying around about Neale Howells the man, before I met him for the first time. He's the enfant terrible of the contemporary Welsh arts' scene. He's an artist who uses bodily fluids in his paintings. He's the man who had his painting taken down by Cardiff Council for painting the wor 'fuck' onto it, for painting cartoo penises onto it. He's the man wh created the album cover for T Manic Street Preachers' Know Y Enemy, and who got into their Ca Bay concert by threatening he'd h his missus sit on the security g

unless he wav them throug He's the ma who went c the radio say tha Welsh art a load rubbish and went c televisio to say again. H sound like th type wild

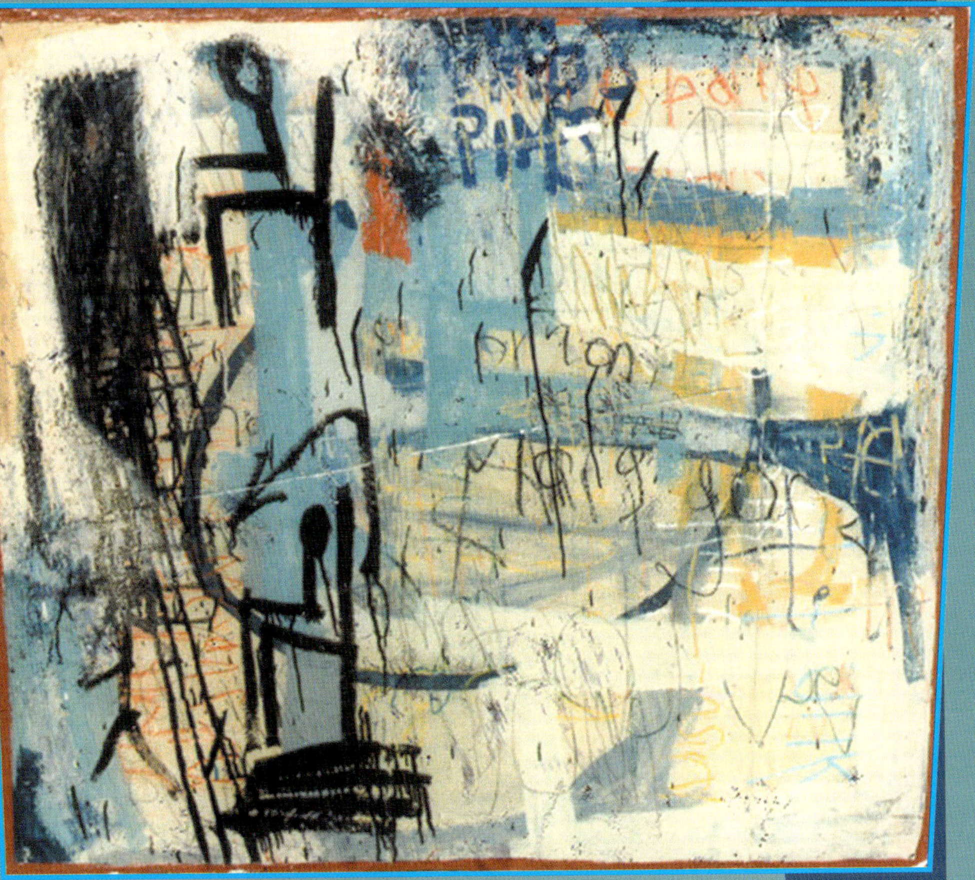

lcohol-
elled, tortured artist I could
et along with. And soon
ough he is the man who I
terview; ring; drink, eat, chat
d visit galleries and public
ctures with, on a regular basis;
ach one of our conversations
eginning in a Neath accent with,
we Are Ewe?'

For our second meeting,
arly on a Monday evening in
tember, Neale invites me to the
ouncing of the short list for the
tes Mundi prize, established to
lebrate visual culture from across
e globe, and based for its first year in Wales. After the film and the speeches there is champagne and finger foods in the foyer. I stand around for a while, sometimes talking to journalists I've known briefly, mostly rearranging the bookstand so that In and Out of the Goldfish Bowl is the only novel visible, with the exception of one copy of Owen Sheers' Blue Book, because I used to fancy him a little bit until he started experimenting with a moustache, although I still think much of his poetry. I go outside to light a cigarette and watch the autumn sun go down over the bell shape roof of City Hall. It's still warm and Cardiff is quiet, except for Neale's voice on the other side of one of the great pillars. He is

regurgitating the Venice Biennale argument from his infamous appearance on BBC's On Show with a middle-aged man from what I assume is the Welsh arts establishment. The man's point is that Neale, by going on television to call other artists 'rubbish' is alienating himself from the arts in-crowd. Neale's point is that he's simply being honest and that his work will speak for itself, thank you. The man leaves with his friends to eat fish in an upmarket restaurant. Neale and I walk quietly to a Castle Street wine bar and drink beer. It may be the beer, but I am sure at this point that if a bomb dropped on the pub, two of Wales' most hopeful artists would disappear with it. We're punks kicking doors in, then leaving them open behind us.

How can you toe the line if you can't see it?

However, what I immediately begin to notice about Neale is that his notions about his chosen career are extremely idealistic and not at all in keeping with his loud mouth media persona. For instance, when we meet for the first time in a Wetherspoon's pub on Neath high street, he asks me who my favourite artist is and I tell him that it's Tracey Emin. Discuss, he says, so I tell him that Emin's work is autobiographical. If I was an artist, I say, my work would look like Tracey Emin's 1995 film, Why I Never Became a Dancer. My novel is a literary equivalent to My Bed. It isn't exactly ladylike, but we're both women who like talking about sex, who like airing our filthy laundry in public.

'Well that's all fucked up to start with,' he says.

'Uh?' I say in my Rhondda Valley accent. Excuse me?

'You said her work,' he said. 'Her work? It isn't her work is it? I never call my work, my work. What's that? Tutor told me years ago in college, what's my work? That's bollocks. I can't stake claim to my work, it's everybody's work. You don't make art, you find it. 'Credit where credit is due,' I say. Sure enough when I'm hard at research later on, I find answers to interviewers' questions where Neale refers to himself as 'we', where he refers to his work as 'ours'. And you may notice this yourself further on in this essay. But it's a universally-known fact that nothing is original. Everything is a reproduction. Neale then goes on to explain that sometimes when he's alone in his studio, it seems as though he isn't working at all, but other artists are painting through him, Jean-Michel Basquait being one of them. This may sound hysterical, but I think I understand it. Often, after a day of writing I'll say something like 'Dylan Thomas got into me today,' to my partner. It means that the day has been fruitful and provided me with eloquence. It's a joke that harks back to the time we visited the Dylan Thomas Centre in Swansea and I thrust my fore and index fingers into the hole where a handle should be on the original door of Thomas' writing shed. My hand tingled for the rest of the day. Without venturing into my beliefs on the supernatural, I'll tell you that I do not want to write like Dyla Thomas. He wrote for posterity and write for eternity. My idol, To Morrison, is still alive and worki on the other side of the Atlantic, Dylan Thomas is dead and ca from Wales. Often I can't believe

I deserve to be left alone in a room to create things all day when it seemed I was destined for a till on a supermarket check out. Being an artist isn't easy, but I love it, and often it's hard to believe my luck, hard to believe that I can do it all on my own. 'Art chose me,' Neale says, but Neale chose art. Everyday, he chooses art. He picks up a brush, and a ghost can't make you do that. It's almost as if he is unwilling to take responsibility for the paintings he paints, as if he wants to hide from his own mind and step out of the way of any possible reproach.

But when he is reproached, when his work is criticised, he publicly defends it with fervour and makes no bones about insulting other people's. When asked, in an e-mail interview he passes on to me to assist with my first chunk of research, if he gets stressed out with preparing and finishing work for new shows, he replies, 'No, I 'ucking don't, you God damn monkey shagger. Come on, I'll rip your arms off you chicken licking panty liner...' which I find daunting. But this isn't the Neale I meet. The Neale I meet is pleasant, mild, thoughtful and mannered, a man I couldn't possibly imagine threatening a security guard. He doesn't even drink that much; since he had children, he says, he hardly ever goes out. In fact he is a born and selfless comedian, a person who knows life tastes pleasant while you're laughing at zany and meaningless things. Here are just two examples: mid January 2004 and the deadline for this essay is approaching. I telephone Neale with my New Year hangover still in place and ask him if he's productive and ready to proceed with another interview. 'We really have to move now Neale,' are my words. 'We're about to hit the deadline.'

'I got a gorilla suit for Christmas!' he says. 'I've always wanted a gorilla suit! I'm dead pleased. I can't wait to go out in it....' Around twelve minutes later we've fixed our next meeting and the deadline doesn't appear as threatening as it once did. On the night of the Artes Mundi short list we enter the auditorium and slowly circle the dusty, stuffed tiger spread on a plinth in the foyer of the museum. I wrinkle my nose at the idea of stuffed wildlife. Neale sees this and regards the animal for a few moments, then, deadpan, says, 'Yeah, they look better dead don't they?' Inside the auditorium, Neale sees one of the artists short listed for the £40,000 prize arrive with their family in tow. 'So what if they win this?' he whispers to me. 'How rich will they be then? Will they be richer than me?' Talking with jealousy about the wealth of his contemporaries shouldn't really leave me with a good impression of Neale or the seriousness of his work, but I realise it's nothing I haven't thought myself. Neale says it with the honesty and insolence of a juvenile. 'Last time I saw them,' he continues, 'the missus was flicking through an Argos catalogue.' I realise later that it is a comment he's also used to poke fun at himself. Trawling through old interviews posted on web sites I notice somebody has asked him if he's involved in art for the money. His reply: 'I wish. I haven't seen my credit card for years and my girl-friend is always flicking through an Argos catalogue. When you forget about the work there won't be any money to worry about.' He reminds me of the quiet kid at the front of the classroom who turns, when faced with a bully, into the class clown, the guy who'll say what you want to hear to stop himself getting hit, forever acting his way out of confrontation and into favour. But at other times he is the bully, mindlessly rebutting his contemporaries' ideas and work, usually without rhyme and almost always without reason.

To describe Neale's work in words, I must mention that it's often likened to the work of Pollock and Basquait. Pollock, best known for his 'drip and splash' style which emerged with abruptness in 1947, was an alcoholic who fixed his canvas to the floor, or wall, and poured and dripped paint straight from a can. He manipulated his work with sticks and trowels and knives and obtained a heavy impasto by an admixture of sand or other foreign material. This manner of action painting was supposed by critics to result in a direct expression or revelation of the unconscious moods of himself. But Pollock was subject to much abuse for his style. In 1956, Time magazine called him 'Jack the Dripper'. Yet he is one of the most famous names in art, the world over. Neale's use of bold colours and abstract images is reminiscent of Pollock's earlier work, but with the confused, choppy and thick diagrammatic style of Pollock's latter work mixed in. Jean-Michel Basquait was a heroin addict, a friend of Andy Warhol and a self-publicist. I think Neale's work is particularly similar to Basquait's, and Neale himself admits that he once used a small design associated with Basquait and then signed the painting with Basquait's initials. Nowhere is this more apparent than in the 1996 Berlin Works. Neale's response to time spent visiting Eas Berlin with its historic and pos modern environments was a series four large panels entitled Berl Work (page 113), Post Berlin, Po Berlin 2 (shown here) and Po Berlin 3 (page 112). They are ra and stirring pieces, seeming

inspired by th graffiti of th

Berlin Wall and making much of his favourite colour (blue). The broken and misspelt words daubed into the discordant array of shapes and colours trail off inexplicably, providing no conclusion, and forcing the person looking at it to create their own. Basquait's Worthy Constituents is a childlike blast of bold yellow and blue colour around stick men and simple line diagrams of abstract shapes and motor vehicles and graffitiesque, nonsensical scrawls of crayon-like text. Neale's Berlin Works are much like the painting, even down to their use of colours. Robert Knafo describes Jean-Michel Basquait in a biography as 'All at once, the ultimate party animal, a wannabe street kid and graffitist, hiding his middle-class Brooklyn roots, an advocate and interpreter of the marginal and dispossessed at the court of the mainstream, an angry and black aspirant to the all-white art canon, a precocious talent, a creature of cynical marketing and a fraud, a proto multiculturalist, an American original.' Neale says he is influenced by nothing. 'The shape of the work will influence exactly what goes on it,' he says. 'I've always been interested in art and that's what it's primarily about, it's about art, it's about painting, it's about finding the hidden painting – it could be anywhere. I don't tackle it with too much of a set idea, I just go straight in and see what I come out with.' Like Jackson Pollock, Neale always seems to be moving away from conscious thoughts and relying instead on streams of unconsciousness. But Neale himself is a mixture of both of these dead artists' personalities, veering at times from brutal honesty to ruthlessness in order to publicise himself and his work.

His current work, since 2000 onwards anyway, is mostly paintings on recycled wood. They're all very similar, in that they're riots of colour and shapes which simply aren't fathomable in the way traditional art is. Their main features are usually stick men with little or no features in their faces, but long, waving, flailing arms and large cartoon hands. Sometimes there are many stick figures, sometimes there is only one. It is clearly American inspired, a kind of mark-making that is urban and male. Most of it is quite exhausting to look at in a way that anything which forces you to think for yourself is. When you stand before one for a time you're in a lonely and desperate place, then when you walk away, sometimes you leave with rage, sometimes with laughter. Essentially, it is the same feeling you get when you find yourself lost in unfamiliar territory. The graffiti on the walls will tell you how close to danger you are; whether the desolate railway station you stand in is frequented by courting couples or violent youth gangs. House Robbed from 2000, for instance, a 183cm x 488cm painting on wood, I find terrifying to look at.

In the foreground, the outline of a naked woman is pasted with blue, a hole for her vagina painted crassly in the centre of her hips. She stands tall and giraffe-necked, taking up the length of the picture, but so tall in fact, her head is outside of the picture. In the background many stick people with bulbous skulls for heads line up in rows. From a distance they look like the numerous cross-shaped graves of a war cemetery. There is one other large figure with no decipherable body shape but long flailing arms and some scribbled but broken words. A daub of red in the otherwise black and white paint drips down the centre of the painting, instantly putting me in mind of blood and violence. At a guess, I would say that the picture

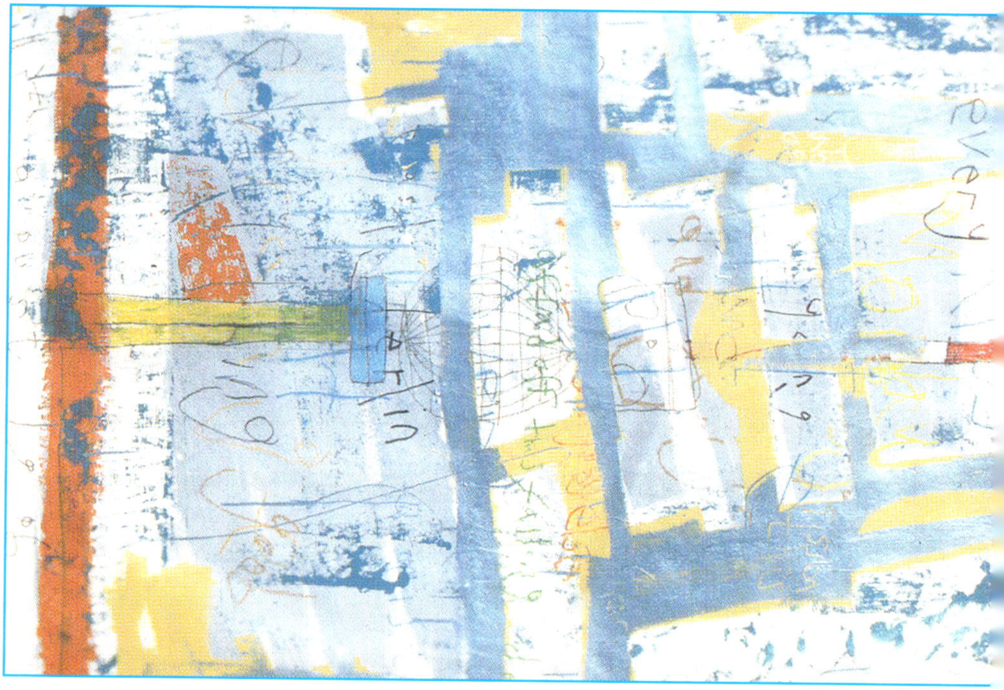

depicts grief. The people in it are scared and without identity, scared by their loss. But I'm not sure how much I'm influenced by the title of the piece. House Robbed quite plainly suggests that the people have been house robbed. What I know for sure is that the painting looks like a nightmare I'd rather not find in my own head. But I also know that I understand and identify with it because at some time or another I have felt that kind of grief, known that kind of nightmare. Similarly, in Cock & Blade from 2003, a stick person stands in the centre of the painting, painted with a white outline while a ruction of colour, abstract shapes and parts of words built up in layer upon layer goes on around and inside him. But the person is scared and taken aback as though he is confronted with something that he would rather avoid, as though he cannot understand any of the confusion and noise around him, as though he is scared of life, his mouth a flabbergasted oblong of stark, white paint. Because the stick figures very rarely have any identifiable features, and quite often no eyes, these paintings look more like landscapes than they do portraits. They are depictions of place around people rather than people filling up and making place. A figure may feature somewhere in the painting but it is the world going o around them that takes up most c the space. They are confusing an strange areas that leave you feelin mislaid, disorientated or abandonec

Interestingly, Neale is unusual i that he creates and exhibits muc f his artwork n abandoned uildings. He as used actories, ospitals, hotels nd telephone oxes as well as he conventional rt gallery. Since eginning to work reatively in 1985 e's worked in he open air, on nountain tops and iver banks and then noving into disused uildings which he alls, 'Fantastic urban laces that are real and ontain excitement,' while galleries are, 'safe nd redundant'.

imilarly the materials e uses are recycled bjects or objects he has ound whilst out exploring bandoned places: other eople's rubbish. He's used ecycled wood, polystyrene, netal, glass, rubber, fridges, ikes, tables, cars and imself. He uses household aints, or paints that people ive him. The only colours he ver buys, he says, are red, lue, yellow, black and white. e never works on canvas ecause he can't afford it. But his aintings are always large panels f wood. Most average 8ft x 12ft ut the longest was 8ft x 24ft nd the highest, 12ft. He likes to nake a statement that can compete with other entertainments like the inema and advertising, music, rchitecture and shopping. Then, or practicality, the paintings are broken up into panels measuring 8ft x 4ft. He says he has no process whilst painting. Sometimes he lies it on the floor, sometimes against the wall, sometimes he paints blindfolded, sometimes in the darkness, sometimes he chooses colour randomly, sometimes he asks other people to draw on it. Sometimes he burns it. And there's the question of bodily fluids. I'm not sure why shit or piss or blood or semen is more enticing than sheer, honest paint, but apparently it is. You only have to remember the outrage surrounding Chris Ofilli's 1998 Turner-winning elephant dung-splattered work to realise this is true. In one interview, Neale is asked if he uses bodily fluids and he says, 'No I only say things like that for attention. My job is to get the work seen, once it's up it'll speak for itself.' In another he says, 'I used sperm once.' In yet another, 'I used sperm once but it was a disaster. I had some sperm in a condom, which I blew up and it exploded and covered everything, and everyone. Some of it went over this woman from the gallery who was a prude, so she cancelled the show.' It is obviously impossible to get a clear picture of how Neale creates a picture because he'll say anything for self-promotion and when I repeat these comments to Neale and ask him if he's ever used bodily fluids in his work, he says, 'You've noticed that I'm a compulsive liar. No, I've never used bodily fluids; I've only ever said I have to get an audience, and it has succeeded. Though saying that, there are two paintings on display with stuff on them. And I'm not telling you which ones.'

Slightly more mysterious is Neale's interest in language, literacy and illiteracy. I have asked Neale if he is dyslexic and he refused to comment. I thought that maybe he was as this would explain his themes of isolation, disorientation and the broken words and sentences he adds to his art work. What he did say was, 'I used to wish I was

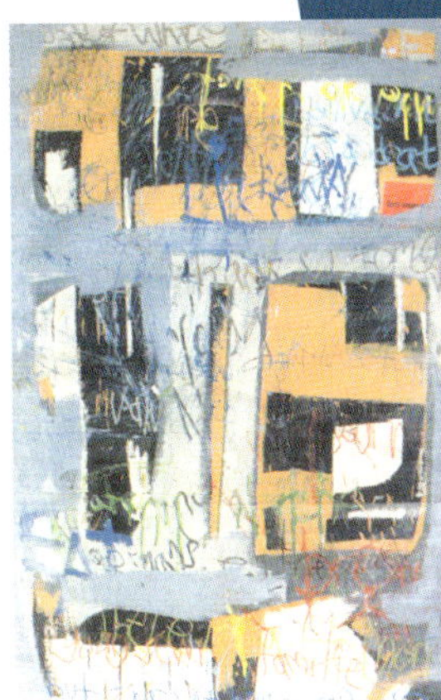

English would simply view the word as art, the illiterate; maybe then I could appreciate the form of a letter for what it really is – a drawing. Being conditioned by education has made me miss out on the beauty of the word. Painting is about being able to communicate through language barriers. I shouldn't have to have a social brief to tell me anything before I view art.' Of course this fits in quite nicely with Neale's claim to being a naïve artist who does not think about or plan any particular effect in his work, but it does not fit in with his continued use of the word 'fuck'. Just to give you some idea of how fond he is of 'fuck', this is an extract from his Censor Or Be Censored essay of April 2002. 'Cunt, fuck, bastard all need airing for our English-speaking selves. I have helped produce, if only known, the filthiest sayings in the work I do, yet they are treated as aesthetic because they are written in shorthand... offence is only an illusion which is supported by frightened individuals whose own understanding may well be based on school yard politics... why ain't we able to write fuck when the majority of people are doing it, they are doing it, and even their mother's done it?' Here he admits that words can mean something, that words have the potential to be filthy and that 'fuck' is part of the English language, so it seems unlikely that he subconsciously scribes words like 'whore', 'tits', 'spunk' and 'fuck' into his paintings, and much more likely that he's considered it at length. For one thing, the use of an English language word in a painting makes the painting impossible to break through a language barrier. Neale may argue that people who cannot understand letters as drawings, but if this is the effect he is trying to achieve it would be far easier to introduce a shape or a simple sketch than use any words at all. As a writer, I do not find these words offensive. I often use them in my own work, sometimes in the dialogue of characters who are in want of better ones, which have for some reason eluded them: maybe rage, maybe lack of education, but always with the knowledge that they have the power to shock. Neale urges us to swear as much as we possibly can then swear words will lose their power, but I do wonder, if that were to happen, what Neale would write on his paintings instead.

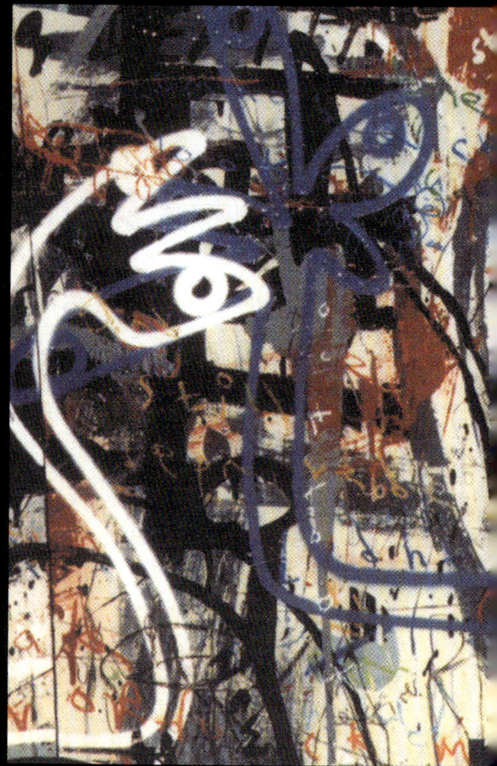

For the record, I think Neale is fairly adept in understanding and using language. In fact or

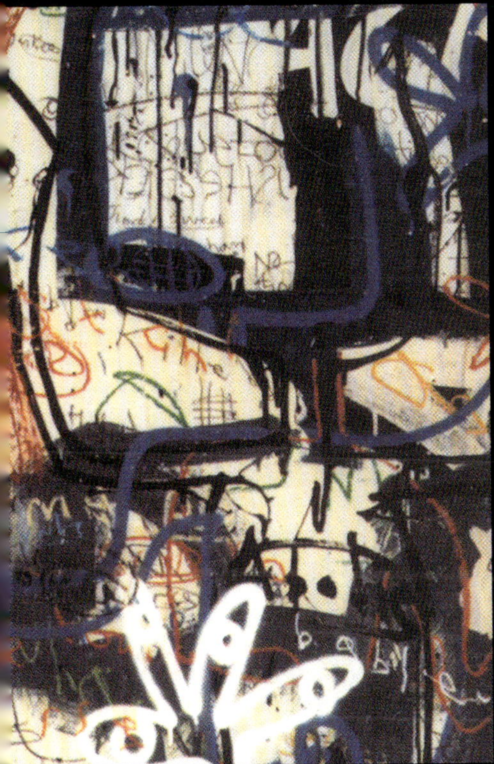

eviewer claims that Jeale is over-reliant on he titles of his paintings. My favourite title is Go On Ay favourite title is Go On Shag The Wife (above). We eedn't look at the content, ust at the title, as much can e deduced. 'Go on...' is an ct of persuasion. It isn't omething you want to do, ust something you should. ts use of slang and use of the isrespectful phrase 'the vife' suggests frustration. Shagging is uggests contempt. omething that simply kills time, it sn't emotional, it isn't an act of ove, it isn't 'fuck', not passionate r even sexy. The wife is an object, omething to be used, something that's not chosen, but taken. It's Neale's voice, but it's sarcastic and self-deprecating, a speech on behalf of the male species in general. He's showing us the landscape he sees around him, a genial and insular man at play with anger, a man grasping for attention with English language words he proclaims art can do without. The same sort of words he writes inside the paintings.

Insecurity & Isolation

You may or may not be aware at this point, that Neale is a master of disguise. He never answers questions directly, but he clearly spends much time and energy on self-promotion which is a creative act and, I've come to realise, as much a part of his art as anything he paints. Early into researching his work I read a review which suggested Neale's major subject is 'being a man.' My looking at Neale's work suggests this is true. Many of the works include stick figures which look like little boys, and the inclusion of cartoon male genitalia and the exclusion of female

is just a little bit of a give away. The cacophony of colour and scribe-like messages that hit you when you stand in front of one of his paintings, is like looking into the mind of a man. Threads of ideas and sentences that are about to hit on something, and never really get there. There is no plan, no organisation and no conclusion, only a basic, frustrated stab at defining an emotion. As a woman, this is what I imagine being a man is like: barren and fruitless. As a woman, emotion and intuition guide me through my life. Men don't have this. Men have something else. What it is, I'll never really know because I'm a woman. As a writer though, I often place myself inside the mind of male characters and it gives me a nagging frustration and yearning for some meaning to my existence, some purpose which isn't simply reproduction, seed-sowing. When I wrote first person as Alex, a 15-year-old boy in a short story called The Jones's, I found myself concealing my real feelings of love and affection and sleeping with the teenage village bike for credit from my male classmates. When I wrote first person as Matt, a 16-year-old in a short story called Fresh Apples, I found myself coerced into arson and a tradesman apprenticeship, when on the whole I would much rather have done something far more sensible. I'm not a man however, and the stories were written with the use of stereotypes. I don't know what being a man is like, but my guess is it's difficult, and my idea of that hardship is what many of Neale's paintings depict.

When I talk to Neale about my opinion he is sitting on my sofa drinking a cup of coffee I've prepared, and he misunderstands my assumptions. He launches instead into a tirade on the weakness of female artists. 'There are no good female artists in the world,' he says. 'That may be a controversial thing to say, but I've looked at women's art and it's distinctly different to men's. Men are naturally harder, naturally more ruthless. Look at Helen Chadwick,' he says. When he has left, I do. I discover that Helen Chadwick was one of the first women to be short listed for the Turner Prize. Her work drew on a variety of disciplines such as anatomy, science and myth. Her photographs, sculptures and installations were considered remarkable for their imaginative and perturbing use of unusual materials, including a lamb's tongue, fur, flowers, meat, urine, chocolate, household cleaning fluids and hair gel. She died in 1996. But back before this, on the sofa, Neale says, 'She used chocolate. Chocolate! How typically female is that? What's that about? Male artists are stronger than female artists because they have female tendencies. They have to have an understanding of everything. That's what an artist does, right? Tries to understand everything. Jessica Stockholder, another one. Did installations with kitchen appliances and cookers. It's a man's world, I know that, but I just don't think about it.'

His claims are, of course preposterous and impossible to agree with, but I think about Neale's comments on women's lack of unscrupulousness against a backdrop of contemporary female artists. On a recent trip to the Saatchi gallery in London County Hall, I looked closely at the work of Jenny Saville (another artist the Manic Street Preachers have worked with). Saville's female nudes are grossly overweight, but painted in a traditional and beautiful manner. Of her works, she says, 'Nearly everyone I know is obsessed with dieting, from anorexics who end up in hospital to friends who take hundreds of laxatives a day.' In her work, I see anger too, but the anger is directed at us, a society which views body image with distortion. Tracey Emin's

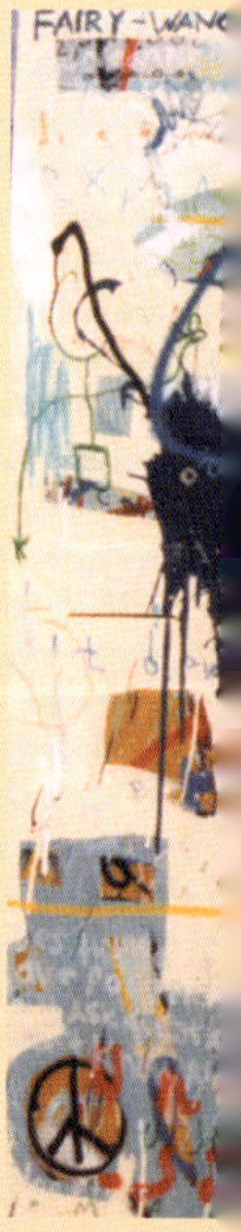

photographic elf portrait, 've Got It All hows her part- aked on the loor, her legs pread while she tuffs a large pile f money into her rotch. I see her as aying, 'I may be ne most renowned iving artist in ngland, with the nost money too, but 'm a woman, and nerefore in your eyes, lways a whore.' I think his is very poignant nd very angry. Shani hys James' oil aintings are clearly ark, despairing and angry. It is obvious that women can be as hard and as seething as men can, it's just that women's anger is delicately considered, worked into projects that say something conclusive about the environments they inhabit.

The fact that Neale does not think about gender is exactly my point. He proves it later that day on my sofa by admitting that some of his work is about the masculine difficulties of expressing his emotions. 'My girlfriend always knows when I'm getting ready to work,' he says. 'We've had a problem and I wind myself up about it, and I'm a man and it's difficult to talk about feelings; relationships are difficult, things are bottled up and I go to the studio and I unleash it. All of my stuff from late 1998 and all through '99 is real, it's personal.' But in the meantime his misogynistic and tabloidesque rant on art has been an attempt to put a smokescreen between himself and his work. While he is desperately attempting to define himself as a man, archetypically potent and strong, his art work suggests that his view on masculinity is that it is weak, soft, ineffectual and thoughtless. I look at one of the paintings he deems personal, The Evolution of Fuck (below) from 1999, a swathe of hand-like paint markings with a small, aggravated-appearing male stick figure in the centre of it, and decide that if it were a self-portrait, as many people

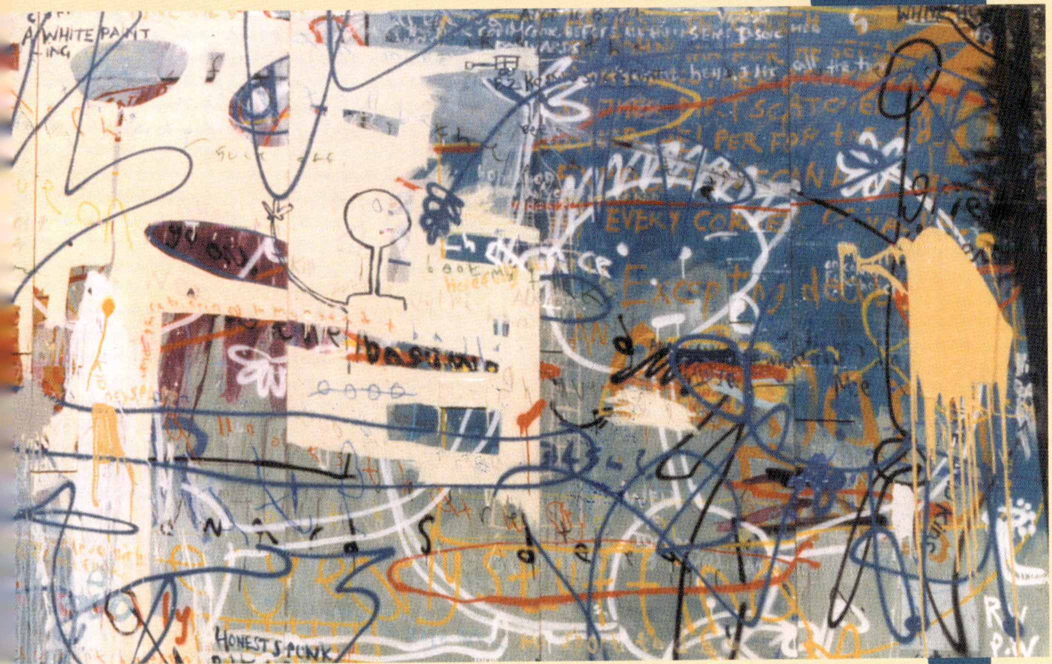

suggest all art is, I would have to say that Neale is boy-like, ignorant and dissatisfied. A man who has painted himself into a vicious circle of frustration he cannot allow himself to escape.

Similar to his view on female artists is his view on all other Welsh artists. It is no secret that his opinion of the arts scene in Wales is a derogatory one. In his opinion, it's all crap. In his opinion, nobody over the age of seven is a reputable Welsh visual artist. In his opinion, the entire country only serves to nurture weakness and mediocrity. 'All of the work here is supported by an intellectual crutch,' he says, 'which explains it in a manner that's not required. What you see is what you get, that's the nature of art. I've seen installation work which is so poor that the accompanying essay does nothing more than make an excuse for the work itself. It looks like art by numbers to me. Too many people are calling themselves artists. It needs to compete on an international stage, and it doesn't. Except the work we do of course. Wales didn't have any great artist of the last [20th] Century. I aim to make sure they do for the 21st.' He also claims that he has never called himself a Welsh artist and if he had the time, he would find every journalist who ever said he was and tell them that he didn't wish to be described so.

I'm no expert on Welsh art or artists. Until this essay came along I probably couldn't have named one, but Neale's main criticism of Welsh art other than his own, is that it does not compete on an international stage. Now, the problem with this is, if everybody knew how to make art that could compete on an international stage, then they would all be doing it, Neale included. The art that artists make doesn't determine how well it will do abroad, their agents do. And the fact is, there are lots of Welsh artists who are doing well, at home and abroad. During the Artes Mundi opening I sat through a film with Neale which showed Welsh artist Tim Davies ship a mahogany floor back to Belize from where it came in the 1830's as timber harvested by slave labour. Shani Rhys James has exhibited and is collected all over the world, as is Ceri Richards and Kevin Sinnott. There are thirty-two art galleries in Cardiff alone and I find it difficult to imagine that they're all filled with rubbish. The art scene in Wales is certainly more various, more vibrant and much stronger than the Welsh writing scene but I could produce a long list of Welsh writers who are creating superb works. Neale is talking nonsense again, but while he talks, his art betrays him. For I do not believe that Neale having worked for the Manic Street Preachers, a Welsh rock band, is purely coincidental. They had released five albums over a six-year period before bassist Nicky Wire visited the Washington Gallery where Neale was exhibiting and invited him to submit a portfolio for consideration. Famed for their anger, the Manics have successfully charted songs about, amongst other things, anorexia, self-mutilation, suicide, sexism (a duet with Traci Lords, a US porn actress) and the death o mining due to Thatcherism. Much c the lyricism from the debut albu Generation Terrorists rages again the empty adolescence the Gwer Valleys gave them. As Nicky Wi himself once said, 'If you built museum to represent Blackwood l you could ut in it would e shit, rubble nd shit.'

These are nemes are sible in all of eale's work. Like e If You Buy Me om 1997 is mixed l, acrylic, pencil nd burn marks. It's landscape of abstract napes daubed in ack on a red and reen background ith nonsensical words ritten in black paint ver one another until one of them are ecipherable. It has been urned to obscure the yer of paint underneath. oupled with its title, it epicts to me a map of a imate where consumerism eans more than humanity, nd materialism more than ducation: a foreign place r a Welsh man of Neale's eneration. The feeling of ienation it sends to me is e same feeling I get from stening to a Manic Street reachers' song. Also, the anics' ongoing theme of self-utilation relates to the way eale paints. He is quite willing burn and slash his work. In ct, he believes that destroying ork is just as creative as not estroying it and that you must be ble to destroy a piece of work efore you can go on. Before uitarist Richey Edwards' apparent uicide, he talked at length about his own self-mutilation and said it was a measure of strength, that he often felt so insecure about the world and other people around him that he attacked himself before others could and therefore retained his own strength. He was harder on himself than anyone else could be. The thick layers of paints on Neale's panels are in a way like welts in skin. They're left to dry, to heal, and then they're recreated, over and over until all that's visible in the end is the thick swirls of the brush, the fast and angry swipes of Neale's hand. I ask Neale, during our first meeting, what he thinks of the themes in the Manics' work and he says that he doesn't know that much about them. 'I'd rather listen to Phil Collins,' he says. No matter, I still believe that what the Manic Street Preachers are getting at, and what Neale Howell's is scratching at, is exactly the same itch. Besides, when asked what inspires him, Neale says, 'Everything that's trashy, tacky, abandoned, lost, untidy, filthy and broke; this is why I like living and working in Wales so much.' If it simply is a coincidence that the Manics chose Neale to represent them, then it's a happy one. The Manics' record company, Sony International, went on to buy three major Neale Howells works for the 2001 Know Your Enemy tour. 'It's gone full circle,' Neale says. 'I can remember going into the careers' office in school and saying, "Look, I'd like to do record covers," and he just said, "Sorry, there's no such fucking job, like."'

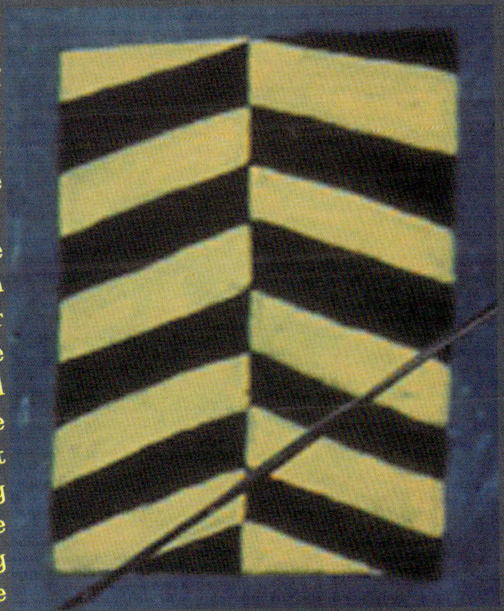

Neale's scorn of the establishment is legendary. We already know from the abandoned places that he chooses to create and exhibit art that he feels uncomfortable working in galleries and with other artists. Before meeting him I came across a review of one of his

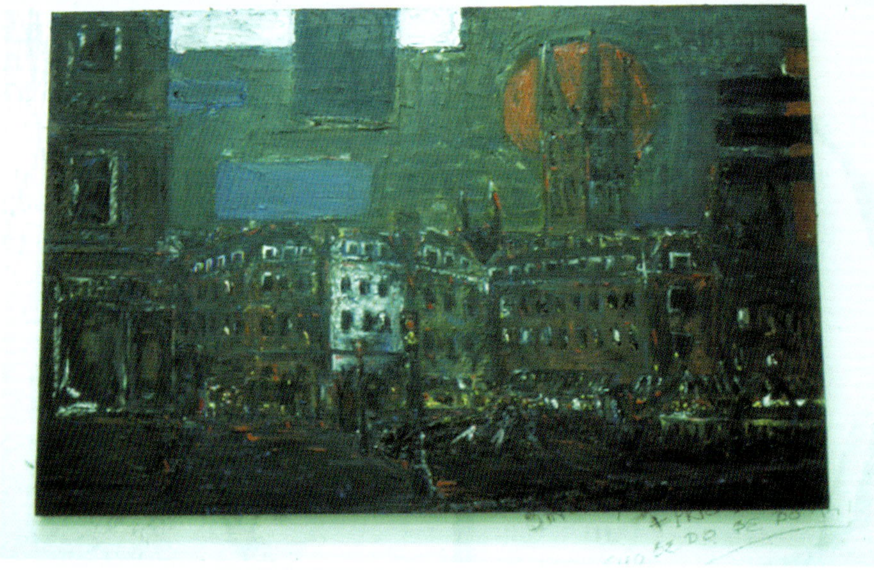

Washington Gallery exhibitions, written by a David Jones MA RCA. It says that, 'Howells' graffiti-based work has no dynamism or brutality, only timidity, rigidity, and worst of all sheer torpor.' More concerned by the reviewer's qualifications than his insults, Neale replied to the review, saying, 'Diolch yn fawr Mr Jones for taking the time to visit the show. I sense that you didn't understand the work there, but that is not your fault. Being trained at the RCA and even announcing an MA after your name says more about your interpretation of public and society. You may find others are impressed by these initials but as with politicians they may have been well educated but that doesn't guarantee anything....' He signed his reply, 'neale howells rac.aa.tesco club card 8990337647.' Similarly, when Cardiff City Council removed the 20ft painting he exhibited on the Millennium walkway to coincide with the release of the Manic Street Preachers' Know Your Enemy album, claiming they'd received several complaints about his use of expletives, Neale said, 'I'm not from Cardiff, but they seem a lot like Neath Council; they're probably made up of very perfect people, people who are generally better than everybody else. They don't live in our world, so anything they don't like they've got the power to take down. These are the same people in charge of Cardiff's bid to become the City of Culture in 2008! Hypocritical or what.' He seems to detest people who assume they are higher in the pecking order than anyone else in the world and he often refers to politicians as 'the orange and stocking brigade'. One day, I ask him if he would ever consider becoming a politician; say a minister for art or culture. 'Yeah,' he says. 'I tried to put myself forward for the Nationa Assembly. By the time I found ou how you go about it, it was too late apply. That's how accessible th make politics for ordinary peop But I'd love to have that power. Fir thing I'd do? I'd strip Wales of all galleries. Wales doesn't deser art.' Here of course there are umber of screpancies Neale's peeches. rstly he tells a viewer that he too educated understand his ork, even though eale's work is eant to be ternational, is ble to cross all arriers, and is eant to be nderstood in any ay anyone nderstands it as he's ot actually fixing for y particular effect. econdly, he claims he ould do exactly what ardiff Council did if he ad their power he would rip all galleries of all art. omething he admits is ypocritical. The operative ords in Neale's rant are, 'I ould love to have that ower.' While he poses as an neducated and natural tist, an outsider who enjoys s solitude, he wouldn't be verse to more control, more me, more power.

Neale is in possession of rmal artistic qualifications. He udied A level Art at Neath ollege and then a Fine Art egree at Bath College. He is pically flippant about this, aking comments like, 'I went to e college and said I'd like to do is A level and they said, sorry you n't do that because you haven't one it before. Well if I'd done it efore I wouldn't want to do it gain,' and, 'Bath College was the first prospectus in the pile in the careers office, so I went there.' But I believe that he truly values it. In November 2003 he takes me to the Washington Gallery to see an exhibition by his friend, Julian Castaldi. Castaldi was for a time the Stereophonics' official photographer. According to the press, that relationship ended in scandal when Castaldi began seeing the lead singer Kelly Jones' girlfriend, and Kelly Jones smashed up his sports car with a telegraph pole, going on to write a song called Rainbows And Pots of Gold about the incident. Anyway, the point is that we're here to see his collection of Polaroid photographs and when Neale introduces me to Castaldi, he says, 'She's going to write my biography, a real sad sob story of how this poor Neath kid got to art college.' Also, Neale often repeats instructions art tutors gave him way back in '87, like the one about not calling his work his work. Hints that have remained cherished in his mind for seventeen years. My favourite Neale Howells work is a construction from 1990 entitled School In Bath (page 118-119), created in his final year at Bath College. It's a partly demolished school, a classroom reduced to grey rubble with the white light of the sky shining in through the busted roof. The only thing which remains intact is the wall the blackboard stands on, and on the blackboard, Neale has oil-painted two sets of bold, diagonal black and yellow stripes. It is by far his most optimistic work. What I see in the construction is that while society and economics may break down, while buildings may crumble, education will always prevail. Two other works from around this period in Neale's life send the same message. Bath City Centre (page 120) from 1987 is oil on wood measuring 92 x 122 cm. It's a landscape painting of an actual place, the buildings and spires of Bath city centre. It even has trees in it. It's a dark painting filled with shadows, moss-green buildings and lawns, but it isn't disorientating or isolating in the way Neale's current work is. The sun shines on one wall of a building which reflects just a little bit of hope, an escape, a way out. And Eisteddfod 95 from 1995 contains the same chess board stripes of red and white paint in its centre as the blackboard in Bath, while all around it are layers on layers of dark blue paint. It's reminiscent of the confusing and riotous backgrounds that are to come later in Neale's work but in the middle the vibrant stripes suggest Neale isn't lost or scared, in fact he's focusing on something positive. Neale does consider himself lucky to have received a formal education at a time when education meant something and he enjoyed his college experience. In the same way, I am extremely proud of my education (although it came much later than Neale's, at a time when practically anyone could have a shot at higher education) because I never felt I deserved it, I was the girl destined for the shop till, but I was the first person in my family to get a degree.

Then, after the Eisteddfod painting in 1995, something changes. The work takes on the anger and loneliness we see in Neale's present work, there are no centre pieces any more and no vibrant eye-catching colours, only colours bleeding into each other or painted over and over one another. During an interview to study an MA at Slade Art College, Neale claims he pissed in a tutor's face. 'As I was escorted away I felt a release of pressure and knew that I needn't please anyone anymore,' he says. 'Artistically I only ever had to please myself.' Of course, I find out later that Neale never actually pissed in anyone's face. He voluntarily left an interview that he knew he was destined to fail. And it's at this point that he begins to become playful with his comments as acts of self-promotion. Shunned by something he once found comforting, he declares himself a bohemian artist, never to respect any kind of establishment ever again. Like Basquait, Neale is a fraud, a creature of cynical marketing, a wannabe graffitist, an interpreter of the marginal and the dispossessed, but also to a certain extent, he is the marginal and the dispossessed; too stubborn or too insecure to conform. But, like Pollock, an action painter who creates stirring work. When I ask Neale what his views on art college and formal education are, he says, quite ironically, 'What's the point in having a degree if nobody ever asks you about it?'

Owe Are Ewe? 2

Neale is undoubtedly a walking contradiction. In a recent interview he claims to hate thinking, saying his current inspiration is the radio because that allows him to think nothing and start painting, yet he regularly writes essays, like Censor Or Be Censored mentioned here, which capture his deep and probing thoughts on art. He

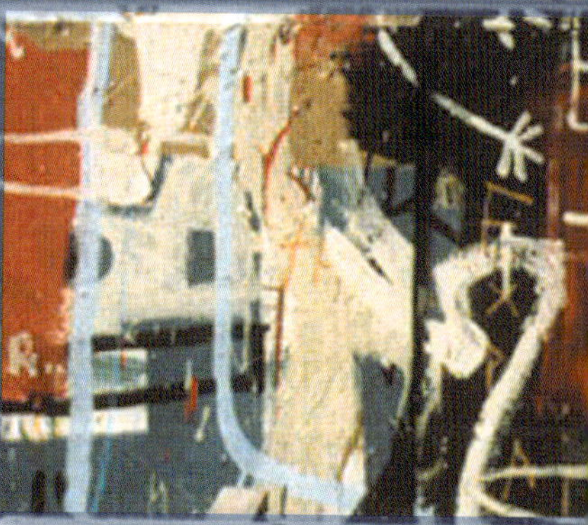

considers himself lazy, but he is forever very busy with too many projects relate, and still always managing get eight solid hours of TV in p day. He's playful, odd and alway

retending to
e the opposite
what he is.
he finds
omething
fficult he'll say
's effortless. He
aims that he has
bsolutely no
nbition but every
ne of his rants, his
levision and radio
ppearances, his
xhibitions, and his
ontinuing to paint
nows that he is
ertainly extremely
mbitious. Yet he's also
ery self-destructive.
t one point I'm
nterviewing him about
nasculinity and he
egins an anecdote about
is appearance on Five
ve the previous day. 'I
old myself before I went
n,' he said, 'I said Neale,
ou can go on here and get
ourself some interest in
ondon art circles or you can
e a clown and blow it for
ourself by doing something
upid, like swearing. Well I
lew it for myself by swearing.
couldn't help it, I'm sort of
ddicted. It's the way things
re. People look and never see
nything. They listen but don't
ear anything. People only start
vatching when the TV goes off.
ou have to hit them to get their
ttention. Everybody wants to play
safe. But it's getting to the point
vhere nobody will want to talk to
ne.' He's stuck in a rut, going
round and around in the same circle; like the strokes of his paintbrush, they never reveal anything new, we see the same dissatisfied stick figures, year after year. It's an addiction though, because he's an outsider protecting himself from the rest of the world. The best form of defence is attack. Fight for his right to be an artist. His disguises are visible in his paintings too. While he paints incredibly moving landscapes of the disconcerting and strange world we live in he adds to its confusion by presenting himself as unresponsive and difficult when he's sensitive and modest. While he's saying one thing, he's painting another thing, his arms and hands making pictures more honest than he'll allow his words to be, like the flailing arms of his stick men, veering off in every possible direction. How RU All Today from 2001 is a simple navy and white painting. Its subject is a stick man with two faces. One face inside another. The first one is a blank face. An empty circle, no eyes, no mouth, no nose. The face inside that though is smiling, its small eyes screwed up in laughter. Strokes of navy paint grasp out in wild directions for his arms, there are some scrawled words underneath – not as many as usual – and there is only a small amount of blue paint daubed into the background. It's not isolating or scary; the general feel of the painting is a playful one, happy, even wicked. I think it's Neale's self-portrait.

Despite himself of course, his art works. His canvases of mad, graffitiesque messages of deprivation and daily violence have a devoted following. They've made a major impact on the Welsh arts scene and their fervour and passion deserve to. They've definitely made an impact on me. I like them too. I like their scepticism, their uncertainty, their colour and humour, decadence and imperfection. Everything I like about Neale. But it's not my job to judge Neale Howells. What I read into Neale's work may not be what you do. As Neale himself keeps repeating, 'Time is my only judge.'

ACKNOWLEDGEMENTS

!!+!
photographs and video stills © eddie ladd

thought and memory
photographs © jeff teare

the wandering eye & its resting place
photographs and images © peter bodenham

shapeshifting
photographs © megan lloyd/india dance wales/araf haq
images © megan lloyd

ow are ewe?
images © neale howells

bIOGS

peter bodenham
is a visual artist; uses a wide range of materials and a number of processes to realise his work, which consists of paintings and drawings, sculpture, site-specific installations, and performance. a central theme for some time has been the journey, both physical and imagined, real and metaphoric. his work is located somewhere between figuration and abstraction, with a touch of the surreal. he has exhibited throughout wales and britain. he is interested in the theory of art and design, teaches part time art history & aesthetics in h.e. institutions in wales.

sarah broughton
is a co-founder of forget about it film & television and wrote the acclaimed bbc 4 documentaries on gracie fields and kathleen ferrier. she has contributed to the new welsh review, mslexia and the big issue. her first novel, other useful numbers will be published by parthian in 2005.

anne cakebread
is an illustrator and designer.

maria donovan
was born in dorset. she trained as a nurse in holland and worked her way around europe for a year, playing the violin. as a magician's assistant the highpoint of her career involved performing a blazing sack escape (with costume change). these days she divides her time between writing fiction and non-fiction, and teaching the same at the university of glamorgan.

neale howells
trained at bath college of higher education. he lives in neath where he has a shed for a studio. he has been named the welsh winner of the only pan-european painting prize, the lexmark european art prize.

eddie ladd
has worked with brith gof, camre cain, hijinx, moving being, taliesin, theatrig, and volcano theatre companies, as well as performing in her own productions, including scarface and club luz. in 1996, she won an r.t.s. award for presenting the bbc wales tv series the slate. in 2003, club luz won a total theatre award at the edinburgh fringe festival. in 2004, she received a fellowship award from the national endowment for science, technology and the arts.

megan lloyd

became fascinated as a teenager with the similarities between seemingly diverse cultures, and in particular between those of her own and that of india. she is now an accomplished practitioner of bharat natyam, indian classical dance, and dances with india dance wales. she is an inspirational teacher working at every level from children to special needs. she is a talented printmaker, specialising in batik. an accomplished storyteller, megan is a founder member of the tales from beyond the border storytelling company.

daniel morden

is a professional teller of traditional stories. his repertoire ranges from the nonsensical to the profound, the ridiculous to the solemn. he works in a huge variety of situations, from education projects for schools and museums to public performances in arts centres and at literary festivals. he was resident storyteller at garden festival wales in 1992. he has adapted traditional stories for the theatre, television and radio. his first book, weird tales from the storyteller, is published by pont.

daniel has travelled widely, collecting and telling stories from hawaii to haiti, from the tropics to the arctic. his tellings (with hugh lupton) of metamorphosis, the odyssey and the iliad have toured literary festivals across britain.

lloyd robson

is a gun-for-hire text operative. as a writer, he is author of cardiff cut and *bbboing! & associated weirdness*. as a visual artist, he produced the sense of city road project.

jeff teare

has worked as an actor, writer, musician and video maker but mainly as a theatre director.

rachel trezise

is a freelance journalist and author of in and out of the goldfish bowl, an orange futures listed novel.

jeni williams

is a cultural critic who teaches art history and literature at trinity college, carmarthen. she is particularly interested in the arts in and of wales.